BLOOD MONEY

NOVAK AND MITCHELL

ANDREW RAYMOND

To the living we owe respect

But to the dead, we owe only the truth

– Voltaire

CHAPTER ONE

SIX YEARS AGO

THE MAN in the front passenger seat of the Escalade SUV with the fake plates flicked idly through the dossier.

'What do you reckon this guy did?' he asked.

'What does it matter?' said the driver. He only had eyes – and thoughts – for the twisting country road ahead, which, in the gathering winter gloom, was in bad need of some roadside lights.

They had been driving for an hour and a half, tracking their target all the way from the underground car park of the ABC Studios at Rockefeller Plaza in downtown Manhattan, navigating the endless traffic up through Washington Heights, where the congestion finally eased. Then briefly crossing the New York state line where Connecticut jutted out across Interstate 684 for a few miles.

The target appeared to have no idea he'd been followed so far north. Not when he crossed back into New York, and the bucolic, quiet roads surrounded by deep greenery on either side that told him he was definitely in Northern

Westchester. Everything out there was slow. Quiet. Peaceful.

Normally.

Slow, yes. Quiet, yes.

But not peaceful. Not that night.

Eric, the passenger, closed the dossier. 'You're not at all interested in what this guy did?'

Damian, the driver, dragged the word out. 'No-ope.'

Parroting Damian's stock reply to most of Eric's questions, Eric said, 'It's the job, right?'

'Something like that.'

Eric brandished the dossier which showed photos of the target taken by Damian on recon the previous week. 'What should I know about this guy that's not in the file?'

'You don't recognise him?' asked Damian.

'Of course I recognise him. Who the hell doesn't recognise Seymour Novak. He's been doing the news for decades. That's my concern.'

Damian shot him a warning look. 'There's no room in here for passengers, Eric. I brought you in on this because you said I could trust you. If you're not a hundred per cent–'

'Hey, I am. I'm just saying, we haven't done anyone as high-profile as this before. This is going to mean headlines. Scrutiny.'

'That's why the client wants it handled discreetly. A man his age dying in a suicide? No one's going to look too closely. Not the way we're going to do it.'

Eric flashed his eyebrows up. 'He must have really pissed someone off.'

'Turn to page eight,' said Damian.

Eric paused as he assessed the number noted on the dossier. 'Too short for a phone number...what is it?'

'That's what they're paying us.'

Eric's eyes almost popped out his head. 'Each?'

Damian snorted in amusement. 'You wish. That's total. If it's not enough–'

'Hell no, it's enough! That's more than I made as a Marine in a year. And this doesn't demand that I drive down Iraqi roads lined with IEDs.'

'That number shows how important this job is to our client.'

'Who the hell *are* these people?'

'They're serious.'

'You worked for them before?'

Damian said nothing.

Eric held up an apologetic hand. 'Of course. Sorry. But I mean, they must be pretty serious to pay that much.'

'Let's just say they're not known for having a sense of humour.'

'This is us.' Eric pointed out the tracker on the target's car beaming on the map, closing in on the final destination. A large white wooden mansion – one of many – among the sprawling estates, rolling meadows, and equestrian farms nearby.

Damian's fingers gripped the steering wheel a little tighter as the target peeled off to the right, disappearing up a leafy, long driveway in his Jeep Cherokee.

Damian drove on. He glanced at the temperature gauge on the dash, then at Eric. 'You feeling all right?'

Eric replied, 'Yeah. Why?'

'Because it's only forty-five in here, you're wearing a

thin ranger shirt and a tactical vest with no insulation, and you're sweating.'

Damian had intentionally kept the temperature cool in the car, so that their reactions would be sharp when they got out. Getting warm and comfortable before an outdoor operation was a fast-track to sluggish responses in a chilly environment like Northern Westchester in deep winter.

Eric dabbed at his hairline above his forehead, as if surprised to learn that there was sweat there. 'Maybe I'm coming down with something.' He leaned forward, trying to make reassuring eye contact. 'Hey. I'm good, man.'

To the untrained eye, Eric might have appeared and sounded at ease. Confident. But to Damian – his senses honed through years of black ops on the battlefield as well as the private sector – Eric was hiding something. Eric might have been in charge of his behaviour, but he was not in charge of his physiology. A true operator can contain those kinds of nerves. It made Damian wonder what they were really about to walk into.

As they drove on slowly, Damian watched through the passing trees as the target parked up in front of their residence. Damian kept driving until they reached a pre-chosen patch of scrub under low-hanging trees. He took out a burner phone and called the only number stored on it.

'Anchor is home,' he said. 'All set for retirement.' He hung up, then he told Eric, 'Let's do this right. Any mistakes, and they'll be sending a couple of guys after us next.'

CHAPTER TWO

THE TARGET, known to Damian and Eric as 'Anchor', stopped by the long mirror in his hallway, catching sight of a light powder streak at his collar line. He grabbed a tissue and rubbed off the mark. 'Sixty-six years old and I wear makeup for a living,' he muttered to himself. He sighed. 'What are you doing, Seymour?'

When he had moved from the newspaper world of the *Tribune* to the bright lights of newscasting on the American Broadcasting Corporation, it had brought him fame and wealth the likes of which he'd never thought he would experience in his lifetime. It wasn't just a different league. It wasn't even the same sport anymore. A life once spent trying to break stories had been reduced to simply relaying them once they had already happened. When he went to ABC, he accepted that he was no longer a journalist. He was a mere announcer. And that's how it had been since he was thirty-eight years old. Until just a few weeks ago.

Since then, Seymour's life had turned upside down.

For the first time, he was considering leaving ABC. Leaving all the bright lights behind. All for one story.

One story that was bigger than anything Seymour had ever lived through.

He poured himself a drink at the well-stocked bar in his study, then he called the only number on the burner phone he kept hidden in the bar.

The recipient was named "RT".

RT answered without a word.

Seymour said, 'I've been thinking about what you said last time. And I've decided. Flights and hotel are booked. I'm all in.'

'What about ABC?' came the reply. The voice was male. Early twenties. Intense.

Seymour paused. 'They're passing. For now. It's complicated–'

'We need to get to Saratoga and get them on record. It's the only way.'

'Calm down. I will. I'll be there this time tomorrow.'

'But where will we take it?'

'We'll take it to print instead.'

'Where?'

'Diane Schlesinger and I go way back. I'll talk to her tonight. We'll figure something out.'

'I don't know. Diane and I don't exactly see eye to eye on a lot of things.'

'Yeah, I know all about that.' Seymour paused. 'Maybe we should bring in Tom on this. He still works with Diane at *Republic*. Maybe–'

'No,' RT snapped. 'Tom had his chance. I'm not handing him my by-line. Not now.'

Seymour nodded then took a steadying drink, considering the road ahead. 'I've taken some precautions that you should know about. To safeguard the evidence.'

'What sort of precautions?'

'A dead man's switch.'

RT paused. 'I know this is big, but–'

'Hey, I know what these people are capable of. And it isn't pretty. This isn't paranoia. This is just being sensible.'

'Okay, then. How will it work?'

OUTSIDE, hiding by the study window and frantically searching through their feed of Seymour's phone lines, Eric crept a safe distance away and radioed Damian.

'We've got a problem,' said Eric. 'He's on the phone and I can't hear it.'

'What do you mean? We've been up on his phone for the last two weeks.'

'I mean, it's a second phone we're not up on. He's got a burner.'

'Shit. Where the hell did he get that? We need to move. Now!'

Eric shoved his radio mic back under his collar, then made his way around the back of the house.

It was time to retire Anchor.

As planned, Damian cut the electricity to the house.

IN THE STUDY, Seymour stopped in mid sentence and looked up at the ceiling, then towards the hall.

'What is it?' RT asked.

'No, it's just...the lights went out.'

'You blew a bulb?'

'No, the lights in the hall too.'

With urgency – and fear – RT told him, 'Check your landline phone.'

Seymour picked up the handset in the hallway and put it to his other ear. 'Dead,' Seymour replied. He knew what it meant.

As did RT. 'Hide the phone in the usual place. Then get out, Seymour. *Run!*'

Seymour hung up, then he scrambled for a small fireproof box he kept in a safe behind an oil painting on the wall. The second it was locked, he collected his regular phone from the hall, then he ran towards the kitchen.

He didn't bother burdening himself with a coat or stopping to grab a 'go bag' that he still kept by a cupboard under the stairs. He didn't want to be weighed down – or slowed down – by anything. This wasn't about having supplies to get through the next twenty-four hours. If they had cut the electricity and phone line, it was about surviving the next thirty minutes.

On his desperate charge through the kitchen towards the back door, he grabbed a chef's knife from the island which was still covered in the various jars of nuts and seeds he had used for his smoothie that morning. He was in good shape for his age, and moved nimbly out over the decking which was already glistening with the beginnings of what would be a heavy frost that night.

He cursed as a battery-powered security light flashed on, prompted by him running towards the trees at the rear of the property. There was no fence or perimeter. Just open woods now. All Seymour's property, and his intimate knowledge of its layout was the only advantage he had over two much younger, and highly motivated, trained killers.

The sudden beam of the security light stretched as far as Eric, who set off in pursuit of the figure that had disappeared into the shadows.

'He's on the move,' Eric informed Damian via radio.

Damian sprinted around the side of the house, vaulting a picket fence then scaling a brick wall beside the double garage with the speed of a gecko racing up glass. For all of Damian's upper-body bulk, he was nimble. In no time, he caught up with Eric in the woods. The pair of them slowed to a stop, taking in the dark surroundings.

Damian raised a hand for silence to stop Eric talking, then he waited. With no visual, sound was their best option of locating Anchor now.

Unseen, hiding behind a rocky outcrop ahead, Seymour sat with his back against a large boulder, his chest heaving. He struggled to get air into his lungs without making a sound, and his frantic panting was sending plumes of steamy breath up into the air.

His thoughts were cluttered. Confused. Everything coloured by fear.

What did they want? Were they going to kill him? Or did they want information? What had he stumbled into?

Seymour took out his phone and called 911.

His hand was shaking so much, he could barely keep it to his ear.

'Nine one one, what's your emergency?' came the response.

Before he breathed a word, Seymour covered the earpiece. He stood up slowly until he could see over the top of the boulder for a glimpse of his attackers.

He immediately shot back down. They were no more than twenty feet away, creeping one step at a time towards him.

Every molecule in Seymour's body urged him to tell the emergency responder what was happening and where he was, but he couldn't say a word. Not with Eric and Damian so close now.

To speak would mean death.

He shut his eyes and hung up the phone before the two men overheard the responder's insistent demands for the caller's location and identity.

He looked at the clearing ahead. Covered in crispy leaves, twigs, branches, and any number of rocks that he could roll an ankle on in such darkness.

It was useless. He wouldn't make it more than fifty yards before they caught him.

With time ticking down until they eventually uncovered his hiding spot, Seymour looked at the phone. It would be so easy to call his son. He had the number memorised. Though it had been a long time since he had used it. Not that Tom was good at staying in touch either.

For both of them, a phone was there simply to convey information. Where were they? What were they working on? They didn't do chat. *How* they were doing. Never had. Never would. It was the way Seymour had raised him. Never an idle moment. Always pushing for the next challenge. Starting the next project. Never sitting around, wasting your life.

But in that moment, if he could even have heard Tom say hello, it would have meant the world to him.

He let out a knowing, gentle snort, as leaves above him rustled. It was pointless running.

'Let's not make this difficult,' said Damian, pointing a handgun at the top of Seymour's head.

'I don't know what you want,' said Seymour, quivering. 'But if it's to kill me, can I at least talk to my son one last time? I won't tell him anything. I just want to hear his voice.'

Damian jumped down off the rock to Seymour's level. He waved with the gun for Eric to come down too.

Seymour glanced at Eric, who had a syringe in his hand. His heart sank, as he realised what the play was.

Death.

Maybe make it look like an overdose. Otherwise Damian would have just shot him already. If they were planning on mere incapacitation, they could have shot a dart by now.

Sensing the end was near, Seymour's voice cracked. 'My son...if it's suicide, he won't get my insurance. Is there any way...you could make it look natural?'

'Sorry,' said Damian. 'I've got my orders.' He nodded to Eric.

Eric stabbed the needle into Seymour's neck.

'Please,' Seymour croaked, feeling the vast scale of the world he had loved so much shrink down suddenly, violently, into something tiny.

Now, the entire universe seemed to consist solely of the few metres of scrub where the three men were playing out Seymour's final moments.

To Eric's shock, Damian took Seymour's hand which was already going limp.

'It won't hurt,' Damian said. 'I'm sorry it worked out this way. Hey, you were a good man. Nothing about what's happening here will change that.'

'But...but they'll...get away with it.'

'I know.' Damian nodded softly. 'They always do. And they always will.'

Spooked by Damian's eerie demeanour, and baffling compassion, Eric retracted his thumb from the plunger once the poison was gone, then he carefully removed the needle.

Seymour's eyes closed, and his head fell to one side.

Damian flicked his head in the direction of the house. 'We'll need to get him a coat and boots to make it look like he meant to come out here. And ruffle those fallen leaves on the trail. It looks exactly like someone was chased through here.'

When Eric returned, they tidied the rest of the scene, sprinkling the detritus and props of a suicide by pills – just as the postmortem would pronounce.

Once the men were back in the Escalade, Damian looked through Seymour's phone.

'Anything?' asked Eric.

Damian took out the SIM and snapped it. 'Nine one one, but no one's going to be looking too hard for a missing phone. Especially at the bottom of the Hudson River.'

'The burner could still be a problem,' Eric said. 'What if he called for help?'

'He didn't know he was in trouble yet when he was taking the call. He wouldn't have known to call for help.' He reached down under his seat, then looked up to face Eric. 'Just like you.'

Before Eric could react, he saw that Damian now had a length of wire wrapped around his hands, prepped and taut.

Damian threw the wire around Eric's neck and pulled

violently, throwing Eric from side to side with visceral strength.

Damian was calm as he tugged tighter and tighter around Eric's neck. 'You shouldn't have tried to screw the op. I know you were up on that burner phone. But I was too...'

Eric fought and gurgled and flailed, but he was powerless against Damian's grip.

'It was a clever move trying to pretend you didn't know about it. What were you hoping to overhear? The location of the dead man's switch. Keep it for yourself, or sell it to the highest bidder?' Damian grunted with effort, sensing Eric's defences fading. 'The thing is, Eric. I don't accept loose ends. And neither does Hilderberg. That's right. You've been working for them this whole time. That's how we operate. That's how we keep ourselves in the shadows. We're everywhere. And nowhere...'

When Eric went still, his final breath leaving his body, Damian let him drop in the passenger seat. He took out his phone and made a call.

'I'm coming back with a plus one,' said Damian.

'What about Anchor?'

'Retired.'

'What about the files?'

'They might be a problem. Anchor arranged a dead man's switch.'

'Then someone out there has everything. How will you get the files back?'

'Same way as always. Persistence. Patience.'

CHAPTER THREE

PRESENT DAY

Senior Security correspondent at *The Republic*, Tom Novak, swung back and forth in his Herman Miller Aeron ergonomic chair. The Rolls-Royce of office chairs, as Novak had put it to almost anyone in the office who would listen – which consisted of mainly junior staff writers who couldn't afford to spend over $1000 of their own money on a chair, and had to put up with the standard IKEA knock-off versions of the Aeron. For them, $1000 was better spent on things like rent. Or a car. Things Novak no longer had to worry about. Despite the chair's exorbitant cost, for all the time he spent at his desk these days it might as well have been a wooden stool that didn't even spin around.

The contents of a two-tier plastic tray spilled over onto his desk. The top level marked "Fan mail". The bottom "Death threats".

As Kenny the mail boy went by with his stacked cart, he handed Novak three envelopes and a small brown box.

'What do we think, Kenny?' Novak asked, holding the mail out in front of the tray.

Kenny considered the packages. 'Handwriting looks quite neat. I'd say fan mail.'

'Yeah, the crazies do get their upper- and lowercase letters a little confused from time to time.'

'Plus,' Kenny added, 'it's a few weeks since your last piece.'

'Thanks for reminding me.'

As his cheeks flushed, Kenny clarified, 'I mean, once your next story comes out, the crazies will find you again.'

'Yeah, they always do,' Novak replied absently. He leaned back, his attention caught by the sight of a young staff writer leaving the chief editor's office, then going straight to his desk, where he packed up the contents of his desk into a cardboard box.

'There goes another one,' said Kenny, pushing his mail cart on to the Metro desk.

Novak threw down the pen he had been spinning across his fingers, and let out a long puff. He stared at the sign above his desk that said, "FACTS or GTFO". Then he lingered for much longer at the picture next to it. A photo of Novak as a six-year-old, sitting behind the *ABC Nightly News* desk – which his father, Seymour, had called his office from the age of thirty-eight, right up until his death six years ago.

In the chief editor's office, Mark Chang leaned towards his computer screen, clicking carefully around a spreadsheet as he shifted cash from one column into another. He and Novak's eyes briefly met.

Chang looked away, then tossed his glasses down on his desk before leaving for the conference room.

A voice behind Novak called to him. Authoritative. English. Female. Unmistakably no one else. That of

Stella Mitchell. 'Hey, aren't you coming to the ten o'clock?'

'Yeah,' Novak replied.

Stella looked at him, then his desk, in confusion. It was free of any paperwork and his computer wasn't even on. 'Because it's ten o'clock. I don't know when you last looked at your watch, but I can tell you that ten o'clock is considered the best time to go to the ten o'clock editorial.'

'Aren't you late as well?' he replied.

'I've got special dispensation. To collect you from your desk and bring you to the conference room.'

Novak trilled his lips – bored and disconsolate at the idea of sitting through the meeting.

'Come on,' said Stella. 'Your empty desk will still be here when you get back.'

Novak got reluctantly to his feet.

As they walked to the conference room just off the main newsroom, Novak said, 'Mark's let someone else go.'

'Yeah, I know,' Stella replied.

'If he keeps this up there won't be a newsroom left.'

'It's not Mark. It's the board.'

'God, not you too, Stel. Mark's a big boy. He knows how to tell the board to go swing if he wanted to. He worked under Diane for years. You're telling me he's lost his backbone?'

From the copy desk, a voice called out, 'Hey, Stella! You put a U in neighbour again.'

'Give me a break, Constance. I barely know what time zone I'm in these days...' Stella lowered her voice again to tell Novak, 'Don't be too hard on Mark. He's not been the same since he came back. Poor sod. A year and a half helping his wife Caroline through chemo, then three weeks after she gets the all clear, she dies by falling and hitting her head by a swimming pool.'

'I'm just saying,' said Novak, 'revenue's up, profits stagnant, but goddamn it if the board doesn't make sure they get their dividends. We're just a cash cow to them, and to hell with it if we're throwing away talented young journalists like we have the last three months.' He shook his head as if a shiver had gone through his body. 'I feel like my goddamn dad. He lived through a ton of these cuts. He used to tell me it was always the talent on the big wages that got it worst from the engine room staff.' Novak looked around as he held the conference room door open. 'Any more cuts, and we might need to start working away from the newsroom.'

Stella stopped in the doorway. 'Yeah. Because the way to prove that you're not elitist is to demand your own office.'

'Yeah, yeah, yeah,' replied Novak, knowing he was in the wrong.

Stella kept on at him until they got to their chairs. 'Maybe you could ask the staff not to look you in the eye...'

Mark Chang, who looked like he had been up for twelve hours already, stood up with his hands on his hips and did a quick visual check of who was there. 'Where is Fitz?' he asked.

Through a smile, Novak said, 'He told me he was going to the gym, and that he'll email you his next piece from a treadmill.'

'Fitz,' said Mark blankly. 'On a treadmill?'

Stella said, 'Apparently he's decided to stop living like he's still twenty-five and take care of himself.'

Mark shook his head in confusion. 'Okay. Well as Sonny and Cher have deigned to grace us with their presence, let's get started.'

Novak looked at Stella, then back at Mark. 'Actually, I always thought of us more like Spencer Tracy and Katharine Hepburn.'

Stella snorted.

Someone at the far end of the conference table who was feeling brave, suggested, 'Try Sylvia Plath and Ted Hughes.'

Someone else piped up. 'As in, she's the talented one.'

Novak smiled. He knew better than to deny it. 'Oh, poor millennial philistines. Denigrate Ted Hughes when I bet you've never even read *Crow*, or *The Hawk in the Rain*. You do realise Sylvia Plath tried multiple times to kill herself long before Ted Hughes cheated on her. She was a genius. She was also doomed years before she ever met Ted Hughes. If you think she wouldn't have killed herself if she'd never met Hughes, then you don't know shit about depression or suicide.'

Novak's diatribe had rubbed Jonathan, the *Republic's* book reviewer, the wrong way. 'And what exactly does Tom 'half a million followers on Instagram' Novak know about depression or suicide?'

It was a glib and baseless comment, said without knowledge of Novak's family history, of which Stella was fully aware.

She intervened, saying sternly, 'Jonathan. Don't.'

Novak took the high ground and said nothing.

'All right, settle down,' said Mark, pushing his hands down towards the table to appeal for quiet. 'Let's go around the room–'

'Oh, come on,' Novak complained. 'There's surely only one place we can start.'

CHAPTER FOUR

Gauging the mood of the room from the expectant faces all turned towards him – including the faces of a dozen field journalists on a TV screen via Zoom – Novak declared, 'There are four empty desks out there. We all know that the board is cutting costs to make us more attractive to whoever is lining up to buy us…'

Mark smiled politely. Nervously. Looking for an ally, he turned in Stella's direction, who offered a sympathetic look in return. She was the only person in the room who knew first-hand how hard it was to chair an editorial meeting with Tom Novak, such was his propensity to suck up all the oxygen in the room.

Novak went on, 'This is straight out the corporate play book: soften up the workforce by letting a number of people go, then attention turns to the key people – namely us, who, frankly, earn the most in the newsroom.'

Mark took a beat, choosing his words carefully. 'The board is in the process of making a number of tough decisions–'

Novak interjected, 'Which you could say no to at any time, by the way.'

Mark tried again. 'There are several buyers interested in acquiring *The Republic*. It's not my job to decide who stays or goes. I just direct the news around here.'

'Do you think that's what Diane would have said when she was chief?'

His invoking the name of the most legendary editor *Republic* ever had, and whose loss was still felt deeply by everyone, was a step too far for Stella.

'Tom,' she snapped. The only thing missing was a motherly mention of his full name to make Novak realise he was in real trouble.

She knew he was just lashing out because of what Jonathan had said, but it didn't excuse attacking their editor who was going through a hard time as it was.

'This isn't about me,' Novak replied. 'It's about all of us.' He turned pointedly to Mark. 'And it would be nice to feel like our chief editor has got our back.'

'I do, Tom,' Mark replied. 'I'm doing everything I can.'

Something about the expression on Mark's face made Novak pause. It wasn't the same Mark Chang from the Diane days. He was a shell of his former self. All the fight had been drained from him during his wife's illness. Now he had no defences left. He was in survival mode, where just getting through the day was enough. Novak could tell, and he wasn't going to push him any further.

Hoping to reroute the meeting, Stella suggested, 'Mark, I think you had said to go around the room.'

Relieved to have her support, Mark nodded. 'Let's do it. Nic, where are we on a hundred days?'

Nicole Santana, White House correspondent, replied, 'The body of it is there. I'm just finessing now.'

Tom and Stella smiled at each other. It was an analogy they both knew well from editorial meetings.

Mark might have felt weak, but he could still recognise bullshit when he heard it. 'We only get one go at a first hundred days piece, Nic. So do me a favour and find me a head and some limbs to go with that body. Is the administration's economic plan still in the toilet? Will the President's Secretary of State ever manage a press conference without a teleprompter? What sort of blowback is the White House expecting from its new financial regulations bill? There's a lobby out there with ten trillion dollars in assets that are ready to fight this thing. What is their plan? Do they even have one?'

Nicole nodded away sagely as if she had already thought of all of that, but was secretly relieved to have some fresh direction.

Stella whispered to Novak, 'So Mark *does* still have a pulse.'

Novak flinched when Mark called his name.

'Tom. Let me guess, you're still on the SCX story.'

A plucky young culture correspondent added, 'Shouldn't that be non-story?'

Novak replied, 'What a shame none of that dazzling wit ever makes it into your pieces, Greg.' He turned to Mark. 'I keep telling you, there's a story here. Four years ago, an Ivy League college kid starts a website for trading cryptocurrency, which becomes the world's leading exchange platform for crypto.'

Mark replied, 'Have you requested an interview?'

Novak smirked, smug about his own ingenuity. 'No. I asked to do a profile. Play up to his vanity.'

'Vanity?' asked Stella. 'He looks like a pretty goofy kid to me.'

'That's all fake,' Novak claimed. 'I'm going online with him at half past. He thinks it's just a puff piece profile. But I'm going to land a bunch of haymakers on him at the end. I want to document the collapse of the whole enterprise. The company stinks. I think it's going to be this century's Enron.'

Mark asked, 'But based on what, Tom?'

Novak paused. 'The fact that nothing is being produced. At least with Enron, there was an actual product. Oil and gas transportation. Broadband. Petrochemicals. With SCX, here's what happens. You hand them over a hundred dollars, and they turn it into what they call a hundred dollars-worth of SCX tokens. Those tokens are then traded on their exchange. There's just one problem: the tokens don't actually exist. They're just numbers on a database. The tokens are only worth a hundred dollars because that's what SCX says they're worth. It's the same with any other crypto token. There's no asset. It's thin air.'

'It sounds great, Tom,' said Mark. 'Except that every major financial institution has invested heavily in SCX, including the biggest hedge funds in the world. Zachary Storm sits on panels with former presidents and titans of industry. And SCX is endorsed by some of the biggest celebrities on the planet. You're telling me they're *all* wrong, and you're right?'

Without missing a beat, Novak nodded. 'Yes.'

Stella struggled to stifle her laughter.

Mark turned to Nasir, *Republic*'s chief financial correspondent, who had been quietly chuckling and shaking his head through Novak's speech. 'Nasir, what's SCX worth last you heard?'

Leaning back in his seat, twirling a pen, Nasir said, 'About twenty-one billion.'

'Oh,' said Novak, in mock surprise, 'you mean the same valuation as Enron before it collapsed?'

Nasir told Mark, 'This isn't a serious story. No one I talk to – and that's *all* the major players in this industry – has a bad word to say about SCX. This is typical Tom Novak. Throw a dozen things at the wall, then when one finally sticks he gets to tell everyone "I told you so."'

Stella fired back, 'And how many times have you been able to tell anyone "I told you so", Nasir?' She feigned counting on her fingers. 'Oh wait, it's *never*. You're great at reacting once a story has already broken. Tom's been out in front of four major stories in the last four years. So maybe once you've done even half of that, you can start directing him. Until then, you don't even get to direct him to the men's room.'

A few chuckles broke out across the table.

Novak said, 'Thanks, Stel. But I can stick up for myself.'

Mark extended a hand to call for calm. 'Why don't we all just cool it, huh? Tom, we all love the passion. But there's another problem: stories on cryptocurrency and Bitcoin are reader-retention poison. Did you *see* the metrics on the last piece you ran? Only a third of readers read past the halfway mark.'

Novak replied, 'That just means they haven't been told the sort of story on the subject to keep them interested. SCX is a story as old as time: financial institution appears to be a huge success, but is actually mired in corruption and fraud.'

'Well, gee, Tom. If only we employed someone who could tell our readers that. Maybe some kind of a journalist...'

'Yes, very clever,' said Novak.

Mark went on, 'There's a reason for that saying in finance: if you think you understand crypto, you don't understand crypto. And the majority of the country – including me – immediately switch their brains off whenever someone even mentions crypto or Bitcoin. People don't care about crypto. *I* don't care about crypto.'

'You should.'

For the first time Mark really raised his voice. 'Then tell me why, Tom!'

Stella smiled to herself. For all of Mark's personal struggles, Stella could tell that deep down he was still an editor.

She gave Novak a look of "he's got you there."

Looking for further support, he told her, 'You like my opinions on crypto.' As the pause that followed dragged out to a few seconds, he added, '*Don't* you?'

Stella replied, 'Actually, I do kind of zone out a bit, Tom.'

He threw his hands up in despair.

Searching for an analogy, she said, 'It's like jazz. It's great fun for the people playing it. But for everyone listening, it's just noise.'

Novak looked to the ceiling. 'Oh my god, Stel. Did you just call Miles Davis, John Coltrane, and Ella Fitzgerald "noise"?'

'She did,' Mark said. 'And now I'm calling *this* noise.'

'I've got an anonymous source, okay?' said Novak.

'Saying what?'

'That SCX isn't doing nearly as well as it's making out. The source actually used the word insolvent. He thinks it'll break this weekend.'

'He?'

'The email read like a "he".'

Stella squinted. 'How does that work?'

Novak made a sarcastic *pipe down* gesture. 'Trust me, Stel. I know these things.'

Stella shook her head.

Mark asked, 'Where did the tip come from?'

'It came into my IronCloud last week,' Novak answered. 'So even if I wanted to, I can't trace the source. I've been researching SCX solidly since then.'

'And what have you got?'

Novak looked at Stella, then back to Mark. 'Nothing.' He raised an urgent finger. 'But I do have this interview.'

Mark sighed. 'Fine. Get me something that even makes a dent in SCX. Stella, give us something – *anything* – else, would you?'

She said, 'I've been working with Ralph...' She indicated the video screen, specifically a middle-aged man wearing a white shirt that still had the creases in it from the supermarket multipack it had come out of just half an hour earlier. His mic was off, but he was clearly engaged in some kind of altercation with someone off camera. It only became clear while Stella attempted to get Ralph to turn his mic on that he was trying to stop a small child from turning off his computer at the mains. During a panicked lunge for the child's tiny hand that was outstretched towards the power socket, Ralph's elbow brushed the button on his keyboard that turned his mic on, filling the conference room in New York with the sound of a four-year-old girl screaming with delight, believing her dad's panic to be part of a hilarious game.

'Molly!' Ralph yelped. 'No! That's dangerous.'

As Ralph pulled her away to safety, Molly's delight turned to anguish and she started to cry.

A chorus of 'aww' went out around the room, which caught Ralph's attention. Realising his mic was hot, he apologised. He pulled Molly up onto his lap, thinking it the safest place for her. Holding a toy giraffe in one arm, she immediately drummed at the keyboard with her free hand, sending Ralph in and out of the audio feed in New York, creating hilarious snippets of parent/child interaction. Everyone tried not to laugh, but it was impossible not to.

Molly finally relented when she saw the room full of people on the computer screen. She waved and said, 'Hiya!' in a cheery and cheeky voice.

'Hi, Molly,' said Mark, waving.

'I'm so sorry,' Ralph said, cheeks flushed in embarrassment. He encouraged Molly to go back and play in the kitchen where he could still see her.

Stella said, 'I was saying, Ralph and I have been working on the Prime Minister's donations in the last election cycle. As part of our new UK reporting arm, Ralph has been using some of his contacts in the private security sector. Now, we're yet to get someone to go on the record, but the message we keep getting is that there's something there. And to keep digging.'

'What are we talking?' asked Mark. 'Going over spending limits?'

Stella replied, 'No, the books are definitive on that.'

'If it's not spending limits, then what is it?'

'We're having to get a little creative to find out. But piggybacking off Tom's story, we do have one lead that might be quite interesting.' She gestured for Ralph to take over.

He said, 'It might surprise you to learn that the biggest campaign donor to the Prime Minister's election campaign was none other than SCX.'

Thinking he had been tricked, Mark shared a confused look with Novak. 'Did you know that?'

A picture of honesty, Novak admitted, 'It's news to me.'

Mark asked, 'Why would SCX be contributing to the British Prime Minister's campaign?'

Ralph replied, 'SCX have been aggressive in lobbying for more regulation in non-traditional financial markets. It was part of the Prime Minister's manifesto.'

Mark turned his head slightly in confusion. 'You mean *de*-regulation, surely?'

'No, SCX are strenuously pro-regulation,' replied Ralph.

Novak weighed in. 'They want a brokerage license-like system for crypto markets.'

'Why?' asked Mark.

'Because it hurts all of SCX's competitors.'

'Why doesn't it hurt SCX?'

Novak deferred to Ralph, who said, 'They've been lobbying for quote, no action relief. Basically, the UK government says, we know you're breaking the rules too, but we'll look the other way because you admitted it first.'

Mark asked, 'How sure are you on the donation front?'

'I've got it triple-stamped now,' said Ralph. 'The last confirmed this morning.'

'*Three* sources?' asked Mark.

'Cast iron, the lot of them. We could be looking at a major corruption story within SCX.'

'There's another one as old as time,' said Stella. 'Major contributor to politician gets them to rubber-stamp laws that make them all tons of money.'

Mark nodded, then pointed back and forth between the video screen, and Tom and Stella. 'I want you three working together on this. Tom, dig into any recent hearings from the House Financial Services Committee. I want to know if SCX has any friends there, and find out what they've been lobbying for. It's small for now, but it could be bigger.'

Novak nodded at Stella, who winked back at him.

CHAPTER FIVE

Twenty-seven-year-old Zachary Storm stood at the floor-to-ceiling windows of his penthouse office in the Bahamas. The view was idyllic. The sand on the nearby beach looked bright white from where he was. The sea a warm azure blue. Tourists frolicked at the water's edge, or sipped cocktails on sun loungers. A playground of the rich.

But all Zach could think was: *I wonder if I'm up high enough to kill myself if I landed on the concrete below?*

He was the only one in the world who knew what he was dealing with internally. The thought of killing himself had become overwhelming in previous days, as the toll of constant pressure weighed increasingly heavily on him. Now his head felt like a dam that needed to burst. But he couldn't do it. The pressure in his head was building each day.

Maybe I could just walk out into the sea tonight, he thought. Weighing himself down by putting rocks in his pockets like Virginia Woolf. Quietly disappearing without making any fuss. But Zach knew that in reality, if he was to disappear as things stood, it would be an international news event. It would only be a matter of time before everyone found out what he knew.

His assistant knocked timidly on the door, then peeked inside. 'Zach, remember you've got that interview in five minutes.'

Zach kept staring out the window. 'Okay. Thanks, Georgia.'

Georgia wanted to pause and ask if he really was okay. But Zach never talked about his feelings. And she didn't think she was in a position to push him on it. Zach had an informal relationship with all of the staff at Storm Crypto Exchange – more commonly known around the world as SCX – but he and Georgia weren't friends. And what Zach needed more than anything was a friend.

Georgia hesitated to leave, then said, 'I know you said no calls, but your mother is on the line.'

Again, Zach continued staring. 'Thanks, Georgia.' He moved languidly to his desk and lifted the phone without saying anything. He never needed to. His mum would start talking anyway.

'Zachary, it's me,' she said. Her voice shook as she ran a fast pace on the treadmill in her office.

Zach knew that the call would have been carefully scheduled by her PA, finding time that otherwise would have been downtime. Anna Storm didn't have such a thing. All that changed was whether she was moving or not, travelling or not.

'Yeah, I know it's you before I answer, mom,' Zach said blankly. 'My assistant tells me who's calling.'

'Are you all set for this interview?'

'Yeah, of course.'

'This isn't just anyone,' she emphasised. 'This is Tom Novak.'

Zach sighed.

'Don't huff at me,' she said. 'I've told you already that I think he's trouble and you shouldn't do this.'

'If I can win over someone like him, that's a huge win. It's just an interview.'

'No,' she warned him. 'That's the danger of doing interviews over Zoom. It feels like you're just having a private chat with a friend. He'll exploit that, believe me. He's taken down Presidents and Prime Ministers. This isn't the mail guy you're talking to. He'll try to disarm you by being light-hearted, but be careful. This is *The Republic* we're talking about. The internet is written in ink, Zachary, not pencil. If anything were ever to happen, statements by you in interviews like this can be used against you as evidence.'

'Evidence? Of what?'

Anna paused. 'You have to protect yourself, is what I'm saying. Remember what we talked about last night. This is all about painting a picture. If you don't like what's being said, change the conversation. It's not about some money-grubbing venture, it's about changing the world. It's not aspirational, it's inspirational. You're selling an *image*, that SCX is the sort of place people want to put their money. How is your hair? Can you let me see?'

Zach rolled his eyes, then took a selfie and sent it to her.

Anna paused while the picture came through. 'Negative,' she said. 'Mess up your hair a little bit. The point, Zachary, is that you're humble. Modest. You're not like these slick Silicon Valley or Wall Street types. Change out of that shirt, too. You look too smart. Put on one of those baggy basketball jerseys you have.'

'I meet people from Silicon Valley and Wall Street all the time, and they all wear nice suits and ties.'

'Those aren't the guys you're trying to court with this interview. You're courting venture capitalists and investors who are a different breed altogether. They see you with the floppy hair, the baggy t-shirts, the cargo shorts, and kind of like you haven't had a shower for a few days, and they love it. Because they think you're so smart that you don't have to care about how you look. And remember to talk about your car. Will you do that?'

Zach sighed. 'Yes, I know, mother.'

'It's a great hook. Eccentric billionaire under thirty drives a crappy Toyota Corolla, and wears clothes like a poor student.'

'You know this is all really dumb. I feel dumb doing this.'

'But it works, Zachary. You're confounding expectations of what someone in your position is like. Remember that line: "it's not about earning to live. It's about earning to give." Effective altruism one oh one. And what do we do if Novak gets political? Which is inevitable.'

We? thought Zach. *Since when was this a team event? Since when was his mother even involved in his business?*

Zach tried not to sigh. 'Regulation, regulation, regulation. We love regulation. We want to run away and make love to regulation. We want to have babies with regulation...'

'Don't be facetious. It's so uninspiring and dull.'

'Actually, I was being fatuous,' Zach replied.

He couldn't take anymore. He held the phone away from his mouth, then said to no one, 'Okay, thanks, Georgia. Tell him I'll be right there.' He spoke to his mother again. 'I'd better go. That's Novak calling now.'

'He's early,' Anna said.

'Yeah, well, anyway, I better go.'

Anna shifted to an entirely different tone. One of sweetness and innocence. 'Okay, love you, Zachary. Call Claudia to let me know how it goes.'

How perfect, Zach thought. *I've to call your PA, not you.* 'Yeah, I will,' he replied. Then he hung up.

He shut his eyes and took a deep breath. Enjoying silence for all of ten seconds, before George appeared at the door again.

'Did you call me?'

'I...um, yeah, but...no.'

Baffled, she said, 'Okay, well, that's Tom Novak calling now.'

Zach kept his eyes shut for a moment, taking a beat. Then he messed up his frizzy hair a bit and unbuttoned his shirt. 'How do I look?' he asked.

'Casual,' Georgia said. 'Unassuming.'

'That's what we want,' he replied, then he accepted the incoming Zoom call on his computer. When he spoke, he was like a different person. He sounded optimistic, in control, and with a little effort, hopeful. 'Hi Tom. This is Zachary Storm. How are *you* today?'

CHAPTER SIX

A FEW MINUTES into the call, Zach had drawn a little stick man holding a gun pointing to the stick man's head, followed by a wild and violent blood spatter exploding out the other side of its head.

At the same time, Novak asked via video call, 'So what is it like having the world at your feet?' He followed it up with a wry chuckle intended to deflect the earnestly flattering question.

Zach folded over the paper he had been writing on to cover it up. 'I don't know that I do, exactly.'

'You run one of the biggest cryptocurrency exchanges in the world, you have a personal net worth – as of this morning – of about twenty-one billion dollars, you're working from a penthouse office in the Bahamas, and you're not even thirty yet. How did you get here? What's the story of Zach?'

'The story of Zach?' He chuckled at the phrase. 'There's not much to tell.'

'Come on, don't be modest. You're the son of Anna

Storm, founder and CEO of Storm Capital. The largest asset manager in the world. Then there's your dad, Noah Storm. An ethics lawyer at Stanford Law, who also runs Move the Needle, a political-donor network. Those are big shoes to fill.'

'It sounds like you know me better than I do.'

'Is it true that you were a millionaire at nineteen?'

Zach couldn't help but smile. 'That's true. I noticed that Bitcoin was trading in the US at ten thousand dollars, but on an exchange in Japan it was trading at eleven. I took out a loan for ten million dollars, buying at ten thousand, then sold at eleven thousand on the Japanese exchange. That one trade makes you a million dollars. I was able to do that every weekday.'

Open-mouthed, feigning that he was hearing the story for the first time, Novak asked, 'For how long?'

Zach shrugged. 'A couple of months before the Japanese noticed what I was doing. I started SCX soon after.'

'Ten million dollars is a lot to land as a loan at that age. Were there other investors involved in the trade?'

'I...had a little help from family members.'

'Your mom?'

Zach paused. 'My mom gave me excellent advice.'

Smiling at Zach's coy response, Novak said, 'Your mom naturally gets a lot of attention because of her profile. But your dad has been quietly accruing a lot of influence himself in recent years.'

Zach paused. 'I'm not sure what you mean.'

Novak pressed on, his tone turning more serious. 'Move the Needle has been a huge contributor to the Democrats, assembling donors that are some of the biggest names in Silicon Valley.'

Remembering what Anna had told him to say the previous night should the issue arise, Zach countered, 'Move the Needle has helped elect politicians on both sides of the aisle.'

'I think it's fair to say, though, that the Republicans it's helped elect have been on the liberal side of very Republican-leaning districts or states. Places where the Democrats have been locked out for decades. Move the Needle has been influential in keeping more liberal Republicans in office in those places.'

Zach paused. 'You'd have to talk to my dad about that. I don't really do politics.'

Novak made his best '*oh, come on*' face. 'Zach you've done multiple speaking events with Democratic former Presidents, you lobby for more regulation in the crypto market, and talk extensively about effective altruism.'

'I don't think effective altruism is exclusively a left-wing issue. What we care about at SCX is regulation. Our competitors don't want regulation, because they make more money in unregulated markets. What SCX wants – what I want – is a crypto market that doesn't have to exploit or cheat anyone.'

'Could you explain effective altruism for some of my readers who won't be familiar with it.'

'Sure,' he said cheerily, happy to get away from politics. 'Effective altruism is the idea that you can use evidence and reason to benefit as many people as possible. Part of that ideology is earn-to-give.'

'Okay, explain that concept for me.'

'So earn-to-give is the notion of becoming rich in order

to give your money away. I want to earn as much money as possible so that I can give it away, and benefit a lot of people.'

'What do you make of the charge that's been levelled at you by some critics who suggest this is just window-dressing to soften the image of someone running a major player in an extremely aggressive and largely unregulated market. There's a lot of dirty tricks in the crypto industry.'

Zach smiled broadly. 'There is certainly that. We like to think of ourselves here at SCX as the good guys, though. We believe there's a way to be successful in this industry while also doing the right thing.'

Novak nodded, pleased that he had just been given the perfect quote for his story if things went belly-up at SCX.

Zach went on, 'It always struck me that if you want to do the most good in the world, how can you ever rest? There's always something that needs to be done. I'll give you an example. When I first thought of the concept of earn-to-give, I was standing in the cereal aisle at Whole Foods. There was the brand name cereal I was used to buying – and I ate several boxes every week – and then there was a cheaper alternative. It was like eighty cents cheaper. I worked out that based on the number of boxes I ate, combined with the potential saving I could have made in the last year from switching to the cheaper cereal, I could have saved, like, three hundred dollars. And that's just on cereal. Extrapolating out all the other combinations of things I could have bought instead of what I had been buying, it ended up closer to seven hundred dollars that I had spent that could have stayed in my pocket, to be given to a more important cause than my personal cravings. It really did a number on me. I was useless for days just thinking about it.'

Novak countered, 'But surely once you go down that path, you have to follow it to the end. Why buy clothes when you could walk around wearing a bin bag? Why pay for basics like deodorant when that could save money too?'

'I've heard that argument before,' said Zach. 'All I can say is that it reminds me of this issue of Superman I once read when I was a little boy. Probably too little to really understand it all. So Superman is flying around the world doing all his usual incredible feats: saving lives, stopping natural disasters, and such. But the world doesn't fully sleep all at one time. It's always daytime somewhere, right? There's always *something* going on in the world that could have been prevented.'

'Right.'

'So if there are, then how can Superman ever sleep? How could he ever pause to take a drink? Or go to the bathroom?'

Novak started laughing, then realised by Zach's expression that he was deadly serious.

Zach went on, 'How can Superman waste a couple of hours dressed as Clark Kent, shooting the shit and flirting with Lois Lane at the *Daily Planet*, when in that same space of time, there have been hundreds of car crashes, kids falling into swimming pools, or buildings collapsing, or earthquakes, or boats sinking...Every time Superman stops means someone dies.'

'That's a little harsh, don't you think?'

'It's the *reality*, Tom. And it was the same with my expensive cereal. With the money I wasted on it, I could have spent it on sponsoring a recovering alcoholic. Or paying for someone's cancer meds.'

'It sounds to me like your mission isn't just to run a place to buy and sell Bitcoin. It's to change the world.'

'For the better, yeah. There's more to life than money.'

Zach sounded so earnest, for a moment, Novak actually believed him.

Lining up his final attack, Novak asked a cheeky softener. 'Does your mom believe that too?'

Zach snorted. 'No comment.'

'What about the future of SCX? The crypto market is changing rapidly. Do you predict any turbulence ahead?'

'I'm a positive person,' Zach said. 'I'm always optimistic about the future.'

'Even with the crypto market down fifteen per cent this morning?'

'Fifteen?' There was a quiver in Zach's voice. 'I had it as down five.'

'Yeah, since we started talking it's fallen another ten per cent.' Novak waited a long time for a response.

Zach tried not to let the horror on his face show on his webcam as he consulted his Bloomberg terminal just out of shot. The crypto market had been so buoyant for so many years now, he had honestly stopped checking it more than twice a day. 'Yeah, well...um, obviously for exchanges that are much less solvent than us, that's a difficult moment. But our assets are fine.'

'What if I told you I had a source on the record who claims that SCX isn't as liquid as it claims to be?'

Zach scoffed. 'Are you serious?'

'Deadly.'

'No,' he said, taking a huge dry gulp that was like a

dictionary image of nervousness. 'Like I said...our assets are fine.'

Novak nodded. 'Okay. Well, I guess that's all I need for now. Will you be available for follow-up?'

Zach sucked his teeth. 'Eh...that might be tricky. Let me talk to my assistant and we can have a look at my time. Because the next few weeks are really busy.'

'Yeah,' said Novak. 'I think they might be.'

The second the interview was over, Zach dialled into SCX's financials. Going back and forth between it and his Bloomberg terminal, he did some cocktail napkin maths. When he reached his conclusion, he mumbled to himself, 'Oh shit...' He yelled, 'Georgia! Get in here!'

She had never heard him sound so shaken before, but didn't think much of it until she noticed that his hands were shaking.

He said, 'Get my mom on the phone, please. Tell her it's an emergency.'

CHAPTER SEVEN

THE MOMENT she saw Novak off the video call with Zachary Storm, Stella wandered over. 'How did it go?' she asked.

'No smoking gun,' Novak replied. 'But he's hiding something, I swear. Speaking of which, did you know Ralph was going to drop that SCX bombshell in there earlier?'

'I had no idea. We talked yesterday, so he must have been working on it overnight.'

'He really doesn't stop.' Novak sighed when he found a note on his desk.

"CALL NATHAN – ALSO, I'M NOT YOUR SECRETARY. CARA."

Novak looked towards a young reporter who was typing away. 'Thanks, Cara.'

She paused just long enough to throw up a wave of acknowledgment.

After sneaking a glance at the note, Stella asked, 'Who's Nathan?'

Novak pretended not to have heard. 'Huh?'

'The note on your desk says to call Nathan.'

'Oh. Yeah. He's helping me with this thing tonight.'

'The archives launch, of course. That's exciting.'

'You're still coming, right?'

'Of course. Fitz is coming too. He just messaged me.' She paused. 'You don't seem overly enamoured.'

He shrugged. 'It's an event celebrating the launch of my dad's archives. A complete paper trail of his entire career. Barring the appearance of a coffin, it's the closest thing to a wake he's had since, you know...' He trailed off, realising he couldn't remember exactly how many years it had been since his dad had died. 'Nathan's been helping me sort out a roomful of chaos and folders and binders and hard drives. You think the Columbia Graduate School of Journalism will ever curate our archives?'

'Not for me,' said Stella. 'Once a story's done, I get rid of as much as I can. I don't want to think about it again, let alone comb through piles of old notes on a Sunday afternoon. What about you? Do you hoard your notes?'

'Yeah,' he chuckled. 'I guess I'm more like my old man than I care to admit sometimes.'

Stella had been looking away, thinking. 'You know, you still haven't told me who this Nathan is. If I didn't know any better, I'd say you were stalling so you could think up a lie.'

'What does it matter, Stella?'

She raised his eyebrows. It must have got to him if he was invoking her full name. 'What's his surname, Tom?'

'I know what you're going to say,' Novak warned her. 'Everyone deserves a second chance. Even Nathan Lugati.'

Her mouth fell open. 'Nathan Lugati? Nathan *Lugati*, Tom!'

Wincing at the volume of her voice, which had attracted the attention of most of the newsroom, Novak led her away from his desk. 'Say it a little louder, why don't you. He's got expertise that I needed for my dad's archives.'

'Then you're more forgiving than I thought,' said Stella.

Novak gestured wearily with his phone, exhausted at the thought of an argument on the subject. 'Look, I better make this call.'

As she walked back to her desk, Stella pointed to him. 'Okay. But Zoom with Ralph in twenty.'

When Novak got through to Nathan, he heard a panicked voice at the other end.

'Tom, I'm sorry to bother you. I think I've found something that...' Nathan trailed off. Purposely. He didn't know how to say it.

Novak waited. 'What is it?'

'It's about your dad, Tom. I think you should come see this.'

CHAPTER EIGHT

NESTLED between two Art Deco buildings off Broadway was a gated entrance to a long tree-lined walkway that led into the grounds of Columbia University. Within a few steps of entering the campus, the hustle and bustle of Manhattan gave way to lush greenery and lawns. A hallowed estate of epic libraries and grand lecture halls.

The Joseph Jamail Lecture Hall in the University's School of Journalism was packed to standing room only, eager graduate students crammed shoulder to shoulder with New York's cultural elite. People were lined up against the mahogany wall at the back, and all down the sides where enormous windows let in soft yellow light from outside. It was one of those perfect New York winter evenings: cold but dry, the night still young, the city transitioning from work into play.

Fleet Street legend and former *Republic* columnist Martin 'Fitz' Fitzhenry stood behind the lectern at the front of the room with meaty hands gripping its sides. His distinctly British, educated voice – a deep, resonant baritone – boomed across the room, driven by the hall's meticulously designed acoustics.

He sounded his usual self, but there were many in the crowd that were surprised by Fitz's appearance. Tom and Stella had grown accustomed to his recent weight loss, seeing him at the office every other day. But most in attendance hadn't seen him publicly for a long time, making the transformation more jarring.

'Why be a journalist?' asked Fitz.

The graduate students in the room seemed to collectively shift forward in their seats in anticipation of the answer. To them Fitz was everything they wanted to be. Provocative, charismatic, erudite. His uncanny ability to tell the world "it's not like that, it's like *this*" on any number of subjects, ranging from politics, to literature, to history, and religion, had made him an unlikely celebrity in the age of YouTube, as his many televised appearances and public debates with his intellectual opposites were viewed in the millions.

Fitz said, 'On the one hand, I became a journalist because I didn't want to have to rely on the press for information...' Riding the wave of chuckles around the room, he added seriously, 'Never underestimate how important it is to know what everyone else *thinks* is the news. Take the risk of thinking for yourself. Much more happiness, truth, beauty, and wisdom will come your way as a result.' He paused, then gave a cryptic smile. 'But I can tell from some of your faces that you would like a little more than that. As I feel like I'm in certain esteemed company this evening, I'll share the response I gave my father when he broke down in tears upon hearing I was choosing to work for a raggedy young upstart publication called *The New Statesman,* rather than following the family tradition of practicing law. I used a lot of words, but it came down to this: I couldn't ignore my personal passion, intellectual curiosity, and desire to engage with the world around me. In the law, one doesn't necessarily pursue the truth. One doesn't even really pursue justice. One merely pursues a man's right to defend himself, rightly or wrongly. And as a young man who saw the pursuit of truth to be above all else, what else could I do with myself? I suspect that the great Seymour Novak was no different...'

Stella, standing in the wings next to Tom, leaned closer to him and whispered, 'I'll never get tired of seeing this in person.'

Normally Novak would have responded, but all the talk of legacy and fathers was getting to him.

As Fitz drew his speech to a close, he gestured to Novak. 'Speaking of the future. I'm sure you'll all agree with me that in celebrating the life and work of Seymour Novak in the opening of this archive here at Columbia, it's worth questioning what's going to become of the profession that Seymour loved so much.'

Novak thought to himself, "*Yeah, he loved it so much he ran away from it for an easy pay day.*"

Fitz turned his hands outwards towards the audience. 'The answer to that lies in all of *your* hands. And this man...' He raised a bottle of water in Novak's direction. 'Tom Novak, ladies and gentlemen.'

The hall filled with warm applause – and a single cry of 'Tom, you rock!' – as Novak strode towards the lectern. Fitz embraced Novak on the way past, pausing and leaning in to his ear, 'He would have been proud of you, Tom.'

For a moment, Novak froze, while Fitz kept walking towards Stella in the wings.

Immediately, she knew that something was wrong.

Novak eventually found his way to the podium, then took three attempts to say, 'Good evening.'

Fitz whispered to Stella, 'What's the problem?'

'Him.' She nodded in the direction of Nathan Lugati, who stood on his own in the east wing of the stage, skulking in the shadows. She added caustically, 'Rasputin over there.'

CHAPTER NINE

STELLA EXPLAINED to Fitz what had happened earlier. With Novak's phone call to Nathan. How quickly Novak had left, and how long he was gone from the office. He missed the Zoom call with Ralph. Then he missed lunch, and a senior staff briefing. All the while, Stella couldn't get through to his phone, which was bypassing even his voice-mail: which she knew from experience meant that he had switched his phone off altogether.

While Novak continued his speech, Fitz leaned in to whisper, 'And what do you think's driven Tom to bring Nathan Lugati back into the fold?'

'God knows,' she replied.

'Did you ever find out what really happened?'

'It was all hushed up by Diane at the time, but she gave me the inside track on it one night when she was three sheets to the wind at a staff party.'

'What happened?'

'Put it this way, he's lucky that all that happened was he lost his job. Diane said he was juggling multiple stories, ran out of time on a deadline, so he made up some quotes for a piece that he thought would be buried online somewhere. Diane liked it so much, she put it on the front page of the next issue. It took less than twenty-four hours for chatter to start about the veracity of Nathan's quotes. It didn't take long for his credibility to get shot to pieces. He kind of ended up in the wilderness after that.'

Fitz said, 'It begs the question: why use Nathan to put together something as sensitive as his dad's archives?'

Stella shrugged and shook her head. 'Christ, this is painful...'

She and Fitz had never seen Novak give such a robotic speech before. Full of improvised platitudes and cliches because he kept deviating from his planned speech.

Novak looked down at the next words on the handwritten speech:

"Seymour Novak is the reason I became a journalist. Without him, I wouldn't be standing here in front of you tonight. That is why opening this archive means so much to me. This archive is a testament to him, and his career as a journalist. [PAUSE FOR APPLAUSE] Ladies and gentlemen, I now declare this archive open."

The more Novak stared at the words, the harder it became to say them aloud. He couldn't do it.

Stella was about to walk out to help him, when Fitz held her back.

'Wait,' he said. 'He'll get there.'

Nervous coughing and throat-clearing broke out around the room. Shuffling of feet. No one could bring themselves to watch, but they couldn't exactly turn their backs on the stage.

Novak finally spoke again. 'I thought I could do this.

But I'm not ready. I'm sorry everyone. This isn't going to happen.' He looked out into the audience for the dean of the university, Calder Lockwood, who was preparing to come up and say a few words next.

'I'm sorry, Calder,' said Novak. 'Pack it up.'

Scandalised murmuring spread across the room as it became clear Novak wasn't joking.

Stella took one step towards Novak, then realised he was exiting to the other side of the stage. Where Nathan was.

'I suppose,' Fitz quipped, 'this would be a good time for me to sneak a fag outside.'

CHAPTER TEN

STELLA FOUND Novak in an auxiliary room behind the lecture hall, far from the confused chattering he had left in his wake. The dean stormed past her, having had it out with Novak.

Alone for just a few seconds, Novak paced, rubbing his cropped hair violently, trying to wipe away the embarrassment of what had just happened. He took a deep breath as Stella entered.

'We don't have to talk if you don't want to,' she told him.

'Good. Because I don't.' He rubbed his face as the reality hit him. 'I don't know what happened. I wasn't thinking out there.'

'Tom,' Stella cautioned, 'I'm not entirely sure that you were *conscious* up there.'

The room was windowless, and had some basic office desks and chairs set up for hot desks for staff members needing to work somewhere on the fly.

Stella lingered by the door, assessing how close she

should come. It seemed like he needed space. 'Tom,' she said softly, leaning against one of the desks, 'what's going on? What's this all about?'

He stopped pacing and put his hands on his hips. 'I spoke to Nathan this morning.'

'Yeah, I know. That's what started all this.'

'All this what?'

Her eyes widened. How could he not know how distracted, how off he had been all day? 'You've been acting strangely ever since he called. You wouldn't talk to me. You've been withdrawn all afternoon, and you bailed on our video call with Ralph.'

Novak took a deep breath but said nothing.

Stella asked, 'What is Nathan even doing on this project? After everything he did.'

Novak scuffed his foot on the floor like a small child. 'Everyone deserves a second chance, Stel. Even Nathan.'

'No, not *even* Nathan. You've said that twice today. What he did was unforgivable.' She paused, wondering whether Novak would demonstrate in any way that he agreed. 'He flat-out made up a story, Tom. He just *made up* sources and quotes, then filed it for publication *knowing* it was fiction. He even handed in notes, for crying out loud. He sat down and invented notes and handed them in. It could have cost Diane her job.'

'Yeah, but it didn't.'

His flippant response only angered her further. 'Have you got any idea how humiliating it is for an editor to have to issue a retraction? I only ever had a minor one to put out, but it hangs around your neck for months, Tom. And it's very hard to shake off. Fortunately Diane was made of stronger stuff than most people. God knows how many other pieces Nathan cooked when he worked at *Republic*. We'll never know. When he was fired, he took his notes and hard drives with him.'

A voice from the doorway spoke up. 'Can I feel my ears burning?'

Nathan entered the room gently, like a doctor who had to tell a patient that they were dying. 'Have you told her yet?' he asked.

'Not yet,' Novak replied.

Stella asked, 'Told me what?'

Nathan said, 'Seymour left an unfinished story behind. I found it among his papers yesterday.'

'He was working on a story? I thought you said he treated ABC like a retirement home.'

'It seems he came out of retirement.' Nathan turned to Novak, as if he was unwilling to say it.

Novak said, 'In the notes Nathan found, there are references to Storm Capital, and political donations they made on both sides of the Atlantic.'

'So Ralph is right,' Stella said.

'Except this was six years ago. And then there's this...' Novak turned to Nathan. 'Show her.'

Nathan took a set of notes out of his shoulder bag and handed them to Stella. They were in a plastic sleeve, like police evidence.

After a brief look at them, Stella held her shoulders up in a shrug. 'Even a few years ago, Storm had the largest assets of any hedge fund in the world. It's hardly strange they were forging political connections. It probably explains why they're so far ahead of the pack now.'

'The difference,' said Nathan, 'is that those notes were in a fireproof box. Everything else of Seymour's was out in the open, left in random piles that I've been sorting out for the past month. What was so special about it?'

Stella handed the notes back, as if she was done with the subject. 'I'm more careful with material for current stories. I'm sure Seymour was no different.'

'He was a TV news anchor, Stel,' said Novak. 'The last time he broke a story, Ronald Reagan was president. The lead story in his first week at ABC was the Chernobyl disaster. Suddenly at the age of sixty-six, he decides to hide story notes in a fireproof box?'

Nathan added, 'Also, he had notes from a few other stories he was working on. None of them were kept in a box. That's not all, though.' He handed Stella another plastic sleeve. 'I also found this in the fireproof box. I charged it up to have a look on it.'

Inside the sleeve was an old Nokia mobile phone.

Stella looked at it in surprise. 'What was Seymour doing with a burner?'

Nathan navigated to the call history then showed it to her.

Arms folded, Novak said, 'Look at the date of the last incoming call.'

She paused, trying to remember. 'Is that...'

'The day he died,' Novak said. 'There's a message history with the number. A source. He was still working with a source in his final hours.'

'Which means what?'

'I have to finish what he started, Stel.'

'Whatever it was, it's six years old now, Tom. What are you expecting to find?'

'Call it closure, unfinished business. Whatever you want to call it. It's something I have to do.'

Stella nodded. Given her recent experiences with her own mother's dark past, she was one of the few people who understood what Novak was going through.

'Where do you want to start?' she asked.

But instead of Novak answering, Nathan spoke up. 'Seymour's notes constantly referred to a source known as RT.'

Novak added, 'It stands for Real Thing. When he was working with Diane, that's what he called sources on big stories.'

Nathan said, 'We need to find whoever RT is.'

'We?' replied Stella. She turned pointedly to Novak.

Novak said, 'The three of us. All we've got to go on are my dad's notes. No one understands the ins and outs of his notation like Nathan. He's spent the last month buried in his papers.'

Stella stared back in disbelief. 'Can I talk to you for a second. Privately?'

It took Nathan a moment to realise before taking his cue. 'I'll go back to the party, I guess.'

'Nathan,' said Novak. 'Not a word of this to anyone.'

He nodded as he put down the notes and burner phone on a table, then left the room.

Stella put her arms out. 'What are you doing? You're bringing him in on this?'

'Stella, the American people just elected a new President, and there's a new Prime Minister in Downing Street. If there's a story about corruption in election campaigning lying in a coma, now is the perfect time to bring it back to life. Nathan's got inside knowledge that could save us days, even weeks, of chasing dead-ends. Plus, we know he's got the chops.'

'He's got the chops, all right,' Stella retorted. 'The chops of a proven fabricator.'

'I saw him work in the field. He made some mistakes, all right—'

Stella scoffed.

Novak said, 'He was running thin with material and needed to break something big. He got desperate. He got stupid. But I know he can work well.'

'My feelings aside, you actually expect Mark to okay this?'

Novak paused. 'Let me worry about Mark.'

'And what about if this goes to press? Are you really going to share your by-line with someone whose reputation is in the toilet? If this is something, the White House and Downing Street have everything they need to pour cold water over it. "Nathan Lugati is a known liar, and is barking up the wrong tree with this one." Nothing to see here, the world moves on within a few hours.'

Novak snapped, 'And what if it's *not* that? Storm Capital have over ten trillion in assets. That's twice the GDP of Japan, by the way. They're the top stakeholder in the seven biggest banks in the United States. It owns most of the American mainstream media. They've got their hands on everything. Healthcare. The German postal system. Airlines. Insurance. And now they're starting to buy and control influence in governments. And now we've found ourselves investigating them independently of whatever my dad had going. Wherever this story was six years ago, it could be a hundred times bigger today. We can't let it get away.'

Stella took a long, heavy breath. 'Tom, I get it. This is personal for you, even if it could potentially be a story that matters. But I'm not seeing it. And I don't understand you bringing Nathan along on this. How did he even end up working on your dad's archives?'

'The dean of the university reached out to me about the archives last year, and I couldn't bring myself to deal with it. I bumped into him at a bar. I knew that he was out of work, and I thought he could help. He and my dad were always close, and I wanted someone who knew him to do the job. I'm not saying let's get him back on staff and give him a by-line. I'm saying, let's use him as freelance for background until we know what this is.'

Stella thought about it. 'No. For you to be this sure, there's something else. Something you're not telling me.'

Novak didn't bother trying to lie to her. He opened Nathan's messenger bag on the desk, and took out some paperwork. He handed it to Stella.

'What's this?' she asked. 'Flights to San José Airport? One night in a cheap hotel in Saratoga.'

'Look at the date,' he implored her.

It took her a few seconds to realise. 'Is that...?'

'The day he died. About an hour from the estimated time of death, in fact.'

'You can't think...'

'Who books a plane ticket and a hotel an hour before killing themselves, Stella?'

She didn't have an answer.

But Novak knew she would ask the next question soon enough.

'Wait,' she began. 'Why *this* hotel in Saratoga? Your dad was well off.'

'Why book somewhere so crumby?' asked Novak.

'Unless he didn't want to draw any attention.'

'And who has their headquarters in Saratoga?'

Stella shook her head.

Novak answered, 'Storm Capital.'

Stella puffed, trying to get her head around things. Novak had been stewing on the material for a while now. It was going to be hard to talk him back. 'This could all be perfectly innocent, Tom. I mean, there *was* an autopsy, wasn't there? I was under the impression there wasn't any doubt.'

'Because I wasn't around to ask the right questions. Maybe it is nothing. But we have to find out what this is. I can't open these archives up to the public before I know. I need closure, Stel. And I want the public to know he still had one great story left in him.' He pointed to the burner phone Nathan had left on the desk. 'We need someone who can reach into that phone and take us to six years ago.'

Stella nodded. 'We only know one person who can do a job like that.'

'Do you think she'll do it?'

Before Stella could answer, Nathan suddenly appeared in the doorway, out of breath. 'Guys...you better come quick. It's Fitz.' Without explaining further, he waved them urgently out of the room. 'He's collapsed outside.'

Novak charged ahead. 'What happened?'

Clearly in shock, Nathan spluttered, 'I don't know...but it's not looking good.'

Stella covered her mouth in shock when they reached a point in the lecture hall where she could see through the windows towards a small patio.

A man was crouching over Fitz's inert body, administering increasingly desperate CPR.

CHAPTER ELEVEN

STELLA WAS in the middle of an argument with a coffee machine on the seventh floor of Lenox Hill Hospital, and the machine was winning. 'Son of a...' she trailed off, then gave the machine a bash with her hand. It was a phrase she never would have thought to use back in London, but she had increasingly found some Americanisms bleeding into her everyday language.

Nathan had been skulking around on the periphery of the waiting area outside the cardiac ward, which Fitz had been moved to three hours earlier.

The bash of the machine did the trick, and Stella's espresso (or at least something that looked like an espresso) started trickling into a plastic cup. Catching sight of Nathan in her peripheral vision, Stella muttered to herself, 'Please don't come over, please don't come over...' She shut her eyes. The next she heard was Nathan saying her name.

'Stella,' he said cautiously. 'I thought maybe we should talk.'

She sighed. 'It's really not a good time, Nathan.'

'I know you don't want me on this story.'

She picked up her coffee cup, which was ridiculously thin. But she squeezed too hard, forcing scalding hot coffee up over the sides. Recoiling in pain, she dropped the cup.

Nathan held out a hand and crouched down to clear up the mess.

Testily, Stella snapped, 'I'll get it.' But she was incapable of doing anything other than clutching her burned hand.

Nathan mopped up the mess with a few paper napkins. He then ushered her over to the water fountain, where cold water was running freely from the tap he held down.

Reluctantly, she said, 'Thanks.'

Nathan repeated, 'I know you don't want me on this story—'

'It's not a story yet,' Stella replied through a wince. the cold water hitting the wound which was already blistering.

'You wouldn't have the story without me.'

Stella knew she should have kept her hand under the water longer, but she didn't want to be in the same space as Nathan. Stepping away, she said, 'It's not yours to give away. It was Seymour's. And whoever RT is. Or was. That's what you've got us chasing. A story where at least one, and possibly both, of the main sources are dead. Chuck in your questionable past, and all I can see is a story that no one will touch with a ten-foot barge pole.'

Nathan squinted. 'I heard Fitz use that phrase once before. What exactly does it mean?'

'As in canals. You know, narrowboats...' She shook her head in irritation. 'I'm really not in the mood to be explaining about English canals, Nathan. The point is, you need Tom and I a hell of a lot more than we need you.'

Nathan said nothing.

Rethinking her tone, she corrected herself. 'I'm just trying to be frank with you. I mean, let's be honest. This is your last shot to get your foot back in the door, isn't it? You've been in the wilderness now for, what, six years? If you don't land a big story soon then it's game over for you.'

He stared back at her, defiantly. 'You have no idea what I've been through. What actually happened back then.'

'Oh, I heard all about it,' Stella replied. 'Diane Schlesinger told me. Novak might have given you an easy ride at the time because his dad had just died. But Diane's career dangled by a thread because of you. Diane bloody Schlesinger. A titan of an editor. Someone to be mentioned in the same breath as Ben Bradlee, Ralph McGill, or HL Mencken. To think that someone like *you* could have brought down someone like *her*...beggar's belief. I won't let you do the same thing to Tom. You pale in comparison to him.' She took a step towards him. 'Let me promise you something. If you ever step out, or do anything that threatens Tom or the credibility of *The Republic,* I will personally *end* you.' She stepped past him. 'He can't see you for what you are.' She added with finality, 'I can.'

Nathan stared hard at her as she walked away, so sure she had delivered some crippling blow. He knew that everything would change when she and Tom found out about what had really happened around Seymour's story and his death.

But for the moment, that was a secret he wasn't just *willing* to keep. His life and theirs depended on it.

CHAPTER TWELVE

IT HAD TURNED into one of those nights that felt like it was lasting for days. When some calamitous event or tragedy occurred that would come to define, if not someone's life, then at least a major part of it. Novak would always remember where he was the night of Fitz's second heart attack.

On his way back and forth through the hospital's endless corridors, Novak noticed the impact of illness on those unfortunate enough to be roaming the corridors at two in the morning. Splashed out on hard plastic chairs, staring at the floor. Or pacing with dread, tension etched on their faces. They all looked so shellshocked. Novak was distraught too, of course, that Fitz might die that night. The difference between Novak and the others was acceptance. The idea of losing someone you love was a new concept to the others. For Novak, he was more than familiar with it. It didn't shock him, or disturb him. He merely accepted it as common. As fact. That's what happens when you discover your mother hanging from a rope inside the garage of your family home when you're seven years old. You don't see the world as full of hope and joy. It's chaos and blind luck. That's all life was to Novak.

In a way, and once the dust had settled on his mother's suicide, he felt lucky. Because his school friends thought that not getting what you wanted for Christmas was a tragedy. Or having a pet die was what loss felt like. He, on the other hand, knew what the world really was: it was dark, dangerous, and was fatal to one hundred per cent of humanity. The only question was when your time would be up. And could you possibly play some part in delaying it, or giving it some greater meaning?

Novak stared out the window of the seventh floor of Lenox Hill Hospital overlooking Central Park. Amid the glamour and riches of Park Avenue, Lenox Hill competed against some of the greatest health institutions in the world. Historically, it had been a glorified community hospital, full of old ladies mostly. But its cardiac ward had quietly become one of the best in the country thanks to the relentless dedication of Dr Frank Blum. Fitz's cardiologist since his first heart attack.

Novak had been standing at the window holding a machine coffee for so long it had gone cold. He didn't hear Dr Blum approaching from behind.

Now into the third hour of waiting since Fitz's transfer from Lenox Hill ER, Novak's thoughts had drifted to the city he loved so dearly. The New York City that Frank Sinatra sang about. That Woody Allen made movies about. That was old New York. And it was over with now.

From a few feet away, Dr Blum said, 'You're the one constant whenever Martin's heart gives out, Mr Novak. I'm thinking of prescribing him ten years away from you.'

With the slightest of smiles, Novak asked, 'Any news?'

'He's stable.'

'What do you think his chances are?'

He paused. 'I don't think it's helpful to start going down that road yet.'

Novak stared into his hands. 'The EMTs said his heart stopped for over six minutes. Brain damage can happen after just five minutes.'

'Really? Gosh, someone should have taught me that at med school.'

Appreciating the dry sense of humour in the circumstances, Novak smiled as he realised how stupid the sentence was given the company he was in. 'Sorry. Yeah. I don't know why I said that.'

Blum playfully scolded him, 'Someone's been passing the time Googling cardiac arrest, haven't they? Seriously, though, you're right. He's not out of the woods yet. We're still running some tests. I thought you looked like you could do with some company.'

Novak looked out of the window again.

Sensing the contemplative moment, Blum stood next to him, quiet for a moment before saying, 'I never liked the East Side. Sure, it's got Fifth Avenue: Tiffany's, Cartier, Saks. The sidewalks are wide, grander. But it all leaves me cold.'

'I don't know,' replied Novak. 'It all seems the same to me now. There used to be subtle differences between the neighbourhoods. Now it's just all for the wealthy. Homogenised.'

'My dad said the same thing to me.'

'Oh yeah?'

'Yeah. In nineteen eighty-seven.' Blum chuckled. 'This is New York City. Things don't change *that* much.'

'I don't know,' said Novak. 'Feels like a lot of things are changing.'

It wasn't just about the city. All the old ways were dying, as far as Novak saw it. The internet and social media had co-opted the profession he loved so much, and bastardised it into a war for eyeballs, for views, for clicks. And in the rush to the bottom, the vortex that had been created pulled in everything and everyone. You couldn't even trust *The New York Times* anymore. All the old institutions either being taken over by Saudi oil money, or quietly going out of business. In Novak's mind, there was no greater example of the old New York business of being a reporter than, ironically, Englishman Martin Fitzhenry. He made literature, politics, and culture exciting, and – even for a man who chain-smoked and had drunk his way through the entire eighties, nineties and most of the noughties – sexy.

Now it was all people half his age that did their entire job on their phones and without ever sitting in on anything as archaic as an editorial meeting. Their idea of a liquid lunch was having a vegan protein shake. And absolutely none of them ever read books. Not that Novak had any actual evidence of that, but it certainly explained a lot about the current journalistic landscape.

'Did you always want to do this?' asked Novak.

'Yeah. Always,' replied Blum.

'Why? I mean, why cardiology?'

'Because my dad was a cardiologist here back in the seventies. It was very different here then. It was a draughty old building then.'

'Sort of the family business?'

'In a way. A bit like you.'

Novak scoffed. 'My dad and I weren't in the same line of work. He was for a while. But he chose money instead. Took the easy route. How about your old man? He still around?'

Blum paused. 'He had a heart attack when I was a boy. He was barely forty years old.' He smiled ruefully. 'Even doctors don't always follow their own advice – even now. I blame the late-night bacon sandwiches, personally. One night, I heard this scream from my parent's bedroom. It was my mother. She kept yelling for me to call nine one one. After I made the call, she told me not to come in. Not to look. All I could see was his feet sticking out past the end of the bed. I knew it was serious when the EMTs arrived. They didn't just run in. They practically charged through the walls to get to him. I know that EMTs see death every day, etcetera. But these guys looked panicked when they got there. I think they knew what was at stake. It was just me and my mother there. You would have thought it was one of their own family members on the line to look at them. Anyway...when they left the bedroom after failing to revive my dad, there was a brief moment when there was no one else in the bedroom. So I snuck in and looked.' Blum shook his head. 'I'll never forget what I saw that night.'

'What did you see?' asked Novak.

'I saw nothing. Just...nothing. How quickly it had all gone. The richness of my dad's life. His beliefs, his desires, his experiences. All gone – extinguished – in a matter of minutes. And then it was all over. No more life, just like that.'

'So you want to save lives for the life you couldn't save?'

Blum snorted. 'If only it were that simple. No. I just wanted to be like him. I was embarrassingly old before I realised that not every son wants to be like their dad.'

'Quite the opposite,' agreed Novak.

Given that Blum didn't have a clue what Novak had been dealing with regarding his own father's demise, the observation hit Novak like a bus. There was Blum, a man of advancing years, still talking in glowing terms about his dad.

Novak said, 'It sounds like he was a real mountain of a man to you.'

'Sure was.'

Novak stared into his hands again. 'I didn't even cry at my dad's funeral. Is that bad? I feel bad about it. It's not like he was abusive or anything. He deserved some tears at least. But I just couldn't manage it. I was too angry.'

'What were you angry about?'

Novak shook his head. 'So many things.'

'Take it from someone who's a little further down the road than you. You've got to let that stuff go, Tom. It'll eat you up inside.'

'What do you suggest?'

'Think about him. Let yourself cry. Let it out. You'll probably surprise yourself once you get started.'

'I don't know…I've felt so disconnected from him for so long. I don't even feel like someone's son anymore.'

As a dad himself, that hit Blum hard. 'That's something you'll always be. No one can ever take that away from you. It's up to you to decide how much of a son you feel.'

Seeing Stella approaching – with Nathan in tow – Dr Frank patted Novak on the arm. A paternal pat. Then told him, 'I don't know what's going to happen, but I promise you, I'll give Fitz everything I've got.' Then he winked at him.

Novak was envious of men who could pull off winks and have it not be creepy or weird. At what age was it okay for a man to start winking? And how did you know when you're ready? After all, just trying it out seemed awfully risky. But a cuddly old bear of a man like Dr Frank Blum could pull it off handily.

When Fitz first went under Blum's care, Novak had taken the time to read up on him to ensure Fitz was in safe hands. According to Novak's research, Blum had walked away from a tenure position at Cornell University to take over the cardiac unit at Lenox Hill. Teaching at Cornell was as good as it got. Still was. Prestigious. Great pay, great environment, great everything. Yet Blum had walked away from it all. At the time, Novak had wondered why. What made someone walk away from that to start over with nothing. A nothing department in a nothing hospital, in a city where being *some*thing is *every*thing.

Now Novak knew the answer: because Frank Blum wanted to make his dad proud decades after he'd been put in the ground.

'Thanks, doc,' Novak told him.

Once Blum had gone, Stella asked Novak, 'Any news?'

'Status quo,' he replied, then sighed. 'Why do I get the feeling that even if Fitz pulls through, we're out on our own now? Mark's an empty shirt as an editor, Fitz is the last of my dad's generation, and Diane's gone too.'

'It's up to us to lead the charge,' Stella said.

'To where?'

Stella looked behind her at Nathan. 'Well, actually, we might have something on that.'

Nathan said, 'I went home to check my notes on your dad's archives.'

'What did you find?' asked Novak.

'RT's phone number.'

'The source?'

Almost licking his lips, Nathan replied, 'Yep.'

Novak glanced at Stella. 'What do you think?'

'I think it's worth a shot,' she said.

Nathan asked, 'You know someone who can run a trace?'

'Yeah,' said Novak.

'Can you get them out of bed?'

'That depends.'

'On what?'

Novak said, 'What time it is in London.'

CHAPTER THIRTEEN

LONDON – 6.07AM

REBECCA FOX HAD BEEN RUNNING HARD since she passed the Oxo tower wharf on the south bank of the River Thames. Dawn sunlight was still some way off, a crisp December chill in the air.

The footpath beside the river that she'd been following – as she followed every morning – was quiet as usual. It had always fascinated Rebecca to wonder what sort of people were up at such an ungodly hour. Dedicated office workers putting in extra time to secure a promotion. Or were they cleaners, cooks, and baristas? Or people who worked in London transport? The people who really got the city up and running in the morning.

And, of course, there were other runners.

Rebecca's dedication to running began as a necessity: pressure at work had meant she was often working sixteen-hour days. Most of it sitting down behind a computer or attending meetings with intelligence officials. Running was simply a way to get moving without having to join a gym – which had been unthinkable to her. But gradually, over the course of the last year, running had consumed her. Now she *needed* it. And if she didn't get a run in, it was like not having a coffee in the morning: everything went to shit, and her head hurt by nine o'clock. She even had the windproof leggings and tiny backpack favoured by so many runners. Now she was one herself, she understood perfectly that it wasn't about looking cool. Like cyclists, it was impossible to look 'cool' in all the right gear. What mattered most was comfort, and not overheating or being too cold.

Rebecca should have been focussed on the path ahead. Instead, she was fixating on a tall, black, athletic man around her age, wearing a dark hoodie. He had been running behind her since Oxo Tower, and had been trying and failing to keep up with her.

When she passed Millennium Bridge, she did a shoulder-check. He was still right there with her.

Upping her pace at Southwark Bridge, she tried to drop him. Her chest was tight, lungs burning, and legs going numb. Crossing Tower Bridge, she was only halfway through her five-mile run and she already felt like death. She had set off much too hard. But the alternative of having the man catch her was far worse than the pain that was consuming her body from the ground up, enveloping her entire body.

On the north side of the river on Upper Thames Street, her vision began to go cloudy at the edges. Darkening. She couldn't stay ahead of him much longer. Every fibre in her body was telling her to stop, but still she pressed on and on.

The construction that had been ongoing at One Millennium Bridge House for the last eighteen months forced her down a small side street, down onto Paul's Walk by the riverside again. A narrower path that was much quieter than the favoured south side for runners.

Rebecca's body tightened. She kept running and gasping for more oxygen, but it was useless.

The man was going to make the catch.

Under Blackfriar's Railway Bridge, the man lunged for her with an outstretched arm.

Rebecca relented and stopped running.

The man charged into the back of her, driven by his own inertia. He was similarly out of breath.

'It really...is...true,' he spluttered, leaning over on his knees. 'It doesn't get any less painful. You just go faster.'

Rebecca paced in circles, regaining control of her breathing.

The man came closer and embraced her.

All Rebecca could manage was draping a limp arm around his shoulder for a second, before letting it drop back off again. 'Pace?' she asked through deep heaves.

He checked his sports watch. 'Four minutes and twenty seconds per kilometre. Fastest ever. I mean, I love you and everything, but all this chasing you every morning is killing me.' He kissed her on the cheek.

'Don't, Leon,' she said, turning away. 'I'm a sweaty mess.'

He laughed. 'And I'm not? Also, about a hundred people just saw a black man chasing a white woman across London. If we don't look like a couple I'll have armed response coming down on me in the next two minutes.'

She pulled him closer and kissed him. 'I'm sure they'll recognise you, Detective Constable Walker.'

'I am incredibly important, yes. And powerful. Very

sexually powerful and magnetic because of how important I am.'

Rebecca nodded sarcastically. 'Of course.' She nodded in the direction of home, back towards Oxo Tower across the river. 'Come on, we better jog back. We're both going to be late.'

As they ran side by side, talking about how manic their days both looked, and the numerous pressures they were both under, Rebecca couldn't help thinking how lucky she was. After everything she had been through with Tom and Stella, and then losing her father, her life was finally on an even keel. And it had been at least several months since anyone had tried to kill her. As far as she was aware.

She knew it wasn't fashionable to talk of feeling safe with a man, but Leon Walker of the Metropolitan Police made her feel exactly that.

A fellow runner checked her watch as she passed the couple, going in the opposite direction. Once they were a safe distance away, she spoke into the lapel mic hidden inside her windproof jacket.

'Target heading south across Blackfriars Bridge. Could be an opportunity to engage at the residence.'

The response was swift. American. Devoid of feeling. 'Negative. We stick to the plan.'

CHAPTER FOURTEEN

THE THREE MEN had been waiting in the anonymous white van for what seemed like an eternity. At least to Damian the American, and Lee the London-native. Because Sean, another Londoner, sitting behind them, hadn't stopped talking since Damian had switched off the engine.

There were a few things Damian looked for in a work associate. Modesty. Diligence. Calmness. Three things that Sean was not. He was also a good five years younger than the other men. Compared to them, he looked and sounded like a boy playing the part of a man. And by the looks that Lee had been shooting in Damian's direction, it was clear that the two of them were on the same page about Sean.

Sean leaned forward, resting his hands on the back of Damian and Lee's seats. 'What kind of piece do you carry, then?' he asked, nodding his head as if he was listening to music. He'd had too much coffee.

Damian shrugged his shoulders in annoyance to stop Sean touching him. 'Whatever,' Damian said, keeping his eyes firmly on the view out the van. Who was going where. Who looked like they belonged. Who didn't. It was hard to describe other than something that was *off*. You knew it when you saw it.

Lee, who had been showing Sean only a modicum of extra patience compared to Damian, answered, 'Glock 17, mate.'

Sean's nods deepened in appreciation. 'Nice, nice. I'm a Beretta 92 man, myself. But that's because I've got big hands, eh.' He laughed in a way that was far too loud for the confined space they were sharing.

Damian turned around and gave Sean a dead-eyed stare. 'Why don't you quieten down.' It wasn't a question. 'Take a few deep breaths and stop talking. You've had too much caffeine. You're jumping about back there like a goddamn jack rabbit.'

Sean pulled back a little, looking this way and that from one window to the next. He was looking at everything, and seeing nothing. Taking nothing in. His thoughts were entirely taken up by what he was going to say next. 'Yeah, love my Beretta. But I tell you, I don't need hardware to get the job done. For real.' He sniffed hard, then wiped his nose with his thumb. 'I even done in this guy in the nick with a shoelace. For real.'

Lee squinted. He couldn't help but be interested. 'Yeah?'

'Yeah,' Sean said. 'Shoved a shoelace down the guy's throat. It was dangling in there while I kneeled on his hands.' He let out another burst of laughter. 'He couldn't do nothing! I mean, this guy was—'

Damian held up a hand. 'Stop talking.'

Sean paused. 'What's up? You the quiet, contemplative type?' He chuckled and looked to Lee for some support.

Lee didn't react.

Damian said, 'No. We're doing this job as independent contractors. The point is that we don't know anything about each other. Not our real names. Nothing. So I question the wisdom of talking about killing someone in prison with shoelaces. If I asked around for a few weeks, I'll bet I could come up with the name of a skinny black guy like you that did someone in with a shoelace. But you didn't think about that when you started your little story, did you?'

Sean was humbled into silence finally.

A beep from Damian's phone pierced the tension in the air.

'Fuck,' Damian said.

'What's wrong?' asked Lee.

'Change of plan.'

'How come?'

'The security guard we need was taken into hospital last night.'

'Is it serious?' asked Lee. 'Can't we just use him once he's out?'

'The client was clear that the job had to be done today. It's time for plan B.'

'What's Plan B?' asked Sean.

Damian scrolled through his phone, then showed Sean a photo of a man in his mid-twenties with short dreadlocks. The photo had been taken from official Home Office documents from UK Visas and Immigration. The name under the photo identified the man as 'WILSON KIPCHOGE.'

Damian pocketed his phone then started the van

engine. The house they had been staking out for the last hour was a bust.

Testing if it was safe to speak again, Sean asked, 'What now?'

'You better get yourselves dialled in,' Damian warned. 'This one's going to get a little messy.'

CHAPTER FIFTEEN

SEVEN TO NINE HOURS, thought Wilson, staring at the mould-ridden ceiling above him.

He put down the wrinkled paperback that he had found on the bus home the previous night: *The Science of Sleep*.

How could he ever achieve seven to nine hours of sleep in such a place?

Wilson looked around the gloomy room. The curtains were paper thin and hanging loosely from the pole. At least the sun hadn't risen yet.

There were six other men sleeping around him on bare mattresses. Like Wilson, they were all immigrants. All from different countries. Not one of them spoke the same first language. Basic English united them. Wilson was the only fluent one, having learned it in school in his native Uganda. No one else could hold down a simple conversation. No likes or dislikes or anything to do with how the men felt. All they had was nouns. Logistics. The names of places. And times. That's what their world revolved around. From one job to another. The endless coming and going and total lack of trying to keep the noise down in the kitchen or bathroom meant that Wilson had been surviving on as little as three hours of sleep a night.

The book spoke of such a sleep deficit over the course of several months in terms of actual torture. That the brain in that state is at a similar level to someone three times over the drink drive limit.

Spooked by the thought that his brain was being eaten away by exhaustion, Wilson put the book down and went to the bathroom.

He splashed water on his face, being sure to run the tap gently so as to not wake his flatmates. If only they were as thoughtful, Wilson thought to himself. Whenever he came back from a night shift, the other men would often clatter plates around in the kitchen, or turn up the television much louder than it needed to be on.

He dried his face on a towel that had once been white, and was now a stale yellow. The only towel in the house. He stared at himself in the mirror, then shut his eyes. He told himself the mantra he fell back on when times were tough. When he was so exhausted pushing a vacuum cleaner around a call centre that he would shut his eyes for several seconds at a time. Or mopping a concrete staircase that he was too tired to climb up.

He whispered to himself, "It's for Lucinda and the boys. For Lucinda and the boys. It will all be worth it..."

Just another three months of sending money back home, and then his wife and sons could join him there.

Then his mantra was interrupted by the sound of four muffled pops outside. The walls were thin in their high-rise building. Was someone slamming doors?

Wilson was about to open the bathroom door, when multiple screams rang out in the bedroom. Wilson staggered back away from the door in terror. What was happening out there? He had never heard such terrified, anguished screams in his life.

In the bedroom doorway, three men in hoods were standing there firing guns at the sleeping men. After the first few shots, the others tried to hide, but there was nowhere to go. Nowhere to run.

One of the shooters pulled back the blankets to see the victims' faces. 'He's not here,' he said.

'He's here,' said Damian, noticing one of the men still moving on a mattress. He pointed to him, then told Sean, 'Finish him.'

Sean hesitated. 'What?'

'There's no reason to leave any witnesses. Finish him.'

The man on the floor had already been shot twice, and was now dragging himself towards the door. He was only a few feet away, but it might as well have been miles. He reached out a hand towards the hall. Towards the bathroom door. Towards the light leaking out under the door.

His last-ever thought was that he hoped Wilson somehow managed to escape. He had always liked Wilson. Appreciated how he kept the noise down. Shared food. Or let him borrow his boots when it was raining outside.

Sean still wasn't shooting. 'He's not the job. This wasn't the job!' He was losing composure now, and it was obvious.

Damian insisted, 'I say what the job is.' Still staring at Sean, Damian fired a bullet into the back of the man's head.

Sean reeled away, spluttering, 'Fuck...' Recoiling in disgust.

It meant nothing to Damian. Killing one, or killing

seven. It didn't make a difference. Because why leave anyone living who can describe your build, or your accent – even through a police translator.

Lee wasn't getting involved. He was too fixated on the light visible under the bathroom door. He tapped Damian on the arm without saying anything. Then he pointed at the light.

Damian nodded.

Lee kicked the door in with a meaty boot. The door flew off its weak hinges, nearly wiping out Wilson who was cowering on the floor in a crouch.

'Please, please,' he begged. 'I have a wife. And two sons. I don't have any money.'

Damian stepped past Lee and stood over Wilson. 'I know,' he said. Then he shot Wilson in the head.

Sean couldn't even watch now. He was too busy throwing up in the hallway.

'For fuck's sake,' complained Lee.

Apparently Sean had been bullshitting about his shoelaces story. And, likely, a lot else.

'Get him out of here,' Damian told him, crouching by Wilson's body. Using a scanner the size of a phone, he took an image of Wilson's thumbprint. When he put the scanner back in his pocket, he realised Lee had pulled out a knife and was facing Sean, who was still buckled over, retching.

With just a look, Lee asked Damian for permission.

Damian pushed his arm down, and shook his head, *no*.

Wilson Kipchoge lay dead on the bathroom floor. The final image of his short life a peeling, mould-covered ceiling in a Hackney flat, over six thousand miles from home.

This was the problem working with hired guns from across the pond, thought Damian. Hiring over the dark web was always a lottery. The nature of the job meant that he needed some locals. Not just for driving in a potential fast getaway on roads Damian had never been on before, but for the next and final stage of the job, he needed someone with a familiar London accent.

Lee had been a safe pair off hands so far, but Sean was clearly a chancer who, against Damian's better instincts, had talked Damian into giving him the job. There weren't any other willing applicants. Too dangerous. Even for the sort that browsed the dark web looking for assassination jobs. Though the really dangerous part was yet to come.

Their base in Wembley was one of dozens of corrugated iron warehouses in a quiet industrial estate. The sort that littered the area. Sean was sick once more during the drive back.

Neither Damian nor Lee said a word. Saving their rage at Sean until they were somewhere they could do something about it.

Lee dragged Sean by the scruff of the neck back into the warehouse. Sean was apologising abjectly. 'Sorry, guys. It's been a while since I had a wobble...'

'You're not being paid to have wobbles,' Lee spat.

'See,' Damian began, ripping off bin bags from a roll, 'the problem I've got, is that I'm leading this job.' He took off his jacket and stuffed it into the bag, then he offered the bag to Lee, who did the same. 'And now I can't trust you to finish the job.'

Sean held out a reassuring hand, standing between Damian and Lee. 'I'm good,' he explained to them one at a time. 'All right, boys. I'm good.'

'I should have trusted my instincts,' said Damian. 'You're a lightweight.'

Noticing his eyes shift slightly, looking towards Lee behind, Sean flicked around in a sudden panic. It was too late.

Lee reached over Sean's shoulder and slid his knife across Sean's throat.

Damian then took the black bag over to the van, which was backed up to a roller shutter door. 'Leave him,' Damian said. 'The job will be over soon anyway.'

CHAPTER SIXTEEN

THE FIVE-STOREY GREY building on the riverfront of the City's Square Mile wasn't much to look at. Few people gave it much thought, if they even noticed it at all amongst the anonymous and dull glass headquarters of various financial institutions. Yet, for a building with no lights on, no front door, and seemingly empty inside, if you looked closely enough you would find it curiously well protected. There were, in fact, plenty of lights on behind the special blackout lacquer painted onto the inside of the windows on the third floor – and plenty of life.

It didn't have the grandiosity of MI5's Thames House, or the conspicuous flamboyance of the MI6 building at Vauxhall Cross, but inside that grey building operated one of the most vital arms of the British intelligence services.

The sign outside said "STANLEY HOUSE" – a respectful nod to the great sacrifices made to the security of the country by Rebecca's own father, Stanley Fox. To those who knew what really went on inside, it was known by a different moniker.

Ghost Division.

The internal affairs department for the British intelligence community. An agency charged with investigating corruption and criminality within the agencies meant to protect the country and its citizens. MI6, MI5, GCHQ, and Defence Intelligence.

Director of Ghost Division, Rebecca Fox, arrived by car despite her home across the river being only a short walk away. It wasn't laziness. It was on the orders of MI5 director James Blakely, who feared for Rebecca's safety. Particularly in light of the staggering levels of criminality she had uncovered within British intelligence since Ghost Division's inception.

She was no longer just a young upstart. She was part of the fabric of the intelligence establishment.

After clearing a black and yellow-striped security barrier that lowered into the ground, Rebecca parked in the recently built underground car park. At the basement entrance – which was covered with dozens of CCTV cameras – she entered a code into a keypad panel which opened electronic doors. The architecture was Brutalist, industrial. More than a hint of Soviet bloc government buildings.

A guard immediately rose from his chair in the nondescript lobby, standing in a booth protected by bulletproof glass. He may have looked like a supermarket security guard in his simple outfit of white shirt and navy sweater and trousers, but he was an Advanced Firearms-trained officer, and member of the Parliamentary and Diplomatic Protection unit. He didn't know exactly what went on upstairs on the third floor, though, where Ghost Division carried out its investigations. It wasn't big enough to demand further floors in the building, though there had been talk around Westminster circles of expanding the department. Especially in light of the Angela Curtis affair, which had prompted widespread protests, months of headlines, and brought the public's trust in politicians to an all-time low.

Rebecca observed the guard with surprise. 'You were on last week, too, Jerry.'

Jerry replied, 'Yeah, Victor was taken into hospital last night. Gallstones. Doctor had to insist. Apparently he was kicking and screaming that he was fine, that he needed to work today.' He shook his head with a smile. 'Can't say I share his enthusiasm. But we'll make the best of it, won't we.'

Although Rebecca was unaccompanied, Jerry followed the strict procedures that Rebecca had put in place. With a swipe of her security pass, her personnel profile appeared on the computer screen built into Jerry's desk. Visible only to him, Jerry was focussed on a window at the centre of the screen. On one side was an expected response flagged as "UNDER DURESS", and on the opposite side "SAFE". In a window above, it said "PROMPT: WEATHER."

'How is the weather this morning, Director?' he asked.

Rebecca replied, 'Clear skies.'

To the uninitiated, it might have sounded a strange response, as the skies over London were a blanket of grey and insistent drizzle.

Checking the UNDER DURESS response of "SNOW MOVING IN" versus the SAFE response of "CLEAR SKIES", Jerry buzzed her through the next set of double doors.

It didn't matter that Rebecca was alone. The process

was in place to protect against all possibilities. Even one that included Rebecca being strapped with explosives against her will and forced to enter the building.

An extreme notion. But if terror attacks since 9/11 had proven anything, it was that intelligence services had to expect the unexpected.

CHAPTER SEVENTEEN

THERE WERE twenty-five employees of Ghost Division, most of them concentrated around a central control room dominated by a vast video wall for live operations. It was a compact office space for a dozen analysts set up in a circular formation to make communication clear and easy. Rebecca's office was accessible to all, and had glass walls, as did the conference room – something she had specifically requested to demonstrate how transparently she did her job, and how accessible she was to all her staff.

The morning briefing took place every day at seven in the conference room, always a lively social affair. A chance for department heads to exchange information, but also to let off steam with each other. The activities of Ghost Division were such that they were not always the most liked operatives in the intelligence services. The 'big four' agencies regularly treated their enquiries with rudeness bordering on abusiveness.

In attendance that morning, as always, were the department heads responsible for investigating each of the intelligence agencies, along with Rebecca and her deputy director. Rebecca liked to keep an informal relationship with her staff, but the tone of the briefing was always one of seriousness. No one knew better than Rebecca what the stakes were in a place like Ghost Division.

Going around the table one department head at a time, the threats were mild – the equivalent of a quiet period.

Marcus, head of the investigation team for MI5, sat relaxed in his chair, under no pressure. 'We're still in the process of clearing Oliver O'Keefe,' he explained.

'You're still on O'Keefe?' asked Rebecca in surprise.

'Word has it that he hasn't told his family yet about his demotion out of Thames House. We've seen before that he could be a candidate for intelligence leaks. My team fancy him for a possible non-traditional threat. He had reasonably high clearance at one time. You know, before the drinking and gambling really kicked in.'

'How high?' asked Rebecca.

Marcus checked his notes. 'STRAP One.'

Deputy Director Melissa Forsyth nodded, pretending to be impressed. 'Wow. A real player.'

A few chuckles smattered across the room.

To the members of the morning briefing, the intelligence classification system was always good for an inside joke, as a person's clearance level was often an indication of the seriousness of the threat they posed. The higher the clearance, the bigger the threat, as they would have been in contact with more sensitive information. The Defence Manual of Security (that, much to the Ministry of Defence's chagrin, had leaked online in its entirety: all two thousand pages of it) designated various levels of classification. From Restricted, to Confidential, then Secret, then Top Secret. A sidebar to these was the STRAP system. According to the Manual, the system was a "set of nationally agreed principles and procedures to enhance the 'need-to-know' protection of sensitive intelligence produced by the principal UK Intelligence agencies."

STRAP One was the kind of intelligence that junior political aides were always leaving on memory sticks on London public transport and finding the story on the front page of a tabloid within a few days. Situations relating to STRAP Two material merited interrupting whatever the Prime Minister was doing. If it was STRAP Three, then the Prime Minister would be whisked straight downstairs to the Pindar bunker under Downing Street for an emergency briefing and often a COBRA meeting, or dragged out of bed in the middle of the night if necessary.

STRAP Three was traditionally thought of as the highest clearance level. But Rebecca was one of the very few to ever see a STRAP Four document.

Going around the rest of the table revealed similarly lightweight potential threats. Certainly lightweight compared to what Ghost Division had endured in recent times. Most notably the treasonous plotting of former Prime Minister Angela Curtis to cover up the false-flag terror attack on Downing Street. As well as the operation led by Sir John Pringle, former Commissioner of the Metropolitan Police, to target everyone involved in the Downing Street conspiracy by any means necessary – even murder and military operations on the streets of London.

But if the department heads thought they were getting a quiet day, they were wrong.

Rebecca leaned forward on the table, cueing up a video

on the laptop in front of her. 'The time has come for us to talk about something I've been working on for a little while now. Something that will require total discretion. What I'm about to show you has only been seen by me, the directors of MI6, MI5, and the CIA and a select few within those agencies. I need your game faces on, guys, because this is STRAP Three.'

A silence came across the room. Smiles disappeared. The time for levity was over.

Rebecca hit a button on a remote control that switched the tint on the glass windows ever so slightly. From the control room, everything inside the conference room now looked murky and fuzzy. The switch had also sound-proofed the room.

She pulled up the video onto the wall behind her.

She explained, 'This was taken last week in Cologne.'

'The BvF?' asked Melissa.

'Yeah.' Rebecca pointed at the man in the still image. He was sitting with impeccable posture, hands clasped, at a table in an interrogation room in the headquarters of German's federal domestic intelligence agency. He was a slight man in his early thirties, and was surrounded by half a dozen men in dark suits, all hanging on every word the man had to say. For most people, such a scenario would have been limb-quivering. But the man had been in rooms with people far more powerful than them – and much more frightening.

'This man,' Rebecca said, 'is Wolfgang Tibor. Does it ring a bell with anyone?'

MI6 Department head, Lucy Aspinall, stared at the image in disbelief. 'The Germans are opening him up?'

'Who the hell is Wolfgang Tibor?' asked Marcus.

Rebecca let Lucy answer.

Lucy was still in shock. 'He was personal secretary to Jozef von Hayek, chairman of the Hilderberg Group.'

Rebecca said, 'He's aged a good deal since he was arrested. He's been bandied around from one high-security facility to another for the last eighteen months. Interviewed and interrogated by every major intelligence agency in Europe thanks to the generosity of the Germans. It must have got to him, because young Wolfgang here has cut a deal to go into witness protection.'

A few scoffs went up around the table.

'Good luck with that,' said Lucy. 'As if Hilderberg can't get to him in witness protection.'

Marcus said, 'But Hilderberg's done. Kaput. Over.'

Rebecca replied, 'The organisation might be officially defunct, but the remaining members were never going to just go gentle into that good night. The arrest of von Hayek drove them underground. The ostentatious conferences might be gone, but I highly doubt the same can be said for their operations. These people have power and influence, and, crucially, connections. That means the intelligence services. That's where we come in.'

'So what has Tibor given up?' asked Marcus.

'According to him, he administered something that von Hayek called the POC list. It stands for political operative cover. Now, the old man has been silent, and he'll probably take most of Hilderberg's secrets to the grave with him – which should be any day now given his current health. But Tibor has detailed a whole range of lists that von Hayek cultivated over the years. I'll let him describe it.'

Rebecca let the video play.

Tibor, who was speaking to unidentified American officials, had flawless English.

He explained, 'They had cover operatives working in politics, as you know. Also the intelligence services. Banking. Big pharma. The mainstream media. They had the entire world in their pocket. And they're all still out there. There are too many to name. Von Hayek never shared them with me. But there was a list. And it's out there somewhere.'

Rebecca stopped the video. 'Tibor goes on to refer to it in German. It loosely translates as "the Directory".'

'What's in it?' asked Melissa.

'The names of every operative Hilderberg owned or sponsored.'

'In the intelligence services?'

'No, everything that Tibor just mentioned. Politics. Finance. Everything. We need to find that list, and find out who's on it. Because the people on that list are the last ones standing for Hilderberg.'

Sounding a lone, reluctant warning note, Lucy said, 'Is that even our remit?'

Marcus added, 'Yeah, shouldn't we just be going after the intelligence operatives?'

'No,' Rebecca replied calmly. 'I'm going after everything. *We're* going after everything.'

There was another long silence. The first person to break it was Melissa.

She asked the others, 'Can you give us the room, please?'

The department heads shuffled quickly out and returned to their teams, heads spinning.

Waiting until the door shut behind the last person to leave, Melissa asked, 'What are you doing, Rebecca?'

'What the British government has asked me to do,' she replied.

'No, they didn't ask you to do this. It's exactly what got GCHQ and NSA into trouble after Tom Novak and Stella Mitchell's reporting. It's overreach.'

'Melissa, when World War Two ended, we didn't stop looking for Nazis. We hunted them down across the world. People made it their life's work to bring them to justice.'

'Hilderberg are not the same as the Nazis.'

'No,' Rebecca conceded. 'But I know what they're capable of. And I don't think we've even seen the half of it. Wolfgang Tibor has given us an opportunity to kill off Hilderberg's remaining forces before they can rebuild. Do you really think that getting Angela Curtis into Downing Street was the culmination of Hilderberg's work? To install a puppet PM for several years?'

'We don't know what Angela Curtis could have done.'

Raising her voice now, Rebecca fired back, 'And we don't know what Hilderberg might have done had it not been for the bravery and ingenuity of people like Tom Novak and Stella Mitchell. What I do know is that Hilderberg were willing to sacrifice my dad's life. And for what? To make more money. To consolidate power and influence. Do you think when von Hayek was arrested they all reformed their ways? Sold up their businesses and went carbon neutral or something? They won't stop, because they'll always want more. We need to be tireless. Dedicated. And, for want of a better phrase, fanatical. If we're going to stop them. And it all depends on finding that list.'

Melissa took a moment to let the dust settle. 'Rebecca,

you know I go wherever you lead. But Five and Six are not going to be happy about this.'

Rebecca took out her phone when it started ringing. 'That's why we're not going to tell them,' she said, then squinted in surprise when she saw the caller ID.

"TOM NOVAK"

CHAPTER EIGHTEEN

As DAMIAN and Lee pulled onto the Stanley House property, halted by the security barrier protruding out of the ground, Lee asked, 'Do you think they'll get suspicious about it being only two of us instead of three. The intel said the cleaning teams were always three. That's why you took on Sean for this too, right?'

Damian did some final checks on his gun. 'Yeah, Sean didn't quite work it, though.'

Facing up to the starkness of their task, Lee said, 'They're expecting one of the cleaners to be a young black guy. I don't know when you last looked in the mirror, but neither of us look like Sean.'

'Trust me,' said Damian, 'we're better off in there as two than with Sean.'

The intercom buzzed, followed by the voice of Jerry the security guard.

Damian let Lee take the lead. As an American, he was going to have to let Lee do most of the talking. He could pull off a rough English accent, but the more Damian spoke inside, the greater the suspicions he might raise. He didn't fear getting caught. Prison – in any country – didn't scare him. After all, he'd run ground patrols in downtown Basra, Iraq. Which, at the time, was deeply in the shit. But what really scared him, was his client.

Lee spoke into the intercom. 'Hi, it's Eriksen,' he said casually. 'Passcode is one four five five romeo.'

Jerry checked the log which showed Eriksen Commercial Cleaning on time as expected, along with the correct passcode. He buzzed them in.

'What now?' asked Lee.

He holstered his gun under his overalls. 'Follow my lead.'

Damian cursed their situation as they parked in the underground car park. The plan should have been so simple. As was always the case with penetrating a location with airtight security, the first weak point was the human factor. Find a compromised security guard – like Vincent – who could let Damian and his two-man crew in as fake cleaners. But that simplicity went to pot when Vincent the guard had been taken into hospital the previous night.

That left them with only one other option. A backup that Damian had never liked, and hoped he wouldn't have to use. But when he was left no other option, he didn't hesitate. Even if it meant killing six other men to get to just one.

Lee and Damian were wearing overalls bearing the name of "Eriksen Commercial Cleaning". They were no ordinary cleaning company. They were one of the few in the country that provided cleaners who were British nationals (not even dual nationalities were permitted) with security clearance. Not that Wilson Kipchoge or any of his many flatmates could ever secure employment with a firm like Eriksen. But Eriksen had offices too, and someone had to clean them. Which is where the far less salubrious Sunnyside Contract Services came in. Every other day, Wilson and two of his flatmates mopped, vacuumed, and cleaned Eriksen's administrative office in South Bank. They had never known the importance of the many files held in the office. Such as codes for bypassing security barriers in places like Stanley House.

Cleaners from Eriksen were never permitted in the control room itself. But for Damian's purposes, all he needed was to get in the building. He had figured, if he couldn't infiltrate a security cleared contractor, then he would have to start lower down the food chain.

With Wilson and his flatmates out of commission, Damian and Lee were free to use the biometrics they had stolen from Wilson to enter the Eriksen offices prior to opening. From there, it couldn't have been easier unless Eriksen staff had left out a manual on how to access Stanley House. Damian and Lee had all the passcodes and electric fobs they needed.

Now only a security guard called Jerry was standing between them and the prize that the client was paying them so handsomely for.

Before exiting the van, Damian checked, 'Are you locked and loaded?'

Lee opened his overalls, showing the gun holstered across his chest.

Taking in the sight of the mysterious building, Damian said to himself, 'Two against everyone inside there.'

'Just think of the money,' said Lee.

Damian replied, 'Or what the client will do to us if we fail.'

CHAPTER NINETEEN

THE FIRST THING Jerry asked Damian and Lee when they entered the basement reception area with their ID lanyards was where their third man was.

Lee answered, 'He's off today. Sore head.'

Jerry held his gaze a little longer than Lee was comfortable with.

Lee wasn't as controlled as Damian. He was a foot soldier, ultimately. The sort of a guy a top-level drugs gang needs as an enforcer. But when it came to staring down a security guard at a top secret intelligence agency, his eyes were all nerves. And Jerry could tell.

He lifted his phone. 'Let me just give Eriksen a call to confirm your IDs...'

Damian reached out towards Jerry. He didn't want to have to open his mouth, fearing his fake accent – practiced as it was – would give the game away. But Lee wasn't capable of arguing their way in.

Before Damian could say anything, Melissa called out from the lift doors that had just opened.

'Morning, guys.'

Her familiarity with the men gave Jerry pause. 'You've let these two in before?'

'Of course,' she said, as if she had seen them a hundred times.

Damian had no idea who she was, or what she was doing. Or why.

Melissa draped herself casually over Jerry's desk, showing what she was certain was a tantalising bit of cleavage. Enough to temporarily short-circuit Jerry's caution. 'Can we get them signed in? The staff room's upside down again. One of the teams must have pulled an all-nighter again.'

Jerry still hadn't put down the phone. But he hadn't dialled yet either. 'I should really–'

Melissa rolled her eyes and took out her phone. 'Fine,' she snapped. 'I'll get Rebecca down. But she's not going to be happy about this happening again.'

'Again?'

'The same thing happened last week.' She gestured towards the lift. 'Look, I'll take them up just now. You can call Eriksen.'

As she led Damian and Lee off to the lift, once they were out of earshot of Jerry, she scolded them, 'You're lucky I knew the other guard was off sick, or you would have been left to deal with Jerry on your own.' She urged them on. 'Come on. I need to kill the power before Jerry gets through to someone that knows you're not meant to be here.'

Lee had relaxed now that Melissa had rescued them. Damian wasn't quite so sure.

When the lift doors closed, Melissa said, 'I thought there was meant to be three of you.'

'We lost one on the way,' said Damian.

Reacting to his American accent, she said, 'You're the one I talked to online, right?'

'Yeah.' He didn't want to talk. Talking took him out of the 'zone'. That mental place athletes talk about entering. Where they don't even have to think. They just do. Everything feels natural. And difficult, even painful, things feel effortless. Damian knew he should just block out the noise of Melissa. The really great ones in his field are able to block out anything. Like a writer in the middle of a crowded cafe, able to keep setting the words down. But Melissa just kept on and on the whole way upstairs to the third floor.

'I'm just glad I get a front-row seat,' she explained. 'You've got no idea the shit I've seen in here. You think you'll be impervious to it, but it renders the real world meaningless when you see what the powerful get away with on a daily basis. They're all getting their pay day. Now I want mine.' She turned around, looking the men up and down. 'It's probably better there's only two of you. It should be easier to sneak you into the control room. And look, I just want to check, because I don't want any dead bodies on my conscience...the files you want aren't terror-related or anything, are they? They're just personnel records, right?'

Damian was relieved to hear the lift ping for the third floor. 'Right.'

When they exited the lift, Lee peeled off to the left towards the electrical room, following the directions Melissa had marked on blueprints sent in advance to Damian via the dark web.

Melissa checked her watch as she marched off towards two consecutive double glass doors that were password and biometrics-protected. To gain access, you had to enter a fifteen-character password that was also simultaneously registering her fingerprints, as well as pulse and levels of sweat to gauge stress levels. It was a failsafe system. Even in the event of a power cut, the doors would still function, running off a separate off-site power generator. It was a system that Rebecca had coded herself, and had since been adopted by MI5 for Thames House.

Damian stood right beside Melissa as she entered her password, which was correct, but the biometrics were flagging her stress levels. Which was to be expected for someone committing treason in an agency whose very remit was catching traitors.

'Calm down,' Damian told her, as if it was a switch she could just flick on or off.

Melissa shut her eyes as she took a calming breath. She whispered, 'And no killing, right? Just darts. That's what you said.'

'That's what I said,' Damian replied.

When Melissa's biometrics flagged a second time, Damian pulled out his gun.

Melissa caught sight of it. 'You said no shooting.'

Damian raised the gun to her head as all the lights and computers switched off all around them. 'Change of plan,' he said.

CHAPTER TWENTY

REBECCA WAITED until she reached her office before initiating conversation with Novak. She closed her door with a backwards heel-kick. 'What can I do for you, Tom?' she asked.

'I'm sorry to bother you, Rebecca,' said Novak.

Short in tone, she replied, 'Uh-huh. What can I do for you?'

'I need the history of a phone number and everywhere it's been.'

She sat down at her desk with a sigh. 'You know, Tom, the resources of Ghost Division and the British intelligence services are not an app you can open up with a phone call to me every time you want to spy on whatever flavour of the month – or week – you're trying to sleep with.'

Novak waited pensively at the other end. He knew from experience that Rebecca felt it necessary to let off some steam before ultimately acquiescing to whatever mad request he made. That was just how it went with people who had gone through as much together as Tom, Stella, and Rebecca had.

'A burner?' asked Rebecca.

'Yeah. Is that possible?'

'All I need is four location points to identify someone. Even with a burner. All a burner really does is anonymise the purchase event. Turn that phone on even for a minute, and if you've got your regular phone on you or someone else has, those numbers are forever associated and I'll find you. One way or another. Give me the number.'

Novak smiled as he gave her the phone number. He knew she could never resist a challenge.

'You sound like you're smiling,' she said.

Novak froze. 'How the hell did you know?'

She smiled. 'You're so obvious, Tom.'

She opened up ELEMENT, the most sophisticated telecoms tracking system ever designed. Only GCHQ and Ghost Division had it. In the war against terror and treason, ELEMENT was like being able to bring a gun to a knife fight.

'Let's see,' she said, eyes narrowing as she pulled up all of the metadata associated with the phone number Novak had given her. Reeling at the wealth of information on her screen, she said, 'Anywhere you want me to start?'

The date was easy for Novak to remember. The day his dad died six years ago.

Novak added, 'I'd also like to just reiterate how terrifying it is that you can do all of that.'

'But you've got no moral objections as long as it helps you out?'

Novak didn't reply.

'All mobiles,' Rebecca explained, 'even burners go

through a mobile carrier. That carrier is involved in every text or phone call that could reveal someone's identity.'

'Don't you need to go through a lawyer or subpoena with the mobile service provider to access that?'

Rebecca snorted. 'The phone companies have been handing over all of that information to us for years now. We don't even have to ask anymore. Here we go...' She pulled up a log on the phone's last active location on the day specified. 'Interesting.'

'What is it?' asked Novak.

'It looks like a pretty rural area. Northern Westchester, New York. I've got one other phone number present at the time. But not really close enough to be considered contact.'

'How close are we talking?'

'No less than twenty metres.' She kept clicking through a timeline of the other phone number she had located near to Seymour's burner. 'It's weird...looking at the next half an hour, this other number, let's call it phone B, goes back and forth a few times to what looks on the satellite view to be a wooded area and a house.'

Novak shut his eyes. A dreadful thought occurred to him, but for now, he wasn't ready to entertain it. Eyes still closed, he asked, 'Is there a history there for phone B?'

After a pause, Rebecca replied, 'Looks to me like classic burner behaviour. It goes inactive later that night. Likely destroyed. You know, if you can tell me who owns the first number I can dig into this a little further. I've still got colleagues at GCHQ that owe me favours.'

'I appreciate it, Rebecca, but it wouldn't do any good.'

'Why?'

He opened his eyes. 'The phone belonged to my dad. That was the day he died.'

Rebecca lodged her tongue in her cheek. 'I see. What was he into, Tom?'

'I don't know. I'm trying to find out.' He was almost scared to ask the next question. 'Do you have a time stamp for when phone B last went out to the woods at the back of the house?'

'Yeah. Seven oh two. Why?'

Novak paused. 'On the satellite image for that location, if you zoom out a little, can you see a red windmill at a crossroad? Maybe a mile south-east from the property?'

Rebecca zoomed out. In an area with not much going on other than shades of green and brown, the red windmill was easy to spot. 'Yeah,' she said in surprise. 'How did you know that?'

Novak let out a long puff of air. 'Because it sounds like you're describing the woods at the back of my dad's old house. Where he committed suicide.'

His inner monologue was going at a hundred miles an hour.

Calm down...

Phone B might have been his as well...

If Phone B's location remained there in the woods, then it was his...

That would confirm that no one else was out there with him...

'Rebecca,' he said, 'I need to know what happened to Phone B. Where did it go?'

His heart was pounding while Rebecca continued the search. Internally, it felt like it was as loud as Rebecca's typing at the other end.

'It was on the road for several miles, heading back to New York by the looks of it. Then it heads west on I-287 and stops by the Hudson River. Then it deactivates for good.'

Novak shut his eyes again.

Then it wasn't his phone...

Someone else was there...

Which means he didn't–

Rebecca gulped hard as she heard Novak crumble at the other end, trying – and failing – to hold back tears.

'Oh my god...' he cried softly.

Rebecca could tell from the metadata what she was uncovering. And what it meant for Tom. Clutching at straws, she said, 'Tom, I know this doesn't look good. But let me–'

She looked out her office, across the control room, wondering why two cleaners were standing with Melissa at the secure-entry doors.

She told Novak, 'Tom, I'm really sorry, but I'm going to have to–'

That was when one of the cleaners raised a gun to Melissa's head.

'No,' Rebecca said quietly to herself. Not believing what was happening. Then louder. 'No!'

The lights went off.

Then there was a loud but muffled crack. The sound of a bullet firing, dampened by the soundproofing of the glass walls surrounding the control room.

The green LEDs for emergency battery-powered lighting that lit up around the edges of the room and in the ceiling were just bright enough for Rebecca to see Melissa's body slump forward through the doorway.

DAMIAN CROUCHED DOWN and grabbed Melissa's thumb, then he lifted it up to the scanner. The elimination of her pulse stopped the biometric alarms triggering this time. The doors opened. Damian and Lee had managed to enter the beating heart of one of the most secretive agencies in British intelligence.

Now every person in the control room was a sitting duck for the gunmen. Trapped in a large glass room with nowhere to go.

CHAPTER TWENTY-ONE

REBECCA GASPED and dropped her phone as Melissa's body tumbled through the doorway, the ominous entry of two men disguised as cleaners transforming the control room into a chaotic shooting range with live targets. They opened fire with eerie calmness, as desks and chairs became makeshift shields. Confused cries and anguished screams curdled together, creating a nightmarish sound.

Amid the pandemonium, Rebecca crouched beneath her desk, reaching for her phone, its connection to Novak drowned out by the relentless gunfire. Panic alarms proved futile, deactivated like the others.

Rebecca held her phone to her ear with a trembling hand.

Novak yelled at the other end, 'Rebecca! What's happening...'

As Damian and Lee advanced, leaving a trail of destruction behind, and facing imminent danger, Rebecca hung up on Novak and dialled for emergency response.

She didn't have to wait for a dispatcher to answer. The

simple act of dialling the number was sufficient. Within thirty seconds of the call, members of the Metropolitan Police's Specialist Firearms Command – MO19, formerly SCO19 – would be running to their BMW X5 armed response vehicles, and powering across the city for rapid deployment.

None of which were going to help Rebecca survive the next sixty seconds. That was all she could think about.

As bullets fizzled over her desk, Rebecca weighed up what few options were available to her. She could either hide under her desk and wait to die. Or she could fight to stay alive and get out of there.

A frantic search for a diversionary tool revealed nothing. Until her eyes landed on an unlikely potential saviour: a fire extinguisher clamped to the wall. Without a second thought, she grabbed it off the wall and unleashed the white powder inside. A thick cloud burst into the air, obscuring everything between Rebecca and the two shooters. She sprinted for the door on the opposite side of her office.

Damian yelled, 'Where did she go?'

Lee caught sight of her dashing around the periphery of the control room, trying to run around behind them. The room was still clouded from the powder, but it was fading fast.

Rebecca hid behind an upturned table, realising she was among very few survivors – if any.

Her fire extinguisher trick had helped extract her from her office, but now she was stuck with no other diversions available to her. That was when more shots rang out. Not from the assailants, but from a mysterious figure systematically approaching.

It was far too soon for Firearms Command to have arrived.

Through the mesh backing of an office chair, Rebecca could see a solitary figure closing in on the control room, alternating between shooting and taking cover.

Damian and Lee struggled to retaliate against the professional tactics.

The two shooters had no choice but to go to ground.

A voice called out, 'Rebecca, go! Go now!'

It was Jerry, stepping over Melissa's body, heroically entering a room that anyone else in their right mind would have run away from.

With Damian and Lee taking cover from Jerry, Rebecca was able to flee, running as fast as she could. Once she had cleared Melissa's body at the control room entrance, she looked around to check on Jerry.

Lee fired multiple shots in Jerry's general direction, one of which struck Jerry in the shoulder. It spun him like a top, and sent him straight into Damian's firing line. But Jerry wasn't done yet. Before he dropped to the ground, he fired off one last shot as Lee rose from behind the desk where he'd been hiding. It struck Lee in the sternum, and sent him straight to the ground.

Damian, fixated on Rebecca – who had managed to override the stress level alarm on the security doors with her director passcode – stepped over Jerry's body and fired further rounds into Jerry's chest. A spiteful gesture for Jerry making him work harder.

Rebecca hammered the button for the lift, momentarily forgetting about the power outage. It was a delay that gave Damian all the time he needed.

Closing in, he grinned malevolently and pulled the trigger.

Rebecca braced herself for the impact.

The chamber pumped twice with a lightweight click.

No bullets had been fired. He was out of ammunition. The last two had gone needlessly into Jerry, and now the one person he'd been sent to kill was able to escape.

Rebecca couldn't believe her luck, and seized the opportunity. She sprinted for the door to the stairs, before trapping the handle shut by snapping it off on the other side.

Damian grabbed impotently at the handle, then reeled back from the door. 'No!' he yelled, his frustration echoing around the hallway.

Descending the stairs with adrenaline-fuelled speed, Rebecca bounded down three, four, steps at a time. Her heart was beating so hard and fast she couldn't even feel it. Her entire body was numb with terror. It was only some basic sense of survival instincts that kept her legs moving.

Bursting out of the stairwell into a rush of cold air, the overcast, muted daylight and distant sirens and blue flashing lights speeding towards her signalled that she was safe.

For now.

CHAPTER TWENTY-TWO

EVEN HOURS after the phone call to Rebecca, at dawn Novak was still shaken and frantic as he and Stella paced down The Mall in Central Park. The wide walkway was lined by two rows of elm trees that, in summer, created a green roof of overarching branches that was almost like the vaulting of a cathedral. In autumn, The Mall was packed with photographers for the trees turning golden brown and orange, as captured so memorably in *When Harry Met Sally*. In winter, as it was currently, the effect lessened with the trees shedding their leaves, but it still provided a sanctuary from the hustle and bustle of the park's most popular spots, like the famous Wollman ice-skating rink, and the hang-out spot at Umpire Rock.

Heavy snow had started to fall, making it harder for Tom and Stella to spot their contact from a distance. Novak knew, though, that the contact would find them first. He always did.

Nathan had done his best to try and tag along, but Novak told him his energy would be better spent going back through Seymour's papers in search of further evidence relating to Seymour's final weeks.

'I'm sure everything's going to be okay,' Stella said, trotting a few steps to catch up to Novak.

'I really wish you'd stop saying that,' he replied, head flicking from side to side for any indication of their contact. There were only a handful of people walking around on their own. Old ladies walking dogs, or men who didn't fit their contact's physical description of big and tall. But for a man of the contact's size, he always found a way to blend in. It certainly helped in his profession.

Stella kept on, 'And you're sure that it was–'

Novak snapped, 'I'm telling you, it was gunshots. Unless someone was letting off fireworks inside the control room of an intelligence agency. And I heard screams.' He stopped walking and shook his head. The path ahead was clear. 'I really don't want to hear screams anymore.'

Just then, a man of six-foot three, in a black winter parka with the hood up, brushed past the pair. 'Keep walking,' he told them.

He looked like a military grunt, which only served to surprise his enemies in the field when he demonstrated his tradecraft and psychological insight.

Stella put a hand to her chest in fright, then had to jog again to catch up with Novak, who had set off after their contact – and close friend – Walter Sharp.

As a Specialized Skills Officer with the CIA, Walter Sharp didn't keep many friends. Preferring a solitary life. It wasn't just that it was safer. It was his preference.

'I'm guessing this is about Rebecca,' said Sharp.

'So you've heard,' said Novak.

'I got word an hour ago. You're lucky I was in the city.'

'I won't ask what for.'

Sharp said to Stella, 'Nice perfume, by the way. It helped me track you for about seven blocks on the way here.'

'Sorry,' she said.

'It's fine,' Sharp replied. 'It's nice. Look, guys. I know I've taught you to be cautious, but we really don't need this cloak and dagger stuff anymore. We're all living out in the open again.'

'Tell that to Rebecca,' said Novak.

Sharp asked Stella, 'What's with him?'

She said, 'He was on the phone to Rebecca when the attack started.'

Sharp's tone shifted to all-business. 'What did you hear, Tom?'

'I don't know.' Novak stopped walking. 'I heard cracks like gunshots–'

Ever a stickler for precise language, Sharp clarified, '*Like* gunshots, or gunshots. You know the difference.'

'It was gunshots,' Novak confirmed. 'Then I heard screams in the background, then the line went dead. That's all I heard.'

Sharp did a quick one-eighty. There was no one else within a hundred feet of them. 'Well, she's alive anyway. She's been taken to a safe house while the Metropolitan Police conduct their investigation.'

Stella said, 'But how can she trust anyone there? The intelligence services have been rotten from the inside out ever since Angela Curtis was PM. God knows how many Hilderberg still have operational in there.'

'What about the shooters?' asked Novak.

'Two of them,' said Sharp. 'One is down at the scene.

The other one escaped. I haven't seen any images yet. It's chaos at MI6 *and* MI5. Attacks on Downing Street are one thing. It's a big, obvious target that's physically easily accessible. But this is a top secret facility deep within the fabric of the British intelligence agencies. The British think anyone could be next.'

'The sense isn't that this is targeted specifically at Rebecca?' asked Stella.

'It's too soon to know. But off the record, there's a *lot* of casualties. Rebecca might yet be the only survivor.'

'What about stolen data? Ghost Division would have been a hive for classified intelligence.'

Sharp shook his head. 'Too soon, Stella. The debriefing process even for Rebecca is probably going to take a day or two.' He took a beat. 'This is still work for me, guys. So if there's anything you know that you're not telling me–'

'We wouldn't withhold from you, Walter,' Novak said. 'We didn't expect anything like this.'

Stella added, 'Though Rebecca obviously wasn't without enemies. A lot of people in the intelligence community don't trust her because Angela Curtis gave her that position. I mean, Curtis created the entire division. It's understandable the reticence about Rebecca's mission there.'

Novak said, 'But there was never any suggestion that Rebecca had colluded with Angela Curtis in any way. On the contrary, she lost everything because of Curtis.'

Free from as deep an emotional connection to Rebecca as the others, Sharp countered, 'Other than a high-paying job and an expensive penthouse apartment for a relatively young woman. Not to mention a great deal of access and power that lifelong spooks could only dream of.'

Stella was horrified. 'You're not suggesting that Rebecca's dirty, are you?'

'Of course not. But that's what's out there. And if someone thinks she can't be taken down through the system, then maybe someone tried another way.'

Novak said, 'You think this was an inside job?'

'It had to have been in some way to have found access to somewhere like that. But what I'm saying is I wouldn't rule anything out yet.'

Novak turned his face to the sky, savouring the cold air. Then his watch beeped. 'Crap.' He told Stella, 'We've got that meeting.' He turned in the direction of Bethesda Fountain, preparing to leave.

Stella stayed where she was. 'Actually, Tom...I was thinking I should go to London.'

'London? How are you going to find Rebecca? She's in a safe house.'

Sharp said, 'Safe house. Not secret house.'

She asked, 'You know where she is?'

'I can get word to her through back channels. Tell her to expect you.'

Novak said, 'Stella, I have to stay here. I have to follow up on this thing.'

'What thing?' asked Sharp. Judging by Novak's sigh, Sharp added, 'Tell me when you're ready.' He turned towards the West 58th Street entrance. 'I'll look out for you.'

He disappeared into the increasingly heavy snow, cutting a lone figure in black against the white background.

'I should go,' Novak said.

Stella nodded. 'I'm sorry, Tom. I'm not abandoning you, am I? I mean, this thing with your dad is so–'

'You're not abandoning me,' he said with an ironic grin.

'If I'm going to find out the truth about what happened to my dad, I'm going to need Rebecca's help anyway. That burner phone trace is just the start.'

The pair embraced.

'Call me when you get to the airport,' Novak said.

'I will,' Stella replied.

As she walked off towards the Fifth Avenue entrance, Novak called to her, 'Hey, Stel...'

Without turning around, she told him, 'Don't say it.'

He waited until she had walked farther away out of earshot. Then he said quietly to himself, 'Be careful.'

CHAPTER TWENTY-THREE

THE ARMED RESPONSE to the Stanley House attack was swift and loud. It may have been a secretive agency, but the response to an armed attack on a government agency property couldn't afford to be genteel in order to protect secrets. Not with a shooter fleeing the scene on foot.

Word quickly spread through Lewisham Police Station – where DC Leon Walker was based – about a massive Specialist Firearms Response happening near Southward Bridge on the Thames. Was it a terror attack? Was it ongoing? No one really knew.

Leon looked up from his tall pile of paperwork, wondering what the commotion was. When someone put up a live track of the police presence in the area of the attack.

'Christ, not another one,' said someone, convinced that the capital was seeing the start of something on the scale of the Downing Street bombing or the armed siege on The Mall that still felt all too recent.

Leon rose slowly from his chair as he stared at the red

beacon on the map on the video wall. The beacon was right over Stanley House's unmarked position on the north riverside.

All around the office, phones rang, and quickly the volume and intensity of the situation went through the roof. Across the sprawling CID office floor, a lone voice called for Leon to pick up his ringing phone.

It was his Senior Investigating Officer, who had been called by someone from Counter Terrorism, confirming that there had been an incident at Stanley House, and that DC Leon Walker should get there as soon as possible. Before he could relay that Rebecca was all right, Leon was already off, running through the office for the car park. The landline phone lay abandoned on his desk, still off the hook with his SIO asking if he was still there.

***

WHEN LEON REACHED the taped-off perimeter at Stanley House, he ran towards the young PC controlling access. Leon flashed his ID from several yards away.

The constable put up a cautious hand to at least slow down to explain himself.

'Detective Constable Leon Walker, Lewisham CID,' he barked. 'Let me through.'

Counter Terrorism were still on high alert, as radical Islamists had increasingly used the tactic of attacking a site, then sending in a following wave in the aftermath. A deviously evil strategy to maximise casualties – especially of soldiers or police.

As a cadre of five Counter Terrorist officers raised their

weapons at him, Leon threw his hands up and reiterated his identity.

'What the...' Leon stopped dead in his tracks. Even as one of the most promising young detective in the Met, he was still treated like an imminent and ongoing threat for being a black man in his twenties.

The SIO quickly realised their mistake and got them to lower their weapons.

There was no time to have it out over the gross overreaction of the officers. Leon shouted, 'I'm looking for Rebecca Fox! Have any of you seen Rebecca Fox?'

The SIO pointed towards the numerous ambulances that had assembled at the front entrance to the building. Paramedics were already wheeling out stretchers. Bodies all covered by white sheets.

'No,' Leon said, when he realised that there were no injured being taken care of. 'No!' he yelled, louder this time. He ran towards the ambulances, calling Rebecca's name.

Then, in a moment of sheer relief and joy, he heard her call his name back.

He found her at the back of an ambulance, wrapped in a blanket. A paramedic had been treating the mostly superficial wounds on her face that had occurred in the desperate scramble to escape the control room.

As he took her in his arms, she sobbed. 'They're all dead, Leon. They're all dead. I'm the only one.'

Leon was still holding her, when the senior Counter Terror officer and a man in a grey suit hurried over. They were flanked by more men in various shades of grey suits, some of them carrying briefcases.

'Rebecca Fox?' asked the man in the suit.

'Who are you?' she asked, stepping back from Leon.

The man showed her a badge identifying him as a Specialist Command officer – a new offshoot of Protection Command that protected the Royal Family and senior politicians. Given ongoing threats in light of the Angela Curtis affair, it was decided that the Metropolitan Police needed a presence specific to the intelligence community in the event of further terror attacks or criminality. The daily business of Ghost Division, and that of MI6 and MI5 were deemed too sensitive to be handed over to regular detectives in the Met. Angela Curtis had changed everything. The landscape was never going to be the same again. That's where Specialist Command came in.

The popularity of James Bond had made MI6 one of the best-known intelligence agencies in the world. But it was easy to forget that as recently as 1994, the existence of MI6 had never even been publicly acknowledged. The way the new government saw it, it was time to put the genie back in the bottle, and rebuild the fabric of secrecy that British intelligence had once enjoyed. Starting with enterprises like Specialist Command.

'I'm DCI Warren Bell,' he said. 'I'll be SIO on this case.'

'Have you got the shooter?' asked Leon.

Bell ignored the question, focussing instead on Rebecca. 'Miss Fox, we need to remove you from this area. It's not safe here.'

'Is there an ongoing threat?' she asked.

'The shooter is still at large, and we need to debrief you.'

Rebecca scoffed. 'You debrief *me*?'

Prepared for this reaction, Bell rocked on his heels.

'Miss Fox, the activities of your agency within Stanley House are one of the most closely guarded secrets this country has. However, the actions that take place within the property are not excluded from the laws of this country. There was a mass shooting event here this morning, and it's my job to bring the people responsible to justice. That requires a debriefing.'

'As the director of Ghost Division?'

'No,' he said. 'As the only living witness.'

A cry rang out from the front steps. 'We've got another one!'

In a wave of groupthink, when a few police officers crouched quickly down, believing that a shooter was still on site, it prompted everyone else within earshot to do the same.

Two paramedics came haring out of the front entrance of Stanley House, pushing a stretcher with a body on it. This one didn't have a sheet over it. 'Weak pulse, but he's hanging in there...'

'Oh my god,' Rebecca said, putting a hand to her mouth. 'That's one of the shooters.'

DCI Bell waved frantically to clear a path along the road for the ambulance. Then he pointed his officers and Counter Terrorism towards their vehicles. 'I want armed guards in that ambulance. He doesn't leave your sight. I want a chopper following...' He pointed to Rebecca. 'And get her out of here. I want her in the safe house within the hour.'

'Safe house?' said Rebecca. 'What safe house?'

'We don't have time to argue, Miss Fox.'

'I'm not going anywhere without Leon. He comes with me.'

Bell stopped to consider him.

Rebecca said, 'I trust him. So either he comes with me, or I disappear.'

'I can't do that,' said Bell. 'I can't. But believe me, I am on your side. I lost two close friends in the Downing Street attack. Trust me, your enemy here is my enemy also.'

Rebecca stood firm. 'Then put Leon on your team.'

Bell scoffed.

'Ask around,' she said. 'He'll make sergeant by next summer, and you're going to need someone I trust to liaise with back in the city. Leon's it.'

Bell stared at Leon, then at Rebecca. Finally, he turned to a woman who had so far been silent, but had stuck close to Bell. Bell said to Leon, 'DC Walker, you're with Detective Inspector Sofia Molina. She's been my right-hand for as long as I care to remember.' He stepped closer, emphasising, 'She tells you to jump. You say how high. Got it?'

'Sir,' Leon replied, then turned to DI Molina.

In Leon's experience, the unwritten rules for pronouns were straightforward. A sergeant was sarge. Inspector was boss or guv. Chief Inspector was boss if you knew them, otherwise sir or ma'am.

Leon asked, 'Do you prefer boss or guv?'

Molina replied, 'I'll take anything above twat, to be honest. Come on.' As she turned to leave, she let out a loud hawk of phlegm, then spat it out to one side. 'Sorry,' she said. 'Sinuses playing up.'

For a vaguely exotic name and the looks of someone who would have been more at home swanning about between tanning salons and a nail salon, DI Molina talked and carried herself like she was watching Sunday League football. The voice that came out of her didn't match how she looked at all.

Before she and Leon left, he embraced Rebecca. He whispered, 'It's going to be okay. We're going to get whoever's behind this.'

Bell gave the nod to two Counter Terror officers who appeared by Rebecca's side. Bell told the officers, 'Miss Fox, we need to get out of here. We don't know what this is yet. Or if it's over.'

CHAPTER TWENTY-FOUR

IT WAS one of Novak's favourite streets in the city. A street that felt more like New York than any other to him.

6th Avenue.

The city rising above you, flanked on both sides by huge skyscrapers. It was a constant source of amazement to Novak that there were enough businesses in the country, let alone the city, to fill all of those offices. It was what New York was all about. Vastness. Scale. Spectacle.

Everywhere he looked there were iconic, unique buildings. The Charles Schwab Building. The Warwick Hotel. Radio City Music Hall with its LED-lit marquee.

Then there was the lit-up marquee of ABC Studios at Rockefeller Centre, advertising as always *The Tonight Show* that had been running for decades with Seymour Novak's name under it. It was sometimes said that the only things to survive a nuclear holocaust would be cockroaches and *The Tonight Show*.

The security guard at the front entrance recognised

Novak immediately and welcomed him. 'Mr Tom Novak,' he said with an actual tip of his hat.

'Hey,' Novak said with humility. Once inside, he muttered to himself, 'Weird.' He was never going to get used to people recognising him in public.

Novak bypassed reception, heading straight for the lifts. One of the upsides to having your headquarters in such an historic building was that little changes over time. Novak still knew from his childhood exactly where he was going. The thirtieth floor. Otherwise known in the building as "Talent and Management."

When he got out the lift, he was met with a reception that blocked all access to the sprawling office floor beyond the windows in the oak doors behind.

'Tom Novak,' he said at the desk. 'I'm here to see Helen Hazelhurst.'

'Is she expecting you Mr Novak?' asked the receptionist.

'Yes,' he lied. He turned away, then added, 'I'm Seymour Novak's son.'

She nodded by way of reply.

He felt like an idiot for saying it, but he wanted to use all the leverage he had to get into Helen's office.

While calls were made to track down Helen, Novak stood against the wall that bore the ABC logo. He felt like a little boy again, standing there like he was waiting for his mother to finish talking to a friend at the grocery store.

When the receptionist informed him that Helen wasn't expecting him, the double doors swung open. Out stepped an agent for one of the biggest pop stars in the world, who Novak recognised.

Behind him was Helen Hazelhurst, who was already on her way back to her office.

As Novak approached the doors, he called out, 'Helen! It's Tom.'

The receptionist hurried over to block his access, but the commotion had caught Helen's attention.

She stopped in the crowded office that was humming with activity and conversation. 'Tom?' she said in surprise.

The receptionist gave way to Novak, who barged past.

'I'm sorry,' he said. 'But I need to talk to you.'

She checked her watch. 'I can't right now, Tom. Talk to Candice. She'll book you in. But I have to run.'

'It's about my dad,' he said.

When she kept walking towards her office, he called out, 'You owe me, Helen.'

She stopped.

To seal the deal, Novak added, 'And you damn well know it.'

Helen relented, her shoulders dropping. 'Five minutes,' she said.

Then she took him to her office in the corner of the room.

The door bore her name and title: HELEN HAZEL-HURST – PRESIDENT OF THE ABC FAMILY

As she fixed them both coffee, she asked, 'What's all this about?'

Novak declined coffee and didn't sit down. 'I need to talk to you about my dad. Specifically, any stories he may have been working on up to the time he died.'

She sat down with a puff. 'Gosh, I don't know. That was a long time ago.'

'Six years,' he said.

'Really? Is that all? Feels longer than that.' She took a pause to drink some coffee.

'I've been working on releasing his archives to Columbia, and a story of his has come to light that I need to chase down.'

'What sort of story?' she asked.

'I don't know. Anything that you can remember might help.'

She took another drink. 'Funny that you mention it, there *was* one story...He kept on at me about it for weeks. I never saw your dad in his heyday, but at the time I remember thinking I had twenty-five-year-olds on staff with less energy and determination than your dad. He was obsessed. Didn't he talk to you about the story back then?'

Novak sniffed in embarrassment. 'I wasn't really around much.'

'Of course,' she said. 'You had the White House beat to cover and all.'

'How often did he bring stories to you?'

'That's the thing. Hardly ever. Our anchors rarely do. It's how we've always done it here. So when he brought this one to me, it took me by surprise.' She hesitated. 'I'm sorry to be blunt, and I don't wish to speak ill of the dead...'

'Helen, just tell me.'

'Seymour was once a great reporter. But not by the time I was producing him. His golden days were long gone. He got up there every night, smart, handsome, well-spoken, prepared, and he read the news. And that was it. He *read* the news. He didn't write it. He didn't get out there and find it. Stories were *brought* to him.'

'What was the story?'

Her eyes narrowed, wondering how much to give away. 'As I recall, Storm Capital.'

'Specifically?'

She sighed. 'Tom, I've been President of this network for three years. Do you have any idea how long ago the newsroom feels to me? Every day there was a crisis, something memorable or important. But what I do remember is that when he told me what he had, I told him no.'

'You can't remember the story, but you can remember you told him no?'

'I know that it's a foreign notion to someone who has never been a producer of any stripe, but ask Stella and she'll tell you: you can't always okay a story just because it's good. There are economics, politics, to consider. At the time, the network was in the middle of negotiating the licences for five affiliate stations on the east coast alone. That meant keeping the stock price buoyant. That meant not losing sponsors like Storm Capital that had invested tens of millions of dollars in several different spheres across the estate. Hell, they own eight per cent of us, which isn't cheap, I can tell you.' Helen stood up, and went to her bureau across the room. She proceeded to rummage through a number of drawers that were filled with hardback notebooks. 'I took the story upstairs. I said it was good. They said no. That was the end of it.' She took out the book she needed then dropped it on her desk close to Novak's side. 'My diary for that year. Go ahead. Open it.'

Novak didn't need to be told twice. He skimmed through to his dad's final month. Then week. He stared at the page, then showed it to Helen. 'This says he had a meeting arranged with Anna Storm.'

Helen put her glasses on for a moment to read. 'Oh yeah, I remember that. Management were terrified he wouldn't get back in time for the show. He never made it, sadly.'

Novak motioned towards the diary page with his phone. 'May I?'

'Take it away with you,' she replied. 'Anything that might help get Seymour's story published now.'

He shoved the diary into his shoulder bag.

She said, 'Tom, I wish I could be of more help, but I really have to run downstairs.'

He nodded and stood up, satisfied that he'd got plenty out of her considering the timescale he was talking about. Before he left, he asked, 'What was he like around that time? Near when he died?'

'Do you mean his state of mind?'

'Yeah.'

She thought hard about how to phrase it. 'The day after his body was found, I watched back the previous night's broadcast, and I remember thinking, that doesn't seem like a man who's about to commit suicide in a few hours.'

'A few people said that,' Novak said.

She paused. 'I know you don't think much of me, and you still blame me for what happened to your mother—'

If Novak had still been sitting down he would have squirmed. 'We don't have to do this...'

Helen raised a hand to ask for more time. 'I cared deeply about your father, Tom. It wasn't just some dalliance we had together. It meant something. But I knew he didn't love me the way he loved your mother.'

'Maybe he should have thought about that before he had the affair. Maybe she'd still be around.'

'Your dad was very special to me too. If there's anything else I should know–'

'I'll tell you,' he assured her. As he walked to the door, he said, 'Not to get too Columbo on you, but there is actually one last thing...did my dad ever mention the name of his source?'

'Sadly not,' said Helen. 'I was aware he had a source, but he never named them to me. There was no need. We never got close enough to airing the story for it to be an issue.'

'Maybe he mentioned someone he referred to as–'

'RT?' She smiled wistfully. 'Yeah, I know all about "Real Thing". He knew the real thing when he saw it, I'll tell you that. So if he called this source RT, you'd best believe he was onto something.' As she walked him through the office, she said, 'I assume that Nathan isn't talking? It was my understanding he didn't know who the source was either.'

Novak froze.

Helen kept walking a few steps before she realised he wasn't there. 'Tom?'

'What do you mean?' he asked, mystified. 'What Nathan are you talking about?'

She said it as if it were obvious. 'Nathan Lugati.'

'How do you know Nathan?'

'He came around here once with your dad. I hadn't met him before, you see, though I'd obviously heard about his implosion at *Republic*. I recognised him and asked Seymour for an introduction. I wasn't wild about him working with someone with a track record of lying. It was selfish, but I was worried about the *Nightly News*, first and foremost.'

'Nathan was working with my dad?'

Worried she had said something she shouldn't, she said, 'Well, yes. Your dad approached him. In the end, they were working quite closely together. You didn't know that?'

Novak shut his eyes. Now so much made sense to him. But it wasn't relief that was flooding through his body. It was anger.

He set off running and didn't stop until he reached the lifts. And when he got outside, he started running again, and couldn't stop.

CHAPTER TWENTY-FIVE

NOVAK HAD BEEN on the warpath all the way to Columbia from 6th Avenue. Normally he would have taken a cab, but his brain was on fire with what Helen Hazelhurst had just told him. He needed the air, to keep moving, to make any sense of it.

He didn't slow down when he reached the stairs leading to the archive rooms, and barely noticed the weight of the heavy double doors behind, which was the dedicated archives suite that Columbia had set aside to house Seymour's papers for the remaining semesters of the academic year.

The doors slammed against the wall as Novak stormed in.

Nathan, standing over a desk covered in folders, binders, papers, stacks of paperbacks and hardbacks with Seymour's handwritten annotations, and yellow Post-Its sticking out every few pages. He jumped at the sound of Novak's arrival, almost spilling the coffee he was holding.

'Are you out of your mind?' Novak barked.

'Tom?' Nathan leaned backwards, then took steps back as well. 'What's going on? What's happened?'

He kept on until he was right up in Nathan's personal space. 'Everything you told me since you came back on the scene. Bullshit. Ironically, only a born liar like you could have pulled it off.'

Nathan placed his coffee down on the ground, to not endanger any of the material on the table. 'I swear, I don't know what's going on. What are you talking about?'

'You must have known that I would find out.'

Nathan had known the moment would come, but not quite so soon. He raised his hands. 'I can explain...'

'You were working with my dad all along, and you never told me. What the fuck is wrong with you?'

'I can explain...'

'Now it all makes sense,' said Novak, backing away, needing room to pace. To prowl. 'You've been working me this whole time, haven't you? Since you bumped into me at that bar. I'll bet that wasn't a coincidence either. You sought me out for this job. You suggested it. God help me when Stella finds that out. She'll string me up at Times Square for not seeing it. For being so naive. It was a shitty job, and you actually *wanted* it. At first, I just thought you were trying to get close enough to my orbit to get another shot at *Republic*. But you wanted in to finish your story. To find whatever Seymour had left, just so you could rebuild your career.'

'It was a *little* like that,' Nathan admitted. 'But only a little. Yes, we were working a story together.' Using his best please-calm-down voice, Nathan said, 'Your dad had found a source within Storm Capital. About political donations that were breaking campaign finance laws. Even in the insane era of money being used as free speech in political donations, Storm had pushed the envelope into a whole new category of illegality.' Seeing that Novak wasn't immediately dismissing him out of hand, he slowly stepped towards him, closing the gap between them. 'He said that he would have come to you, but that you would never have shared a by-line with him. So he came to me asking for help. He had been out of the game so long, Tom, he had no idea what he was doing. I set up meetings and I had to take them. Think about it. He was Seymour Novak for god's sake. He couldn't be running around New York City causing a stink about a major hedge fund. The story would have blown up before he got a single thing on the air or in print. Nobody knew who the hell I was, so he was happy to use me. It was a *quid pro quo* thing, Tom. We were helping each other. I actually think we made a really good team.'

Novak let out a long exhalation. Slowly, his barriers were coming down. 'What happened in the final week?'

'We were making good progress, and thanks to his contacts, he'd set up a meeting with Anna Storm.'

'At their headquarters. Saratoga. That's why the plane ticket and hotel booking.'

'A guy like me doesn't get to sit down with someone like Anna Storm,' said Nathan. 'It had to be Seymour. But we never got a smoking gun. Nothing we could use anyway.'

Novak sat on the ground. When he bent his legs, he realised how far he had actually walked from Central Park.

Nathan sat down in front of him, and continued. 'I was all in. Diane had given me a deadline, and there was no wiggle room. When Seymour died, I was left with nothing. No backup, nothing else to file. So I got desperate, pulled some B material on a bullshit Washington process story, botched some quotes and made up some sources to give it bones. All the while, I was running around travelling off the books to keep chasing Seymour's story. Then, when the shit hit the fan about the bullshit story I filed, I bailed on the whole industry.'

'You could have just told Diane the truth,' said Novak. 'Or me!'

'I was scared!' Nathan cried. He lowered his head. 'When I heard he had died, and how, I knew that there was something wrong with it. I just knew. I did everything I could to make the pieces fit, but I couldn't. I had my suspicions about what had really happened to Seymour, but I couldn't risk bringing you into it as well. Not without proof. Even I wasn't sure, and I didn't want to dredge everything up. Bad enough you lose your father. Then someone comes along and wrongly claims that there were suspicious circumstances.'

Novak kept processing the version of events and trying to press on something that didn't stand up. So far, he had failed to find anything. But he wasn't done yet. 'Why wait this long? And why come back now? What's changed?'

'When I saw what you and Stella have done at *Republic* the last few years, I realised that I had thrown away my real calling in life. What you've done is what I should have been doing all these years. So much wasted time, bumming around south-east Asia, working in kitchens and tending bars in Australia. Just trying to forget. But I couldn't forget. The Goldcastle Papers made me want to come back. When you gave me this job I found my sense of purpose again. I knew that I let your dad down in not finishing his story for him.' Nathan reached out to him. 'And that I let you down in not pursuing the truth about what happened to your dad. So I begged for the job so I could start digging again. With the right access, I was sure I could prove everything.'

'What do you mean?' asked Novak.

'Do you think I've spent the last three months just organising and filing things?' Nathan got to his feet and indicated the vast paper trail on the table. 'I was a reporter, Tom. And I still am.'

Novak joined him at the table. It was only when he started looking carefully at what Nathan had laid out that he understood what he had actually been doing with his time.

Nathan explained, 'I've been piecing together every fact, every detail, I can about your dad's final days.'

'Short version first,' said Novak. 'Do you think my dad died because of suicide?'

'No.'

'Do you think you've got evidence of foul play?'

'No...' Before Novak could ask him to explain, Nathan added, 'I don't "think" I have. I'm absolutely convinced of it.'

CHAPTER TWENTY-SIX

WITH HIS EVIDENCE literally laid out on the table, Nathan set about tackling it all piece by piece. 'This could get a bit grisly,' Nathan warned him.

'If there's a truth to be faced, then bring it,' Novak replied.

Nathan turned to the first piece of evidence. 'The autopsy on your dad states cause of death as blood loss with contributing overdose. But the seven doctors I've spoken to have all cast doubt on that conclusion. The blood vessel severed was the ulnar artery, which as you can see from the illustration here is about the width of a matchstick. For the autopsy to prove accurate, it would mean your dad dying of a haemorrhage by losing nearly three litres of blood. The doctors I've spoken to all say this couldn't have happened.' Nathan raised a finger to prevent being interrupted. 'Say we put that aside. We shouldn't, but say we do. There's not enough blood at the scene where the body was found.' He took out photos taken from forensics at the scene. The ground was covered in leaves, and the blood that had been photographed was minimal. 'Do you see three litres of blood there?'

Novak shook his head, shaken by his first-ever look at where his dad had died. When he'd thought Seymour had killed himself, it was painful enough already to think of him feeling so dejected to choose to die by his own hand. The thought of his life being taken against his will was even worse.

'So we have question marks over blood loss,' Nathan said. 'What about the overdose?' He took out further paperwork that illustrated his points to come. 'The autopsy notes state that an excessive amount of coproxamol coupled with a silent coronary artery disease your dad was unaware of at the time played a part in bringing on death. But the doctors I've spoken to tell me that the amount in your dad's system is at the low end of the range measured in people who have overdosed fatally on that drug. Then, of course, you've got the psychological angle.'

'In what way?' asked Novak.

'You spoke to Helen Hazelhurst this morning, right?'

'Yeah. She said that my dad was energetic, determined. Not seeming much like someone on the brink of suicide at all.'

'Which is exactly the testimony I've managed to find from over a dozen other witnesses who either saw him or spent time in close proximity in the last forty-eight hours of his life. And that's not even counting the live network broadcast he performed the same night he died. But I've got some other inconsistencies I want to show you.'

Novak shook his head slowly as the abundance of mate-

rial Nathan had compiled became apparent. He had definitely been busy.

'Questions,' said Nathan. 'Did you know that your dad
apparently cut his left wrist? And the cut was made from
right to left?'

Novak did a double-take. 'You mean left to right,
surely.'

'No, it was right to left.' Nathan showed him the photo-
copy of the autopsy report where the cut had been illustrated and indicated on the outline of a hand. 'Who the hell
would cut their wrist like that? It's like pushing a knife,
rather than dragging it across your wrist. And your dad was
surely smart enough to know that cutting the wrist that way
was a much slower way of bleeding out. You don't cut
across, you cut up.'

Novak had been shaking his head with increasing
vigour while Nathan spoke. 'Hang on, hang on...you said
he cut his left wrist. So with his right hand.'

'Well, yeah,' Nathan replied. 'You can't cut your left
wrist using your left hand.'

Novak shut his eyes – almost in anger at the mounting
proof. 'My dad had damaged nerves in his right arm. An
old golf injury from hacking a ball out of the rough. He
couldn't even cut a steak with his right hand. He had to
hold his knife and fork in reverse.'

This came as news to Nathan. 'No shit,' he said in
fascination.

'Is that it?' asked Novak. 'Or is there more?'

'There's more, Tom. But if you still need convincing
then maybe we're not on the same page. If I haven't
convinced you by now...'

'No, no. You've got me,' he assured him.

'What's next?'

'Next?' Novak picked up the autopsy report, noting the location of the medical office where it had been performed, and the pathologist who had performed it. 'We need to talk to this guy.'

CHAPTER TWENTY-SEVEN

Rebecca had been taken to an MI5 safe house in the Buckinghamshire side of the Chiltern Hills. Had the events that brought her there not been so harrowing, she might have considered it one of the most beautiful places she had ever seen.

The safe house was more of a country farmhouse, but with thousands of pounds of security upgrades throughout the property and surrounding area. Known in MI5 simply as the Farm, it had been built at the top of a small rise in quintessentially English countryside, of rolling hills, sparse woods, and in front of the Farm, mile after mile of empty hay fields. No one was going to sneak up on the Farm without making it obvious to the MI5 and Specialist Command officers guarding the property.

DCI Warren Bell and his team were now entering their third straight hour of debriefing, combing over every last detail Rebecca could think of. They had spent so long talking, they had changed venue three times – from the open-plan kitchen, to the study, and finally to the main lounge, where Rebecca had found a deep, soft sofa to sit on with her feet up, nursing yet another cup of tea.

'I told you already,' Rebecca said, her frustration evident, 'I've never met, nor recognise either of the shooters. We didn't have any intel of anything in the pipeline. Nothing. And if you ask me again about possible motives, I'm going to scream. The nature of everything we do at Ghost Division invites enemies.'

One of Bell's detectives showed him a video of something on a phone.

Rebecca leaned forward, eager to see, straining to hear.

DCI Bell asked, 'Would you care to revise that statement, Rebecca, in light of this?'

'What is that?' she asked.

He handed her the phone.

The video played from the start, showing Melissa intervening at reception.

Bell said, 'The security guard, Jerry Wozniak, attempts to run further checks on the two men. Until your deputy just happens to appear and leads them away.'

Rebecca covered her mouth in shock. 'She couldn't be...'

'Melissa Forsyth is the reason those men entered the control room.'

In full denial mode, Rebecca thrust the phone back to DCI Bell. 'No. You're wrong. You must be wrong.'

Bell scrolled through the phone to a series of photos. 'These were found on Melissa Forsyth's home computer an hour ago. Does that surprise you?'

Rebecca nodded and handed the phone back. The screen showed a picture of Rebecca out running in the morning. Along with a whole host of other mornings.

'Why was your deputy director surveilling you, Rebecca?'

She corrected him, 'It's Director Fox. And I don't know. I don't know why she would have done that.'

'Our tech forensics found all sorts of other interesting stuff.'

'Like what?'

'Anonymous posts on online forums, railing against the political establishment and the intelligence services for allowing criminals to escape punishment if it served the country's interests. She cited examples ranging from Russian oligarchs to Saudi princes. That was six months ago. But then there's this...' He showed Rebecca an iPad which had photo evidence taken of Melissa's computer. 'These are cryptocurrency deposits left in an account she opened a few months ago. There's over a hundred thousand pounds in it. I'm assuming that's not her salary.'

Rebecca's head dropped. 'Oh my god...'

'She was on the inside of an agency that knew firsthand the reality of dealing with traitors and criminals. And what she saw was a nest of corruption, of people getting away with huge crimes all the time in exchange for intelligence. She saw them all getting paid. I think she decided she wanted her pay day too.'

Rebecca couldn't speak. She was replaying so many moments with Melissa that now made sense. Her railing against the various injustices that Ghost Division couldn't right. Of cutting deals and accepting pleas.

Bell went on, 'We know the shooters must have had help to get in there.'

'How did they do it?' she asked.

'By assuming clearance codes given to cleaning staff at

Eriksen Commercial Cleaning. We're still unravelling how they managed to infiltrate that, but we've managed to trace back the van they used to reach Stanley House to a street two minutes away from Eriksen's offices.'

'What about the other shooter?' asked Rebecca.

'He isn't saying much. Yet. But with his accomplice still on the loose, he's holding all the cards. We need the second shooter much more than anything we can threaten him with. Is there anybody you can think of that might have wanted to harm Ghost Division. Or you?'

Rebecca scoffed. 'Only the majority of the intelligence community.'

'Your work isn't appreciated, then.'

'Not exactly.'

DCI Bell said, 'You don't have to tell me. I worked in anticorruption for three years. I didn't become a copper to arrest other coppers. But that's what the job demanded.'

'I'm still waiting for a question.'

'We've hit a brick wall with Melissa Forsyth. We can't access her work computer. Everything's locked up, encrypted. Twenty-character passwords on everything.'

Rebecca shook her head witheringly. 'I can break whatever Melissa put up. But that's going to take time.'

'What do you suggest?' asked Bell.

'Whatever might be on Melissa's work computer could be compelling. Maybe even incriminating. But I doubt it'll help you track down the missing shooter.'

Bell folded his arms in impatience. He wasn't going to ask again.

Rebecca said, 'ANPR. This is all about tracing whatever vehicle they were in. At some point this morning, the shooters came together. An operation this big, you don't risk someone missing a meeting point.'

'How does number plate recognition help? We don't know what vehicle they had been in before they were at the Eriksen office. One witness thinks they may have arrived in a white van before that, but we can hardly search ANPR for every white van in the area. Say we do find the right vehicle. We can't trace everywhere it's been in the last twenty-four hours.'

'I wouldn't be so sure about that.' Rebecca leaned across to her laptop, which had been idling. She opened up ELEMENT and signed into all of her security suite applications.

'But ANPR only does active searches,' said Bell.

Rebecca said nothing.

DCI Bell leaned forward in anticipation. 'And you know that.'

'Actually,' said Rebecca, 'Ghost Division and GCHQ have been making a few revisions to the ANPR system recently. In light of Angela Curtis and Goldcastle et al.'

'What are you talking about?' Bell asked belligerently.

Whilst typing quickly on her laptop, Rebecca said, 'Come on, DCI Bell. The whole country was brought to a standstill thanks to a terror attack that could have been avoided with better preventative measures and tracking. The Goldcastle conspiracy could have been brought to light months earlier with more powers. ANPR is no longer just a live-tracking event. It's retrospective as well.'

Bell's jaw almost hit the floor. 'Director Fox, are you telling me that ANPR is tracking the movements of every vehicle in Britain. Logging everywhere a vehicle goes? Live?'

'It's only to be used in matters of national security.'

'You mean for whatever you decide is a national security event.'

'Someone has to decide. Personally, I would rather it was someone like me rather than another Angela Curtis.' She turned her laptop around and showed DCI Bell. It showed the ANPR logs for a white van travelling from the Eriksen offices to an industrial estate in Wembley. 'Don't go congratulating me yet, Detective Chief Inspector. By the satellite image, I'd say there's nearly a hundred units on the site. But if you send in enough officers, you might be able to flush out the missing shooter.'

Bell called DI Molina back in the city. 'Sofia, we've got a lead. I want every available body on this.'

CHAPTER TWENTY-EIGHT

LEE HAD BEEN TAKEN to St Thomas' Hospital by Westminster Bridge – the same hospital the Prime Minister was taken to in the event of an injury, or other health emergency. The staff in the South Wing were well versed in security protocols, and used to having armed police officers walking around during the numerous tests they ran to be ready for an emergency. For many, the memory of former Prime Minister Simon Ali arriving and soon after being declared dead was still fresh.

The doctor overseeing Lee's care had given DI Molina and DC Walker five minutes to attempt to get something out of the suspect.

But they didn't get anywhere.

'I thought the nurse said he was becoming responsive,' she said.

Dr Linda Upshaw was a trauma specialist with twenty years experience. Just walking the corridors of the hospital she stood out from the other doctors with her dark red scrubs, and name embroidered on her V-neck top.

Patience running thin, Dr Upshaw folded her arms. 'I'm not a police officer, DI Molina. I'm not here to get answers. I'm here to preserve life. And, frankly, if you want to bring this man to justice, he can't see the inside of a courtroom if he's dead.'

Leon thought better of saying what was really on his mind. Namely, that he couldn't give a monkeys whether Lee saw the inside of a courtroom or not.

Molina was less discreet in her response. 'I'll live with that, doc.' She touched Lee on the shoulder and gave him a firm shake. 'Oi...wake up. Come on...'

Dr Upshaw stepped in. 'No, no, no. This is ridiculous. I know that you want answers, Inspector, but I draw the line at shoving a man who's been shot in the sternum. He's lucky to be alive.'

Leon retorted, 'He won't feel quite so lucky when he's being wheeled into an interrogation room at Lewisham Police Station, answering for the twenty-odd dead bodies he and his pal left behind at Stanley House.'

Upshaw looked at Molina, as if to question whether DC Walker was allowed to talk that way about an injured suspect.

'Don't look at *me*,' Molina told her. 'He's just saying what I'm thinking.' She stepped away to answer her phone. 'Molina.'

While Molina took the call, Leon asked Upshaw, 'What are his chances of surviving this? To the point that he could talk?'

Upshaw threw up her hands. 'How long is a piece of string? You should give him a few more hours.'

'I'm not just sitting about waiting for someone to talk. We've got a fugitive gunman on the loose.'

'Bodies don't generally respond to a firm tone of voice, DC Walker.'

'You'd be surprised,' he replied.

Molina spun around and snapped her fingers at Leon. 'We need to go. Now!'

Leon set off after her, running at full pelt down the corridor. 'Where are we going?'

'Industrial estate in Wembley. Possible hideout. The gunman could have gone back there.'

WHILE MOLINA DROVE like a madwoman through the streets of Westminster, Mayfair, and along the Westway – what Leon believed to be one of the most miserably busy roads in existence – Leon had time to make calls with the management of the industrial estate.

Once he was finished, Leon scribbled down notes in a pad, the inertia of Molina's rapid overtaking and wild veering across lanes throwing him from side to side.

'Okay,' he said, 'there are eighty-six units total on the site. Only seven have been taken up in the last three months.'

Molina shook her head. 'No, that's too long. They wouldn't risk being seen around any one place for that long. Try the last two weeks.'

Leon did some quick calculations based on the information he'd been given about each of the seven units. 'That narrows it down to three units.' He circled them on a map.

Despite navigating through dense traffic at a rapid rate, Molina took a moment to look at the map. She pointed to a unit on its own. 'That one.'

'How do you know?'

She pointed again. 'The other two are next to each other. They wouldn't take on a unit which someone else could have been using while they were around. The other unit's more hidden away too. Near the back of the estate, so there's less traffic going past it.'

Leon couldn't fault her logic. 'All right. Sounds good. Will I call it in?'

'Call it in? Armed response are ten minutes behind us. And that's if they left right this second. No, mate...' Molina floored the accelerator as the road cleared ahead. 'We're going in.'

CHAPTER TWENTY-NINE

MOLINA PARKED a corner short of the cul-de-sac where the suspect unit was.

'What's the plan?' asked Leon.

Molina reached into her jacket pocket and checked the magazine of a Glock 17. 'We go inside and take whoever's there.'

Leon stared at the weapon. He could never get used to the sight of guns. 'You're armed?'

'That's an armed suspect in there,' said Molina. 'And you've come along for a ride in Specialist Command.' She opened her door. 'Do yourself a favour. Stay behind me.'

With no choice but to follow her in, Leon sighed, then said to himself, 'Shit...'

He kept low, following closely behind Molina who showed zero fear in approaching the building. Her weapon was drawn, but pointing down, at her side. She wasn't relishing the prospect of having to shoot someone, but she was clearly comfortable with a gun in her hand.

She directed Leon to a side door of the warehouse,

rather than attempting to open the large roller shutter at the front used for pallet and van deliveries.

Leon stood with his back to the corrugated iron wall, then gestured with open hands. *What now? I'm unarmed.*

Molina mouthed in reply, 'Follow my lead.'

She stole a glance into the warehouse through the narrow window pane in the door. Not satisfied that she had absorbed enough information to go inside, she stole a second look.

'Anything?' whispered Leon.

She shook her head, no. She held up a finger to indicate "one". 'He's down.'

Before Leon could respond, Molina readied her weapon, then threw the door open. 'Armed police!...'

Leon felt helpless running in after her with nothing more than his bare hands to use as weapons should they come under attack. But as they ran to the middle of the room, the only threat was lying face-down on the ground with his throat slit.

Molina pointed to him. 'Check his pulse.' She kept her weapon trained on whatever possible threats might still be around the warehouse.

There was a banged-up blue van behind the closed roller shutter. Other than that, there were no other hiding spots.

Molina closed in on the van, operating on the assumption that there was someone in there with a weapon: the only sensible approach in the situation. The van was unlocked, having been used for reconnaissance two days earlier with no plans to use it again.

Molina called out, 'Clear!'

Leon, hands bloodied from checking the dead man's

pulse, sat back, kneeling on the ground by the body. 'He's gone,' he confirmed.

Molina holstered her weapon. 'Looks like someone had a dramatic change of heart about his involvement.' She began searching for any clues. 'Give me a hand here,' she said, rummaging through the back of the van.

Leon put on latex gloves before checking the front. Two takeaway coffee cups were in the cup holder by the gear stick, along with the usual detritus of a work van: old newspapers, receipts and random bits of paper and rubbish piled up against the base of the windscreen. 'This thing's a tip,' Leon said.

Then he opened the glovebox.

Inside was a plain brown envelope. Leon took out the photographs inside, all of the same thin, black man with short dreadlocks.

Leon held them up for Molina to see. 'Do these look like surveillance photos to you?'

'Could be a target,' she said, taking a closer look.

Leon tipped the envelope up, and out dropped a printout from Google maps with an address circled in pen.

Molina got straight onto Protection Command's control centre in Lewisham. 'Hey, it's Sofia. I need all hands to a flat in Hackney. Be advised: possible shooter on site.'

BY THE TIME Molina and Leon had navigated the A1 west across the city, looping around the top of Hampstead Heath, then south into Hackney, there were already two police vans and Counter Terror's neon BMW X5s parked outside Wilson Kipchoge's high-rise flats. And, curiously, a forensics services van.

'How did they get here so fast?' Leon wondered aloud.

'Yeah, that's weird,' Molina agreed.

There was no sense of urgency in any of the officers around the area. The sense was that DI Molina and DC Walker were late to the party.

In the surrounding flats, residents watched from their balconies, pointing at the huge police presence and speculating with neighbours about what had happened. The assumption from the military look of the Counter Terror officers was that some radical Islamist had been captured. Even the people on Kipchoge's floor didn't know who lived in there.

Molina and Leon entered the flat that was still largely in darkness. The only light source was the open front door.

Leon put a hand to his mouth, recoiling from the sight of so many dead bodies in the bedroom.

As weathered an officer as Molina was, she was still shocked. She stopped walking the moment she saw the bodies. 'Fuck me...' she gasped in disgust at how anyone could commit such a gruesome crime. She checked with Leon, 'There was only one guy in those photos, right?'

Leon looked to his right, into the bathroom where a forensic specialist was examining Wilson Kipchoge's body. 'Him,' he pointed out.

'Then why kill the others?'

In the bedroom, a photographer's flash cast a shocking and painful burst of light in the dark room.

Molina remarked, 'Wrong place, wrong time? Looks like a shared flat for immigrants. This number of people all living under the same roof.'

Leon couldn't get his head around it. 'But...killing all these innocent people. For one man?'

'Because why leave a living witness?' Molina replied. 'That's how these people roll, Leon.' Following voices at the end of the hall, she rounded the corner to the kitchen where two officers were huddled in close conversation. When Molina saw that it was Superintendent Sue Thornley standing with an unknown sergeant from Counter Terror, Molina said with surprise, 'Ma'am?'

The sergeant stepped back slightly, as if aware that he'd been looking conspiratorial.

'Sofia,' replied Thornley. 'What a bloody mess, eh?'

Molina was still clearly confused as to why Thornley was there – and how she had got there so quickly. But there was no way to question her on the fact without sounding impertinent. 'I was going to say shit show, ma'am. But yes. Bloody mess about captures it.'

'I was just saying to Sergeant Webb here...'

The man next to Thornley nodded in acknowledgement to Molina.

Thornley continued, 'It looks very professional. Mostly single shots. Instantly fatal. Where did the lead come from?'

Molina indicated DC Walker, who was examining the bathroom scene closely. He flagged up Sean's vomit to a senior officer.

'We should get this checked,' said Leon. 'I don't see any signs of vomit on any of the victims. Nothing around their mouths. Unless the shooter wiped up on their way out.'

Molina nodded in appreciation. 'DC Leon Walker, ma'am,' she told Thornley. Expression steeling, she added, 'Where did your lead come from?'

'I'm sorry?' said Thornley.

'Forensics look like they've been here at least fifteen minutes. They didn't get here off the back of our lead, so something else must have come up.'

Sergeant Webb cut in. 'Anonymous tip over the phone to the station. Reports of a man with a gun fleeing the scene this morning.'

'I would have thought DCI Bell or myself would have been made aware of that the moment it came in, no?'

Webb said nothing.

Thornley led Molina out of the kitchen. 'The important thing is we get one step closer to catching this guy.'

'There's been about ten people living here,' Molina said. 'It'll take days for forensics to confirm elimination prints and DNA.'

'Let them worry about that for now.' She called on Leon, who dutifully joined the women in the hallway.

'Ma'am,' Leon said with a firm nod, only too aware of the esteemed and decorated officer standing in front of him.

Thornley explained, 'It looks like we know how this whole thing was put together now.'

'How so, ma'am?' asked Molina.

'The young man in the bathroom is Wilson Kipchoge. He was a cleaner at Ashcroft House, which several businesses work out of. Among them, Eriksen Commercial Cleaning.'

'The cleaners' overalls,' Molina said in recognition.

'There was a biometric scanner in the Eriksen van left at Stanley House. It has Kipchoge's fingerprint logged in it.'

Leon said, 'That's how they acquired the passcodes to get in.'

'It seems the others here were just collateral damage.'

'It's messy, though, isn't it?' said Molina.

'Doesn't appear to have been plan A. The security guard that should have been on site this morning at Stanley House, Victor Kemp, was taken into hospital with gall-stones overnight. We paid a visit to his ward to ask him some questions, but he was tough. Bastard took at least ninety seconds to confess. Couldn't shut him up in the end. He'd been paid to let some people in for what he was told was data theft. Said he didn't' see the harm, if you can believe that. He's spilling his guts on every detail to trim any second he can off the presumably hefty prison sentence he's got coming his way. But I doubt any of it will lead to anything. These guys have been too careful so far. And as we've seen here: unrelenting in covering their tracks.' Thornley looked towards the front door, where an officer was holding a phone aloft and calling her name. 'What is it?' she asked.

The officer called back, 'St Thomas, ma'am. The injured shooter's waking up.'

Molina leapt on it. 'We'll take that, ma'am.'

Thornley widened her eyes to emphasise the importance. 'Go! I'll update DCI Bell.'

As Molina and Leon took off towards the door, Thornley shouted after them. 'I want names, DI Molina...'

When they got onto the landing outside, Leon could tell that Molina wasn't happy about something. 'What's wrong?' he asked.

Molina jogged on, shaking her head. 'I don't know...the whole scene back there. Something's not right.'

CHAPTER THIRTY

NOVAK WASN'T ENTIRELY sure what made somewhere a 'hamlet', but Regis Point in the deepest countryside of Northern Westchester certainly seemed like one.

Nathan, sitting in the front seat of Novak's grunty engined Ford GT, said, 'How much business can there really be for a pathologist all the way out here? Is this one of those opioid counties where everyone's dropping like flies behind closed doors?'

'Not quite,' said Novak, checking house numbers along Main Street to see how much further they had to go. 'It's mostly wealthy retirees around here. Hence why my dad was living nearby. The pathologist who did the autopsy on his body used to work at Northern Westchester Hospital. He moved out here a few years ago apparently.'

They pulled up in front of a tiny surgery on Main Road, a converted bungalow next to an Italian restaurant that looked like it had seen better days.

Nathan leaned down for a better look out his window. 'This is it?'

'Yeah,' said Novak. 'And just a reminder. I'm not going in there accusing anyone of anything, okay? There's no faster way to get someone to clam up around here than acting like some New Yorker big shot. We're just here for clarification.'

'Got it,' said Nathan.

A bell dinged above the door when the men entered, finding the reception empty, and no one in the waiting area.

After a few seconds of waiting for someone to appear, Novak called out, 'Hello?'

A woman in her late fifties limped in behind the counter. She didn't say anything until she had comfortably sat down, giving a weighty sigh of relief at getting off her feet. Her name badge looked decades old and said "Dorothy".

With a wide smile, she said, 'So...what can I do for you...gentlemen?' She trailed off. It wasn't often that two men showed up together for an appointment.

Nathan hung around awkwardly in the background, leaving Novak to do all the talking. It had been so long since he'd last done anything like this, he didn't know what to do with himself.'

'I'm Tom Novak,' he said. 'I'm looking to speak to Dr Blackford.' He gestured to himself. 'He's an old friend of the family.'

Dorothy pursed her lips tightly, her smile gone in an instant.

Novak added, 'He was my dad's physician.'

'Oh, I'm sorry, dear,' she said. 'Harry passed on just a few weeks ago.'

Nathan came over, suddenly intrigued. He shared a suspicious look with Novak.

'What happened?' Nathan asked.

'A car accident out by the old boathouse. You know how misty it can get around there this time of year.' Interpreting Novak's lack of reaction, she added, 'Oh, you're not from around here.'

'Close,' Novak clarified.

Nathan pressed on, 'Was he hit or something?'

'No,' Dorothy said, 'he just went off the road.' Despite there being no one else in the surgery except the new doctor down the corridor, Dorothy lowered her voice and made a drinking motion with her hand. 'He'd had a few too many. Blood alcohol was off the scale, the police said.'

'Really,' Novak said, failing to mask his scepticism.

Getting overexcited at being back chasing a lead, Nathan kept pushing, 'What about–'

Novak put a hand to Nathan's chest to stop him. 'No, it's okay. We don't want to cause you any upset. But I'll tell what I'm looking for. I'm putting my dad's affairs in order, and Dr Blackford had promised he would look out a copy of his autopsy report on my dad. He, um, committed suicide, you see. And there have been some life insurance issues recently.'

'Those sons of bitches,' said Dorothy. 'I've been there. But I'm going to have to see some ID. You're next of kin, right?'

'That's right,' said Novak, passing over his New York State driver's licence.

Satisfied that everything was in order, Dorothy set off towards Blackford's office.

Novak put his hands in his trouser pockets, feigning casualness. The moment Dorothy was out of sight, he whipped around to Nathan.

'Drink driving, my ass,' Novak whispered.

'It sounds suspicious,' Nathan agreed, 'but we can't make assumptions.'

'Ordinarily. But Blackford used to visit our house, and the first thing my dad did – every time – was offer him a drink, and he always declined.'

'That's not strange, is it? He would have been working.'

'I'm talking social visits. They played golf together, Nathan.'

Nathan shook his head. 'You're reaching.'

'No, I'm not saying that Blackford didn't drink much. I'm saying that he couldn't have. The reason I always remember that Blackford never took up my dad's offer is that Blackford had chronic persistent hepatitis. It's non-progressive liver inflammation. He couldn't have been so drunk that he drove off the road. If he'd blown a point one on a blood-alcohol test, he couldn't even have made it to his car let alone drive for miles before crashing.'

'But she said that thing about the mist.'

'Bullshit,' Novak fired back, struggling to restrain the volume of his voice. 'If his blood alcohol was that high, he would have already been dead before he could start the engine, Nathan. Now, in the weeks before you discover that burner phone, and all of this other stuff about my dad comes out, Blackford just happens to die by means that don't make *any* sense whatsoever.'

Nathan had been off the scene for a while. Seeing Novak's passion up close was inspiring. And also a little intimidating. Like an average rookie trying to keep up with the star player on the team.

Dorothy brought back the autopsy report, saying from a distance, 'Got it.'

Novak had to restrain himself from snatching it out of her hand and speed-reading it right at the desk.

Once they were back in the car, Novak was free to read it. 'This is different,' he said. He flicked through the pages with increasing urgency. 'Look,' he pointed out a particular drug found in Seymour's blood. 'That wasn't in the autopsy report Blackford originally showed me.'

'He changed it?' asked Nathan.

'He must have.' Novak tucked the report into his bag in the back seat. 'We'll need to get a second opinion, but it's documented evidence at least that the autopsy results were changed. But that will need to wait.'

'Why? What's next?'

'We need to take the meeting that my dad wasn't allowed to get to. Whatever Anna Storm was going to tell my dad, she can tell it to us.'

'Us?' Nathan checked.

Novak sped off from the kerb. 'My dad trusted you, Nathan. That's good enough for me. So yes. Us.'

'But how are we going to get the meeting. We can't just show up at Anna Storm's office demanding an interview.'

Novak sighed. 'I'm going to have to call in a favour. But it's not going to be easy.'

CHAPTER THIRTY-ONE

Rebecca stood by the old wooden fence in the back garden of the farmhouse, drinking a cup of tea and watching the sun go down behind the hills in the distance. She had been cold for a while, but didn't want to break the mood of the view by leaving to fetch a jacket.

The intense quiet felt strange to her ears which had become accustomed to the endless hum of the City. It was the landscape she had once been familiar with, growing up with her father, and later, in the surrounding hills near Cheltenham where she had spent so many years working for GCHQ.

It was the landscape of Ralph Vaughan Williams' *Lark Ascending* concerto. Of Elgar. Of gentle strings and peaceful flutes. But Rebecca knew that it was all temporary. Eventually she would have to face the city again. And whoever had gone to such lengths to try and kill her and Ghost Division. Because one thing was clear from the attack: they meant business.

Rebecca turned around upon a car crunching up the gravel driveway.

An unmarked police car with one of DCI Bell's sergeants driving – as demanded by Rebecca. She wouldn't have had Stella Mitchell's safety compromised for anything. Not after everything they had been through.

Stella threw the car door open before the car was fully stopped, then dashed to the garden where she could see Rebecca. She threw her arms around her.

'I'm so glad you're all right,' Stella said.

'I think the jury is still out on that one,' Rebecca replied. 'Can I get you a coffee?'

'God no. I'm wired. I had about four on the flight over. How are you doing?'

'All right, considering.'

Stella looked over her shoulder, seeing DCI Bell standing at the french windows at the living room, watching them. 'How have the police been?'

'Reasonable so far. That won't last, though. Christ, what I would give for just one easy year. Is that so hard to ask?' Rebecca took up her position leaning over the fence again, beseeching the dark orange sky that was crystal clear, promising a harsh frost that night. 'I see other people walking around every day, and it all looks so easy. So simple.'

'I'm sure it just looks that way,' Stella replied. 'You don't really know what people are dealing with underneath.'

'I know. But for the most part, most people don't have to deal with the sort of things we have. Being chased by gunmen through the streets of Pimlico. A paramilitary assault on the Mall, and the same again in downtown

Manhattan. What is it about me that I don't get a quiet life. A peaceful life?'

'Because you chose as your career something bigger and more important than yourself.'

'What I would give for a year of no great traumas. No disasters. No drama.'

Stella smiled.

'What is it?' asked Rebecca.

'It reminds me of a story I once read. It was a cold winter's night, and the Glen Miller Band were on their way to a gig when their bus breaks down in the middle of nowhere. So the musicians grab their instrument cases and start walking. Before long, they come across this picture-perfect, cozy little house. It's like something out of a Norman Rockwell painting of classic Americana. Inside, there's a family sitting around a dinner table, talking and laughing. They're digging into this steaming apple pie that the band members can taste through the window it looks so good. It's been raining so they're all soaked through and shivering watching this idyllic scene. Finally, one of the musicians turns to another and says, 'Jeez, how do people live like that?'

Rebecca was too down-hearted to laugh outright, but her smile was warm.

Stella concluded, 'The normal life isn't for people like us. There's a reason for that.'

'What's the reason?'

'Anything of worth in this life demands sacrifice. And what we do has worth.'

Rebecca looked back out across the endless fields. 'I don't know anymore.'

Stella turned around as she heard DCI Bell approaching.

He asked her, 'Can I talk to Rebecca for a moment?'

Stella didn't budge. 'That's up to Rebecca.'

Rebecca said, 'I'd rather she stayed.'

'You might not like everything I have to say,' said Bell. 'Some privacy might be preferable.'

'Ask what you have to ask, DCI Bell,' Rebecca said.

'DC Walker. You two seemed very close back at Stanley House.'

Rebecca snorted knowingly. She said to Stella, 'I wondered how long it would take before they tried this line of questioning.'

'He is several rungs below you, is he not?'

'What's that supposed to mean? What rungs?'

'It's a pretty obvious fact. He's a detective constable. You're the director of a major intelligence agency. Until recently, he was living in a single-bed shit hole in Lambeth. Now he's living in the clouds with you in a penthouse apartment.'

Impatient, Rebecca said, 'Get to the point, DCI Bell.'

'How much do you really know about Leon Walker?'

'I know he's a hero and a decorated police officer.'

'That's the public profile, though, isn't it. What about underneath? What about in private? He's never going to earn as much as you.'

Rebecca tossed the remnants of her tea over the fence, then started back towards the farmhouse. 'I don't have to listen to this shit.'

Bell stayed exactly where he was. 'So you know about his secret savings account?'

Rebecca stopped and stared at the house in confusion before turning back. 'What?'

'An account in his name was opened last month, and two hundred thousand pounds was deposited in it.' He leaned forward slightly for the kicker. 'Last night.'

'I don't know where you've got your information, but you're mistaken,' Rebecca said. 'I know what you're thinking. But if you're suggesting that Leon was involved in any way with what happened at Stanley House, you're wrong about that too. Leon's never known any specifics about Ghost Division. Not procedure. Not protocols. Passwords. Nothing. And he's never asked, DCI Bell. So I'd check where that information has come from.'

To stop Rebecca leaving again, Bell said, 'It came from the injured shooter in St Thomas' Hospital. From the mouth of the only suspect captured so far.'

Stella couldn't help but interject with some sarcasm. 'So a totally trustworthy source.'

'How would he know Leon's name?' Bell countered? 'More to the point, why would he be calling it out.'

'Calling it out?'

'His doctor was in the room doing tests while he was asleep. He called out DC Walker's name several times before passing out again. The doctor just called me. Apparently he's woken up again. I'm sending in DI Molina and DC Walker to question the suspect. I'd be damned interested to hear what our suspect has to say in Leon's company. I think you might too, Director Fox.'

CHAPTER THIRTY-TWO

STELLA RAN INSIDE after Rebecca to check she was okay. She found her in the living room, hunched over a GCHQ-issue military-grade laptop that gave her access to Ghost Division's off-site servers.

Stella cautioned, 'You know he's just trying to push you because he's got nothing else to go on. Don't let him get to you.'

'He isn't remotely getting to me,' Rebecca replied. 'But I'm worried about Leon. We don't know who we're dealing with yet, and I don't want Leon to end up as collateral damage. We've seen that too many times already. That's why I need to move fast on some things I found earlier.' She beckoned Stella next to her on the couch.

'What am I looking at?' asked Stella.

'Melissa Forsyth's home computer. Courtesy of some old friends at GCHQ.'

'I won't ask.'

'And I wouldn't tell. She was a regular on the dark web.'

'Business or pleasure?'

'A little of both, it would seem,' said Rebecca. She navigated to a site that looked like an unsophisticated, much older, version of Facebook. It was called CrookBook.

'Catchy name,' said Stella.

'That's the one thing that isn't lacking on the dark web: honesty. It's like a classifieds website for criminals. You can advertise jobs you want done, or offer your services – whatever they might be. It's terrifying to think what business is being transacted on a daily basis there. Based on our research at Ghost Division, the job requesters outnumber the hired hands by about three to one.'

'So there are more jobs needing done than there are criminals willing to perform them?'

'I don't know whether that reinforces my view of humanity or destroys it. I'm not sure.'

'Which was Melissa doing?'

'Offering services. Specifically, using Ghost Division's systems for illicit tracking and data gathering. Spying, basically. For a fee. Which was a bit of a niche on CrookBook, because very few people have access to the sort of systems that Melissa had access to. It was easy for her to prove her worth. She could just dial into ELEMENT when no one was looking, and find out every detail about someone's life and relay it to them by encrypted chat. Once the buyers knew she was for real, she pushed the envelope further and further with what she was offering. Until she pushed thing so far, she was willing to help two men enter Stanley House in order to steal thousands of documents. So they claimed. On the dark web, their sale could have been used for wholesale identity theft. One of the most lucrative markets on

CrookBook these days. But they didn't tell her the whole story.'

'There must at least be some comfort knowing that Melissa didn't willingly let them in to shoot the place up.'

'She turned into everything she claimed to detest. Forgive me if I'm not buckled over with grief at her loss.' Rebecca clicked out to a tranche of log files from ELEMENT. 'You won't know ELEMENT yet, but suffice to say it's like Google on steroids for telecoms tracking. It gives us everything you could imagine. Now, what got my attention was one number here.' She highlighted it with the cursor. 'See that number there? It's the same one Novak asked me to check this morning.'

It took Stella a moment to catch up, because it didn't make sense to her. 'Seymour Novak's burner phone? Nathan only found out about it yesterday. When did Melissa look up the number?'

'Last week.'

Stella shook her head slowly in confusion. 'There's no way Melissa could have known about it.'

'Unless someone else asked her to look into it. Someone else who knew about the phone.'

'But who could that have been?'

'The search has to be connected to the attack on Stanley House, Stella. Seymour died six years ago. That's a long time in telecoms. Pre-NSA Papers, when it just wasn't known how information from your phone was available to government agencies.'

'What was Melissa doing with the data about the burner?'

'Deleting phone connections associated with it. She started it, but never finished. Seems she was holding out for more money. Once she let the shooters in this morning, she was probably going to hold the data hostage over it. But look...' Rebecca clicked further through the data. 'I've traced one of the phones in proximity to Seymour's burner the night he died to a location in and around Seymour's property, and near his time of death. Unquestionably someone who was involved in Seymour's death. Now, that phone ends up in the Hudson River later that night. It's been inactive ever since. But I did a check on that location of the river over the following few weeks. I found this.' She clicked open a story from the tabloid *Bastion News*. A grisly salacious headline and photo showing a bagged body being pulled out of the Hudson River. 'The deceased's name was Eric Bogossian. First hits I got on him were all military. And that's when I found this...' She then opened up a photo of a US Marine unit taken in Iraq. 'Look familiar?'

Stella leaned in for a closer look. 'I can't tell...Who am I looking at?'

'This guy,' said Rebecca zooming in further.

Once he'd been pointed out, Stella could see it straight away. 'Oh my god...is that...? It can't be...'

'It is,' Rebecca assured her. 'There's a good image of him that I managed to clean up from an exterior CCTV camera. Click between them if you like.'

Stella clicked from one photo to the other. The likeness was undeniable. 'That's the other shooter. For sure.'

'His name's Damian Oxley. And if his record is anything to go by, we're dealing with one twisted, and extremely intelligent individual.' She paused, waiting for the implications to become clear to Stella. 'I'll bet everything I have that Damian Oxley was involved in Seymour's death. He's a clear link between the two crimes. The question is, why did Oxley – or someone employing him – arrange the attack on Ghost Division?'

Stella let out a long puff. 'I don't know how you do it.' She got to her feet, then wondered why Rebecca was still sitting. 'Aren't you going to tell DCI Bell?'

'Yeah, tell me something,' DCI Bell announced from the doorway.

He was flanked by two Protection Command constables in uniform.

Bell continued, 'Tell me, for instance, why your fingerprints, Rebecca, were just found at Wilson Kipchoge's address.'

Rebecca was the epitome of confusion. 'Who the hell is Wilson Kipchoge?'

'A weak link in the security chain between the Eriksen cleaning company and Stanley House. Wilson was found dead this morning.'

'DCI Bell, I have no earthly idea what you're talking about. I've never heard of Wilson Kipchoge, and I've got an alibi for my entire morning.'

'Would one of them be DC Leon Walker? The man who one of the suspects in custody has just named as an accomplice?'

Rebecca's stomach churned. She could see where Bell was going now. 'Leon's an accomplice now?'

'According to the suspect. Who we now know is called Lee Patterson. Name ring any bells?'

'None,' Rebecca answered.

'It should ring some bells with Leon. He arrested him for burglary last year, then charges were mysteriously dropped. Was Lee repaying Leon for the favour today? Did they keep in touch all this time, Leon waiting for the right time to use him?'

'That will be easily refutable with the wealth of data I have at my disposal.'

'And what if it isn't?' asked Bell.

Rebecca didn't respond.

'DI Molina will be observing Leon and Lee closely when they go to question him. After that, Leon will be taken in for questioning.'

Stella said, 'Rebecca, as hard as it is to hear, you have to accept there's at least a chance that DCI Bell is right about this.'

Rebecca thought about it, then shook her head. 'No. I know Leon. And he knows me. DCI Bell, you're wrong. All you've got so far is one man's unofficial statement.'

Bell retorted, 'And one set of fingerprints that places you, Rebecca, at the scene of a murder that made the attack on Stanley House possible.' He turned back to Rebecca. 'And so far, your only alibi is a man who a suspect has named as an accomplice: your own boyfriend. You've been looking for traitors, Director Fox. Might I suggest you take a look in the mirror. You've left me no choice.' He gave the nod to one of the officers at the edge of the room. Then he said, 'Rebecca Fox, I'm placing you under–'

The lights went off all around the house. The only light source was Rebecca's laptop, which was running off the battery.

'It's him,' Rebecca said, eyes flicking from one set of windows to another, waiting for the inevitable dark figure outside to appear. She said to Bell, 'If you cuff me, you'll be killing me.'

Bell, still confident that he was controlling the situation, moved towards Rebecca to restrain her. Then he saw one of the Protection Command officers grab his sidearm weapon, preparing to fire at Rebecca.

The light from the laptop was enough for the officer to see what he was doing. But before the officer could fire off a round, Bell lunged for the laptop, slamming the lid shut and plunging the room into total darkness.

He yelled to Rebecca, 'Down!' He then threw himself towards her, right at the point of the trigger being pulled.

The sound of the gun firing and Bell's cry of agony as a bullet pierced his side, were almost simultaneous. Bell had blocked the bullet from hitting Rebecca, who he shoved aside to safety.

Stella couldn't see anything, crawling along the floor trying to get behind a sofa.

The officer kept firing blindly into the darkness, hoping to hit Rebecca. But now the second officer had managed to grab and restrain him. As they rolled on the ground, another two shots rang out. Now both DCI Bell and his one loyal officer were down. The traitor was met by Damian in the kitchen, who had burst in during the melee.

Damian scolded him, 'I told you to wait for me.'

'I had the upper hand,' the officer replied. 'It was worth a shot.'

Damian shone a torch into the living room, where DCI Bell and his colleague were on the floor. Both unresponsive.

Rebecca and Stella had fled, escaping out an auxiliary room door to the stables at the side of the farmhouse.

Following the only road to the nearest village would have been suicide. Instead, they ran through the hayfield out the back. Both gasping for air, and running for their lives.

'Don't turn round,' Stella told her. 'Don't stop...'

Rebecca's voice shook. 'Is he dead back there? DCI Bell.'

'I don't know.'

Once they were satisfied that the shooter wasn't chasing them through the field, Rebecca slowed – only slightly – to make a phone call. 'Call Leon!' she told the AI assistant on her phone.

The call went to voicemail.

'Leon,' Rebecca cried desperately. 'Wherever you are, get out. It's a trap. Someone's framing us...'

CHAPTER THIRTY-THREE

THE CITY WAS SMEARED with rain. Black clouds overhead bringing a premature darkness to the day as DI Sofia Molina and DC Leon Walker pulled into St Thomas' Hospital.

Molina made repeated attempts to reach DCI Bell on the phone as they ascended the building to the ward where Lee Patterson was being kept.

'Everything okay?' asked Leon.

'It's probably nothing,' Molina replied.

'How do you want to play this if he's talking?'

'I'll take the lead. The boss has given me a few questions he wants answered.'

It was only now that they were in the momentary calm of the lift that Leon realised he had a voicemail on his phone – missed when they were at Wilson Kipchoge's flat.

'Sorry, two secs,' Leon said as he listened to the voicemail.

Before he could appreciate that it was Rebecca's voice, he registered the panic, the sheer terror, in her voice.

'Wherever you are, get out. It's a trap. Someone's framing us...'

Leon waited several seconds after the message had ended before he reacted in any way. Calmly pocketing his phone, he told Molina, 'Just Rebecca checking in.'

'All good? Anything about the chief inspector?'

'No, she didn't say.'

'But she sounded okay?'

'Yeah. Fine.' Leon kept his eyes locked on the LED ticker showing what floor they were on. He felt that if his eyes met DI Molina's, he'd crumble like a Jenga tower.

What the hell is going on? he thought.

Did Rebecca mean that the two of them were being framed for the Stanley House attack? If so, who was framing them? And what should he do about it?

Despite Rebecca's warning, he didn't think he had any choice but to stick with Molina until he could work out what the shot was. If he ran, where would he be running to? Who could he trust? The only person who might be able to make it all clearer was a short corridor away, handcuffed to a hospital bed.

The moment they reached Lee Patterson's ward, Molina knew something was wrong. There was no police presence outside the room as had been arranged.

Barely slowing down, she barked at the reception desk, 'Where's my police guard?' Frustrated at the nurse's slow response, Molina emphasised, 'At Patterson's?' She pointed at the offending private room.

Mystified, the nurse at the desk shrugged innocently. 'They just left about fifteen minutes ago.'

'Where are they?'

Irked by Molina's tone, she replied, 'I don't know. I'm not responsible for what police officers do around here.'

Molina shook her head at Leon, as if to say, *amateur hour.*

She stormed into Pattersons's private room hoping to find the police officer that should have been standing outside. Instead, she found Dr Upshaw winding up one of five sections of blinds that had been covering the windows.

Leon registered it with confusion. Why would she be rolling a blind up as daylight was fading? But he didn't say anything, as Molina was swallowing up all the oxygen in the room.

She pointed disdainfully at the door. 'Where's the armed guard I had posted here?'

'I have no idea,' Upshaw replied, moving over to Pattersons's bedside. 'I've been a little busy keeping people alive.'

'What's he been saying, then?' asked Leon.

'It's been a little scattered,' Upshaw said. 'But I thought DCI Bell would want to know. I mean, you never know what could end up being important, right?'

Molina said, 'But he's named names, hasn't he?'

'He said one name. Leon Walker.'

Leon looked at the pair of them with incredulity. 'What? That's impossible. He couldn't possibly know my name.'

Upshaw shrugged, equally mystified. 'I don't know what to tell you.'

Molina asked Leon pointedly, 'Why would your name be the first thing he says?'

'Yeah, exactly?' Leon gestured to Patterson, who still looked groggy. An oxygen mask over his mouth. 'May I?'

'Go ahead,' said Upshaw.

Molina pushed forward ahead of Leon. 'I'll handle this,' she said. She crouched down by the bed. 'Lee Patterson? I'm DI Sofia Molina. Do you recognise the man with me?'

Leon turned away, shaking his head. 'This is crazy,' he said to himself.

Molina tapped Patterson's hand, but got no response. She said to Upshaw, 'The point of us coming here is that we were told he was talking.'

Patterson started talking, muffled, beneath his mask.

When Molina reached to take it off, Upshaw stopped her, taking over herself instead.

'Lee, can you hear me?' she asked.

'Look,' said Molina, 'we really need him to talk. Is there anything you can give him to help him along?'

Upshaw looked first towards the closed door, then back at Patterson. She lowered her voice. 'I shouldn't do this, ordinarily. But...'

It was a phrase that had been magic to Molina's ears so often in her career.

'Give me a minute.' Upshaw rummaged through a metal drawer on a medicine trolley, then returned with a syringe of something.

'What is that?' asked Leon.

'You want him to talk, right?' She checked the needle, then plunged it into a vein in Patterson's arm. 'He'll be singing "You Are My Sunshine" any minute.'

But before Upshaw could fully retract the syringe, Patterson began spasming in a leg. Then both legs. Then his torso as well.

'Shit,' muttered Upshaw, lunging for the phone attached to the wall behind Patterson's head. 'Crash in room two!' She hit a large red button that set off an alarm that seemed much too loud to be in a hospital room.

'What's happening?' asked Molina, backing away quickly from the bed.

Upshaw grabbed defibrillator paddles from the crash box behind the bed, then Patterson's heart monitor emitted a long, terminal beep. 'What does it sound like...'

While Upshaw prepared Patterson for shocking, and a team of nurses piled into the room, Leon noticed a small red light dancing along the ground. Just a small dot, like a laser. As quickly as it had appeared, it was gone. Then a few seconds later, Leon saw it again. This time on Molina's back. Unmistakably, a red laser sight.

Molina was watching the desperate efforts to revive Patterson, when Leon remembered about the blind being opened. And how it had struck him as odd. Now it made sense.

But by the time Leon made all those calculations and realised what was really going on, the red dot had moved upwards. Now it was at the back of Molina's head.

Almost in slow motion, Leon cried out, 'No!'

A bullet shattered the window behind, then DI Molina was sent hurtling forward onto the ground. A single bullet entering the back of her head.

Almost instantaneously, blood from the entry wound spattered across Leon's face. The young detective constable remained rooted to the spot, in shock at what had just happened in front of him.

Dr Upshaw whipped around at the sound of the window breaking behind her. She was still holding the paddles over Patterson's chest. She had tears in her eyes when she looked at Leon. 'I'm sorry,' she said.

Leon understood now. He threw himself out of the sight line of the window, as another shot fired through the already broken window. He rolled to one side, praying that the sniper didn't have a shot.

They didn't.

Upshaw dropped the paddles and made a run for it, as the sniper took blind shots in desperation, hoping to get lucky by firing bullets through the windows that still had blinds lowered over them.

Leon's first instinct was to chase Upshaw. But when he saw the other nurses cowering for cover, he slowed his escape from the room by helping them to the sanctuary of the corridor.

Only once the nurses were safely out of Patterson's room, and out of the sniper's sight, Leon set off after Dr Upshaw. She was already far along the corridor, fleeing towards the stairs.

Leon called in the emergency. 'This is DC Leon Walker. Shots fired at St Thomas' Hospital. Officer down! Repeat, officer down!'

Back in Patterson's room, it was eerily calm.

Molina and Patterson's dead bodies lay unattended. The only sound that of Patterson's flatlining heartbeat, and wind gusting through the shattered window.

As Leon closed in on Upshaw, she bolted for a staff-only stairwell. Access to it required a staff swipe card. Leon watched her fumble with the card, delaying her progress.

The door began to shut behind her, inching closed on a slow spring-loaded mechanism. Leon knew if he didn't catch it and keep it open, he would have lost Upshaw for good, disappearing into a labyrinth of corridors in the adjoining wings.

He pumped his arms as hard as he could, straining to move his legs fast enough to get there. He threw out a desperate hand to catch the final inch of the door being open. But he couldn't get there in time. The door slid shut, and Upshaw escaped.

Leon hadn't given up, though. As he turned to find an alternative route out, a fire alarm went off along with sprinklers. No doubt Upshaw's work, Leon thought.

The sprinklers drenched him in no time as he ran back towards the ward reception. There, he was met with an intimidating sight of armed police officers.

They were all shouting his name, and instructing him to get down on the ground.

Leon showed them his hands and lay down on his front. 'I'm unarmed!' he yelled.

In the moment, he didn't care about the indignity of being accused of a crime and arrested. All he wanted was Upshaw in custody so he could question her.

As he was surrounded by black boots of the armed response team, Leon accepted his fate – however temporary.

An officer cuffed him, and began reading him his rights. 'Leon Walker, you do not have to say anything...'

CHAPTER THIRTY-FOUR

NOVAK'S BRAIN was still buzzing after his and Nathan's visit to the pathologist's in Regis Point. As night fell, they decamped to the archives room at Columbia University, which Novak had a key for.

The campus was a peaceful place to be at night. It reminded Novak of times when he had been in school after normal class times. Parents' night, or a school show, when in the aftermath you could wander the building freely. There was something illicit about wandering those dark corridors, and Columbia was no different.

In the archives room, Novak was sitting cross-legged on the floor, riveted by the autopsy report. He combed through it in greater detail than earlier, while Nathan sifted through boxes and crates and carefully annotated notebooks, which detailed the contents of every container in the room, pulling together everything he could find on Seymour's story notes.

'You were right,' Novak announced without looking up from the page.

Nathan huffed, as he put down another weighty box just to find a single document within it that he thought might be of value. 'What about?' he asked.

'You said that the original autopsy stated cause of death as blood loss with a contributing factor of an overdose. This report here concludes the same as the seven doctors you spoke to who said my dad couldn't have haemorrhaged three litres of blood from the wound on his arm. There's even a possibility that the wound was made post-mortem, though it's not conclusive.'

'We can't use it, then,' Nathan said, returning to work.

'We have to keep it in our pockets though.'

Nathan replied, a little irritably, 'I don't think we should use anything that we're not one hundred per cent on.'

Novak stared at him. 'I get it. You're gun shy. It makes sense. But Nathan, pull back your lens here and look at what we've managed to get in a short space of time.' He stood up and showed Nathan the report. 'This report verifies that there was nowhere near enough blood found at the scene for the sort of blood loss that had to have occurred for my dad to die the way the original autopsy report claimed.'

'But we shouldn't rule out the possibility that it soaked into the ground.'

Novak couldn't believe what he was hearing. 'What?'

'I'm saying, the smart thing to do is to go there, and run our own experiments on the ground. See if we can replicate what the original autopsy report claims.'

'You can't possibly recreate it. We have no idea how hard or soft the ground was that day. Also, it's winter now. It's, like, five degrees colder than when my dad was killed. I don't understand why you're getting gun-shy all of a sudden.'

Nathan replied, 'Because there's a lot to lose now. Before, I was just a guy with a story that no one wanted to hear. But now, there's something actually at stake.' He paused. 'That's the first time you've described your dad's death as anything other than suicide.'

'Surely you don't still believe he killed himself?'

'No,' Nathan replied. He backed away, running his hand through his hair. 'I'm just tired. And more than a little scared. When we publish this, Tom, everyone's going to come after us. Including Stella. And *Republic*. I'm not sure you've thought that through fully.'

'Of course I have. But we have to remain objective. I don't want you making the same mistakes I made. It won't end well.' Nathan put down the box he was working on. The thought of everything he had gone through making him melancholy. 'Look, it's going to be a long night, so I'm going to get a coffee. Do you want one?'

'Sure,' Novak said. 'Want me to carry on with what you were doing?'

'Uh, yeah...' Nathan pointed to the box he had been looking through. 'There's a document called 4F in there somewhere. Can you see if you can find it?'

Novak rummaged through, finding the 4F document folded over, stuck inside the plastic sleeve of another document. He took a moment to look around the room, and the copious amounts of documents that Nathan had sorted through. It was an impressive achievement.

Then, he noticed a small laptop in a plastic bag. Nathan had noted on the front, "NO WORK – JUST

PERSONAL – MAKE SURE TOM GETS THIS BEFORE ARCHIVES OPEN"

Intrigued, Novak powered the laptop on.

The desktop was empty, as well as the hard drive. Thinking that some things might have been accidentally deleted, he checked the recycle bin. That was when he heard the disc drive booting up.

It had been so long since he had used one, it hadn't occurred to him that there might be a disc in there.

The drive icon on the desktop lit up. The name of the disc showed as "XMAS 87"

'What the hell?' Novak thought.

He clicked on it, and a video file opened up on the laptop media player. The screen showed an extended wave of VHS-tape static. The audio came on before the static cleared, the sound of Paul McCartney's "Wonderful Christmastime" playing slightly muffled, as chatter and laughter played over the top of it.

Then there was a voice. One that Novak hadn't heard in such a long time, but that still lived in his head after all these years. Dormant. A sound that he was attached to like no other. The sound of his mother laughing.

The static rolled up and down, then finally cleared, revealing the scene: Christmas Day, post-dinner at the Novak residence.

The footage had been taken in the lounge, which was only ever used for special occasions. The house had another living room that the family used on a daily basis. To save on heating, Seymour always turned the radiators fully off in the room, as no one needed to go in there. Though Novak often sneaked in to listen to Seymour's high-fidelity stereo, sifting through his collection of cassettes, ranging from Dire Straits to Queen, and many other English rock bands that Seymour was partial to.

One of Novak's most treasured memories was of sitting in there when no one else was around, the room freezing, a pair of headphones on listening to his dad's music.

He remembered the Christmas well, as it was his mother's last. Seymour had not long bought a camcorder which had become the latest craze, and had taken to filming almost everything that went on around the house – no matter how monotonous.

At some point, Seymour must have digitised the old VHS footage, which Novak knew was a laborious process. As he pulled the cursor down to raise the volume, he noticed a pop-up menu appear that showed various metadata points. One of which was number of plays, which was listed as 24. It touched Novak to think of Seymour in his cavernous country mansion, sitting alone watching old Christmas videos so often.

Novak worked out that he was six in the video, and by the looks of it, he hadn't changed much. He held his arms out in embarrassment as he realised he was wearing almost the same type of shirt as in the video. What was different, though, was his smile. In eighty-seven, it seemed incandescently joyful. The sort of smile that makes your cheeks hurt if you keep it up too long. He couldn't remember the last time he had smiled like that.

It started to make him feel sad. All that brightness and naivety. No idea of the freight train of grief and loneliness and alienation that was going to take over his life the very next year.

Watching the large family scene, with multiple generations all mingling and chatting and laughing as the fire roared in the corner, and the Paul McCartney song played – a song that at the time Novak had found silly, but now sounded sweetly innocent. It seemed impossible that the family he was watching, looking so joyful and united, could implode in such a way as the Novaks would. That the man who seemed like such a caring father would fail Tom so terribly in the coming years after his mother's death. Behind the facade and fancy clothes and nice house, there were a lot of demons and secrets hiding.

It reminded Novak that the truth wasn't always on the surface. It was often buried.

Nathan returned with two coffees, pleased to see Novak engaging with some of the material on a personal level.

'That sounds like a nice time,' Nathan said.

'Yeah,' Novak said wistfully. 'It was. It never got better than that, in fact.' He shut the laptop screen and shook his head. He looked slowly around the room once more. 'Why didn't I do this?'

Nathan handed him his coffee. 'It's a pretty laborious job, Tom. I doubt you could take a whole month off just to–'

'No, not just the archives, Nathan. I mean the journalism. I call myself a journalist, yet I didn't do the work. For my own dad. I should have been the one to care. Where was I during all this? When my dad needed me to actually be a son and stand up for him, to bring the people who murdered him to justice. I wasn't there.'

Nathan crouched down next to him. 'You're here now, Tom. That's the point.'

'All these years I criticised my dad for not being there. But I did the exact same thing.' His eyes filled with tears for a moment, but they didn't spill down his cheeks. He took a deep breath, composing himself. 'You know, now that I can see everything that he was working on with you, bringing this to you to try and blow it wide open, I respect what he was trying to do. I just wish it hadn't taken this to happen for me to understand that.'

Nathan patted him on the arm. 'All the more reason to keep going. Don't stop until it's out there. Finish what he started.'

Novak wiped his eyes, then returned to the autopsy report. 'Speaking of which...we should really get our hands on the original report that was shown to me by Dr Blackford.'

'Where can we get that?'

'It should be on file at Westchester Hospital.'

'We should get it ASAP. Hard copy's always good to have for a reference point.'

'Yeah,' said Novak, picking up his phone which was ringing. 'Stella,' he answered. 'Where are you?'

She sounded as if she had been through the wringer. And recently. 'It's a little complicated,' she replied.

CHAPTER THIRTY-FIVE

REBECCA STUCK CLOSE to Stella as they walked through the dimly lit streets of Romford in the east end of London. The journey from Buckinghamshire had been fraught for both women. Every pair of eyes that landed on them felt like those of a conspirator. It was only when you were on the run from both the police and shadowy unknown forces that you realise how hard it is to travel anywhere in the modern world without your face being seen on a security camera, or having your movements tracked via your debit card or your phone.

Rebecca had tried to reassure Stella that the people who were hunting them probably weren't in control of the entire apparatus of the intelligence services. At best, they might have a mole or two here or there, but their faces wouldn't be flashing up on any intel officer's computer screens thanks to facial recognition technology. It wouldn't take long for it to become standard, but the UK still didn't have such technology working seamlessly.

'And you're sure we can trust this guy?' asked Rebecca,

admiring how warm and cosy all the living rooms looked on the terraced street they were walking down. All lit by the glow of televisions.

Stella replied, 'Trust him as you trust me and Tom.'

When Ralph Ogden opened his front door and saw the two women drenched from steady, fine rain – the kind that somehow soaks you through much more than a real torrential downpour – he beckoned them in immediately. He put a finger to his lips. 'Matilda and Molly aren't long asleep, so you'll need to keep your voices down in the hall.'

Stella shook the rain off her coat in the porch. 'I'm sorry, Ralph,' she whispered. 'But we didn't know where else to go. There wasn't a way to book into a hotel without it flagging our cards.'

'Don't be silly,' he replied, showing them through to the kitchen. 'You two look like you could do with some dinner.'

Rebecca almost cried with joy. 'That would be fantastic. Thank you.'

Ralph stole glances at her while he took out some eggs and bacon from the fridge. 'Christine is working late shift this week at the supermarket, so it's just me tonight.' He put a frying pan on the hob, then shook his head. 'I'm sorry,' he said to Rebecca. 'I have to say what an honour it is to have you here.'

Rebecca flashed a look at Stella as if to say, *is he being serious?*

'When Tom and Stella broke the Goldcastle story, my old website Verax did a whole series of articles on how GCHQ made it possible.'

Rebecca nodded shyly. 'I know who you are, Ralph, and everything you did with Verax. But thank you.'

After breaking some eggs into the pan and starting the bacon, he set to work on cups of tea for everyone.

'When I was a kid,' he began, 'the smell of this used to drive me crazy. My bedroom was across the hall from the kitchen, and my dad was often partial to a late-night bacon sandwich. Not much that's worse than lying in bed struggling to sleep because a bacon sandwich smells so good. There's something about the smell of bacon that manages to creep under doors and permeate concrete walls.' After a pause, he said, 'I'm deliberately not asking what's brought you here, but if you want to tell me...'

Stella said, 'We were in a safe house that I'll be reporting under the Trade Descriptions Act.'

By the time they had caught Ralph up on their progress, their plates were almost licked clean, and their cups of tea had been refilled twice already.

Ralph shook his head slowly in wonder. For someone who was still relatively new to the world that Tom and Stella had inhabited for many years, the notion that someone out there wanted to kill you was no small matter. After a narrow escape with the Russians on Tom and Stella's previous story, it was a world that he had no intention of re-entering.

By now, he had pulled out all of his research on the political campaign funding story he and Stella had been working. He stood over the kitchen table which he had cleared of dinner plates, and laid out what he had.

He said, 'For someone who doesn't like Zoom much, it's a real blessing to have you both sitting here. Saves me holding pieces of paper up to a shitty webcam.'

'What have you got?' asked Stella, browsing through it all.

'I got it wrong,' Ralph admitted. 'It's not Storm Capital that's been funding political campaigns. Well, they have. But not on the same level as SCX.'

Stella turned her head slightly in confusion. 'You mean that the other way around surely?'

'That's what I thought initially. But the numbers check out.' He showed her the Freedom of Information filings that proved it. 'For the last General Election here in the UK, SCX outspent Storm Capital on campaign donations two to one. Now, how is it possible for a crypto exchange to outspend a multi-trillion-dollar hedge fund?'

Stella stared at the numbers until she finally accepted them. 'I agree. That's insane.'

'It's not the only thing here that's insane.' Ralph passed Stella another document. 'Take a look at SCX's balance sheet.'

'Where did you get that?' asked Rebecca.

'Anonymous source within SCX,' Ralph replied. 'Someone junior. But I'll tell you, I had potential contacts from three other departments. Whatever is going on in there, a lot of employees are starting to speak out.'

Stella handed the document back to Ralph. 'I don't see what's wrong with this. Plenty of cash in the bank. Accounts look healthy.'

'I agree, the overall picture looks fine,' he conceded. 'Until you dig into the numbers. Look at this here. This shows the breakdown of SCX's assets. And this shows that the majority of their assets are made up of SCX tokens.'

'I'm going to regret asking this, but what's an SCX token?'

'It's a kind of Bitcoin specific to SCX. When you trade with them, say, one hundred pounds. You transfer one hundred pounds from your bank, and they convert it into one hundred pounds' worth of SCX tokens.'

'Who decides the value of the tokens?'

'That's where things start going loopy. And note that I say "start" going loopy. Because you're about to see that there is a whole lot of loopy going on at SCX. It's SCX that decides the value. It's just made-up money. All these assets on SCX's books should be cash. But as it's not, where has it all gone? They're one of the biggest exchanges in the world. The money that millions of people have traded with them has to be somewhere.'

Stella said, 'If it's not on their books, where is it?'

'That's where it gets really interesting.' He handed over another document. 'I added up the assets missing from SCX's balance sheet, plus or minus a few hundred thousand – which you would expect given fluctuations in interest rates, etcetera. It comes to the same amount donated to these two politicians' election campaigns in the last cycle.' Ralph circled the names then slid them across the kitchen table to Stella.

Stella read them, then scoffed.

Rebecca leaned over to have a look. 'No way,' she said.

Ralph said, 'The US President and the new British Prime Minister.'

'I know what you're thinking,' said Stella.

'What am I thinking?'

'You think SCX is, at worst, laundering money – or, at best, running a glorified Ponzi scheme – to fund politicians.'

'It's like you said in the briefing this morning, Stella. It's a story as old as time. Financial institution plays fast and loose with accounting in order to commit fraud.'

Stella took a moment to let all the information settle in

her head, putting on her editor hat. 'If SCX outspent everyone else in the last election cycle, what do they want? The Financial Regulations Bill will have far bigger repercussions for the likes of Storm Capital than anything SCX could ever do. They operate on a scale that's an order of magnitude greater than SCX, in entirely different spheres. It's not about billions for Storm. It's trillions. I don't see how SCX will ever see a return on the investment they've committed to funding political campaigns. Sure, they might get some new regulations passed that helps fend off the competition. But the Securities and Exchange Commission will eventually cut them down to size if they end up with a monopoly. They've spent way more than they could ever earn from a single new law.'

'That's not SCX's only problem,' Ralph said. 'I think they're going to collapse in the next twenty-four or forty-eight hours.'

Stella leaned forward in surprise. 'Huh?'

Ralph pulled out the SCX balance sheet again. 'Remember all those SCX tokens that are sitting as assets on their books? Well, the company looks very successful if the value of those tokens keeps going up. Which the crypto market has been doing for quite some time now. Until the last week. And today was the biggest drop in years. By my calculations, if the crypto market falls by only nine per cent, the company will have less in liquid assets than potential...' He decided to phrase it a little simpler, as Mark Chang was always reminding him to do. 'The value of the company will be significantly less than the money it owes.'

Stella who had got to her feet to pace around, said slowly, 'Okay...so if crypto values fall...' She trailed off intentionally.

Ralph said, 'More people will withdraw their money from SCX. And if the total amount that SCX traders want to withdraw is more than the actual cash the company has, it will have to declare bankruptcy.'

Rebecca said, 'Ralph, you said there would be problems if the market fell by nine per cent. How much did it fall by today?'

He paused for dramatic effect. 'Twenty-two per cent,' he answered.

'Jeez,' Stella said.

'Yeah, pretty much, jeez. We're talking bigger-than-Enron collapse.'

'But wait, that would also mean that campaigns that were successful thanks to huge cash injections were paid for by...what would you call it?'

Ralph, who had been sitting on the information for a few hours, and had processed it all, emphasised, 'Illegal means, Stella. It's not much different to a diamond thief selling something they stole, and then using the money to help elect a politician.'

Stella sat back down again and covered her mouth. They had brought down politicians before, even heads of state. But not two at the same time. 'We have to talk to Tom about this.'

Once Novak picked up, he asked where she was.

Her head still spinning from Ralph's revelations, Stella answered, 'It's a little complicated.'

CHAPTER THIRTY-SIX

ONCE STELLA HAD FINISHED EXPLAINING to Novak everything that had happened, there wasn't any time for respite. She had to take him straight into what Ralph had uncovered about SCX and election funding.

'As much as I love an opportunity to say I told you so,' said Novak, 'this is a great story. It's just not the story that we've been chasing.'

Stella asked, 'What exactly did you have in mind, Tom?'

'We know that my dad was digging around about Storm Capital six years ago. But SCX didn't even exist when he was working on this. We have to find a way to connect these two stories. Do we have, say, anything that links his death with the Ghost Division attack?'

Rebecca and Stella looked at each other in confusion.

'Why does there need to be a link, Tom?' asked Stella.

Novak paused. 'My dad didn't kill himself, Stel. He was murdered.'

Nathan chimed in, 'We got our hands on an autopsy

report that's nothing like the one Tom was shown six years ago. I've assembled a whole lot of evidence that casts major doubt on suicide.'

'It doesn't just cast doubt, Nathan,' Novak interjected. 'It proves it. Six medical experts all say that there's no way my dad could have died the way I was told he did.'

'Jesus, Tom, I'm sorry,' Stella said.

'Yeah, I'm sorry,' Ralph added.

Novak appreciated the sympathy, but he wanted more than that. 'Storm Capital is a constant between the story my dad found, and what we've been chasing between the three of us. But we need some kind of concrete link between the two if we're going to prove conspiracy.'

Stella said, 'Rebecca's found a bunch on that actually.'

Rebecca took over. 'Using the burner phone that belonged to your dad, I was able to track down another mobile in the area around the time he died. I traced that second phone to an eventual location in the Hudson River. Dumped, no doubt. However, I found reports of a body found in the area in the following fortnight. His name was Eric Bogossian. A Marine turned private contractor. I've found a photo of Bogossian with his former troop in Iraq. I recognised one of the other men immediately. His name is Damian Oxley. The second shooter on site this morning. Who's still armed and dangerous and on the loose.'

Novak said, 'And he's apparently got police contacts too. You said this officer who fired at you is Specialist Command?'

'That's right,' said Rebecca. 'A new offshoot in the Metropolitan Police.'

Stella raised her eyebrows. 'Someone influential must have turned him.'

'You don't mean Hilderberg, do you?' asked Novak.

She sucked in air. 'Well...'

'Stella's got a point,' said Rebecca. 'You brought a lot of people in Hilderberg to justice. But it would be naive to think that you caught absolutely everyone.'

Novak argued, 'But if Damian Oxley is a connection between my dad's murder and the attack on Ghost Division, there has to have been some major catalyst for both crimes. Why kill my dad and make it look like suicide? Why attack Ghost Division? There has to be some overlap in what we were investigating and what my dad found out. Rebecca, I know you can't go into details about everything you've been working on. But can you think of anything that might tie in with Seymour's Storm Capital story?'

Rebecca had to think long and hard about bringing it up. It was barely ready as a piece of actionable intelligence, let alone part of a news story. But there was a reason she and Stella were sitting in a terraced house in east London, on the run for their lives.

'Actually,' she began. 'There might be something that we all have in common. Do you guys remember Wolfgang Tibor?'

Novak did a double-take. 'That's a name I haven't heard for a while.'

'The Germans have been farming him out to foreign intelligence agencies. He's ready to turn a witness against Hilderberg and give up valuable intel in exchange for disappearing into witness protection.'

'Yeah,' chuckled Novak, 'like Hilderberg won't be able to get to him there.'

'That's what my guys said.' Rebecca had a lump in her throat and had to pause to swallow, as the gravity of the situation hit her fresh. She didn't have any "guys" anymore. They were all dead. 'According to Tibor, Jozef von Hayek kept a comprehensive list of Hilderberg agents and operatives across many fields and disciplines. Including politics and the intelligence industry. The complete list translates to something roughly known as the Directory. And Tibor seems to think it's out there somewhere.'

'Are you thinking what I'm thinking, Tom?' Stella asked.

He said, 'What if that's what my dad found?'

Ralph remarked, 'That would be worth killing for. And if they somehow found out that you, Rebecca, were starting down a path to track it down, it would be motive for the attack this morning.'

Rebecca shook her head, unconvinced. 'I've been working on this on my own.'

Novak asked, 'Not a word to Melissa Forsyth? Not a single document she had access to?'

'I only told my senior staff this morning,' said Rebecca. 'We know that the hit team were already making moves by then.'

Having made some quick calculations, Nathan asked Novak if he could say something.

Novak held the phone out for him to talk on speaker.

'Nathan here,' he said. 'If the Directory does exist, and did exist when Seymour was working, then it stands to reason that Angela Curtis would have been on it. Along with every other collaborator.'

Novak asked, 'The question still stands: why go after Ghost Division? Angela Curtis is dead, and her plot was foiled. What's the damage in what Rebecca wants to track down?'

Stella said, 'Because it could expose current politicians who are bought and paid for by Hilderberg. The next generation of collaborators.'

Ralph offered, 'How about the new President and British Prime Minister?'

A silence followed that seemed to go on for an age.

'When you think about it,' said Ralph, 'I've found evidence of huge donations from SCX to both of them. Seymour was looking into Storm Capital doing the same thing. SCX is obviously linked to Storm Capital by Zach and Anna Storm. What if she's using SCX to keep financing Hilderberg-backed candidates?'

'She runs a multi-trillion-dollar hedge fund,' said Novak. 'She doesn't need a crypto exchange to hide something like that.'

'No,' said Ralph, 'but she does need one if she wants to put some distance between Storm Capital and lobbying for softer measures in the upcoming Financial Regulations bill. It's currently going through the House. Second draft. It's expected to pass next week.'

Convinced that he knew more about American politics than Ralph Ogden from Romford, East London, Novak said, 'The Securities and Exchange Commission will come down on them like a ton of bricks. We all agree that SCX doesn't have long left. No way the SEC won't see market manipulation in how the company is collapsing. Storm Capital won't get away with it.'

Ralph pulled up a few bookmarked webpages for this very argument. He turned his laptop around. 'Tom, I'm currently showing Stella and Rebecca an official online profile for SEC Chairman Larry Friedkin. Stella, would you be so kind as to tell Tom what it says in the third paragraph of his biography?'

Stella read it aloud. '"Graduated from Stanford Law before working on Wall Street." I don't get it.'

'What's missing from the biography is the name of Larry Friedkin's ethics professor at Stanford Law.'

'Who was it?' asked Novak.

'Noah Storm,' Ralph answered. 'Zach's dad.'

The revelation put Stella into a tailspin. 'Hang on, hang on,' she said. 'Let's not go down the no-smoke-without-fire rabbit hole.'

'You don't think there might be a conflict of interest ruling on a company owned by the son of your former law professor? What if this has been the play all along? For SCX to aggressively outspend on donations. Buy influence with lawmakers, and get them to change laws not for them, but in favour of Storm Capital.'

Stella started to nod. 'That...actually makes sense.'

'Think about it,' Ralph continued. 'A new law that helps SCX might make them a few hundred million. Maybe a billion. But a hedge fund with investments across so many different spheres, and at a scale that no one else can match? That could be worth hundreds of billions. And it gives Storm Capital total cover, because SCX is the one handing out all the money to politicians.'

Novak was less convinced than the others. 'It's a great plan. Except, it couldn't have been the plan six years ago. SCX didn't exist.'

'I never said it was the plan back then. But I think it's the plan now.'

'There's nothing else for it,' said Rebecca. 'We have to find that Directory. Seymour could have been killed for it then, and now what's left of Hilderberg are going after it again. If that list gets out and Anna Storm's name is on it, Storm Capital is over, along with her career, and everyone she's conspired to bribe.'

Novak said, 'Nathan and I have made some moves tonight to try and get some face time with Anna Storm tomorrow.'

'How did you swing that?' asked Stella.

'I had to call in a favour. But it's not certain.'

'I don't know if that's a good idea. If you go into Anna Storm's office and give her any clue about what we know, she'll bolt the door. And the only likely way of getting our hands on a silver bullet is something from within Storm Capital or SCX themselves.'

'Not necessarily,' said Nathan.

Only Novak could see Nathan's body language, which was curiously guarded: Nathan was perched on the end of a table, surrounded by Seymour's papers. Whatever he had to say, it seemed to be weighing heavily on him.

He went on, 'That's not your only possible source.'

'Are you going to tell us?' asked Novak. 'Or do you want us to guess?'

The fact that Novak was managing to be lighthearted about it all was only going to make it worse. Of that Nathan was sure.

'You need the dead man's switch,' Nathan said.

Stella quipped, 'What, are we in *Pirates of The* bloody *Caribbean* now? What the hell is a dead man's switch?'

Both Ralph and Rebecca spoke over each other, about to explain it. Ralph deferred to Rebecca.

She explained, 'It's a backup plan in case you become incapacitated or die. There are a number of ways to do it.

You could have an email auto-send if you fail to log in after several days–'

The others at the Romford end had no idea, but Novak was staring at the laptop across the room that he'd been watching the old Christmas video on.

'What about a video file?' Novak asked. 'Could you prompt for a passcode or something at a certain point in a video file to trigger the dead man's switch?'

Rebecca bobbed her head. 'A little clunky, perhaps, but it's possible.'

Novak went over to the laptop and searched through the video file.

'You won't find anything,' Nathan told him.

'It's worth trying.'

'Actually, it's not. The files have already been sent. There's no evidence of them left on the video file. Each time it played, it showed a different four-digit code. An email would ping to an address chosen by Seymour. You enter the passcode, and you receive the dead man's switch files. Simple.'

Rebecca said, 'That's actually a very decent setup. Double-factor authorisation. Multiple safeguards in different–'

Novak didn't care about any of that. He was fixated on something else. He asked Nathan, 'How do you know all that?'

Nathan prepared himself for the onslaught he knew was about to come his way. 'Because I was the one who received the files when Seymour failed to log in the day after he was killed.'

Novak raised his hands to his head as he realised what

Nathan was telling him. 'You're RT. Real Thing. You were my dad's source.'

'If he didn't watch to a certain point of the video, the files would auto-send. It was his system, but they were my files.'

Novak's heart sank further when he realised that that was the only reason the Christmas video had so many views in a short period of time. It was because he had to.

Nathan looked at him with tears in his eyes. 'I'm so sorry, Tom.'

CHAPTER THIRTY-SEVEN

Novak didn't know whether to be raging angry, upset, or relieved. Unable to make up his mind, he went through a range of all three to varying degrees, standing stock still with his phone in his hand hanging at his side.

Stella's voice could still be heard distantly. 'Tom? Are you there...'

Novak snapped out of his daze. He held the phone only vaguely near his face, telling Stella, 'I'll call you back.' He hung up, then dropped the phone on the table.

Nathan took a deep breath. He had known whatever was brewing in Novak would eventually come out. He had just hoped it might have taken a little longer. He still didn't know what to say to try and mollify him. Nathan had entertained all sorts of possibilities for Novak's reaction, including at the extreme end where Novak simply beat the crap out of him.

'I don't know what to say,' Nathan said softly. 'I should have told you.'

Novak exploded, 'You *think*?!'

'I'm just trying to be honest.'

'Yeah, *now* you are! First, you weren't involved. You were just working on the archives. Then you *were* involved in the story, but my dad just brought you in to help. And now you're saying it was actually your story *all along*, and on *top* of that, you were actually his initial fucking *source*. Where does this end?'

A hand extended, pleading, Nathan said, 'I was trying to protect you. But I am telling the truth now. I'll tell you everything.'

'I think I'm owed that much.' Novak turned away from Nathan and paced around, the physical distance between them helping to bring down his temperature. But only slightly. 'So go on. Tell me everything.'

Nathan took a seat at the table where he'd laid out Seymour's papers. From Novak's vantage point he looked like a suspect being interviewed in a police station.

'I had been working on Storm Capital for a while,' Nathan began. 'There was something about them that always seemed off. I had been working on a piece for Diane about the revolving door of politicians joining Wall Street firms, after apparently being fundamental to regulating them years earlier. It didn't take me long to establish links between Storm Capital and several former members of the Senate Financial Services Committee. To flesh it out, I investigated how much Storm Capital had donated to those politicians in the past. I couldn't find much. The strange thing was that they had donated to campaigns, but relative to the company's value, they were way behind the rest of the pack. Except in the case of one particular politician. Tucker Adams.'

Novak's eyes widened. 'Senator Tucker Adams. He

was Hilderberg through and through. Until he switched sides and went to the Russians.'

'That was much later in his career though. Back when I was investigating, he was Hilderberg's candidate eyeing up the White House. You and Stella were right on the money on that one.'

Novak recalled, 'Adams got pissed off when Hilderberg decided to throw their weight behind Bill Rand.'

'But I didn't know any of this back then. All I knew was that Tucker Adams was deep in the pockets of Storm Capital. No one else came close to their level of investment in him. It didn't make sense to me. Why was one senator being given the lion's share of donations from a behemoth like Storm? So I did what you taught me to do: I kept digging.'

'Why didn't you bring it to me? We could have worked it together.'

Nathan chuckled darkly.

It threw Novak for a curve. What the hell did he have to laugh about in such a moment?

'You really don't remember, do you?' Nathan said. 'I caught you after an editorial meeting one morning and asked you if you wanted to come in on the story for me.'

Novak stammered. 'I...I don't really...What did I say?'

'You said, quote, it sounds like a good story for you, but it's not big enough for me. Then you told me to work with one of the junior staffers on it.'

Novak shook his head. 'Christ...yeah. I remember now.'

'I knew I had enough to convince you, but you'd looked at me like I was such a nothing...In the end, the last thing I wanted was to bring you in. So I stopped trying.'

'Nathan, if you told me half of what you've told me now–'

'Hey, don't blame this on me, man!' Nathan fired back. 'You had your shot at the story, and you told me where to jump. Because you were Tom Novak, who was going to do great things. Remember where you were six years ago compared to me. You were White House correspondent, blowing the lid off national stories as a matter of routine. I was still living out in Iraq for months at a time, embedding with Marine units and nearly getting blown up by IEDs. I finally got out of the desert, and found a story that could have been front page stuff.

'Then why take it to my dad?' asked Novak.

'I needed help. Contacts. My name didn't open doors. But Seymour Novak's did. So I worked him for a while in the lead-up.' Trying to neuter Novak's disgust at the admission, Nathan said, 'I'm just trying to be honest. I'm sorry.'

Through gritted teeth, Novak asked, 'How did it work?'

'I found out that you two had drifted apart, so I played up the idea that I had a story you would have wanted. The thought of beating you to a story was exciting to him.' Nathan shrugged with innocence. 'He was an old man settled into his *Nightly News* retirement home. He knew he wasn't cracking anything else in his career unless someone brought it to him on a plate. When I showed him what I had, he was all in. I mean, I actually had to get him to cool off. He was ready to go on air way before the story was ready.'

Novak shook his head and snorted disapprovingly. 'He wanted the win.'

'And so did I,' said Nathan. 'Working with your dad was the best thing that had ever happened to me and my career. I'm sorry to talk of it in those terms, but it was. I went over not only your head, but Diane's. I wasn't aiming for the front page of *The Republic*. I was aiming for top story on the *Nightly News*. Which, let's be real, is on a whole other level. Back then, your dad was still pulling in ten million a night. *The Republic* hadn't sold ten million copies in its lifetime.'

Novak sighed. He wasn't looking forward to this part. 'So tell me about the final weeks. Final days.'

'The higher up the chain we got with Storm Capital, the more paranoid I got. I took to communicating with your dad via burner phones alone. I couldn't risk being seen with him. He was too recognisable.' He paused. 'In the days leading up to your dad's...' He couldn't bring himself to say it now: murder. 'I was pretty sure I was being followed. So I damn well didn't want to go near your dad. But I wanted to warn him. We were talking one night after his show. He had been working on getting a sit-down with Anna Storm.'

'The Saratoga hotel booking?'

'Yeah, their headquarters were still out there before they moved to New York. But he told me ABC was passing. Your dad said it was complicated, but I assumed that management got spooked about hurting their ad revenue. No one wanted to piss off Storm even back then. They spent too much money in the mainstream media. And now they're majority shareholders in most of it. Anyway, your dad wanted to take it back to Diane at *Republic*. We needed someone with courage to get the story out there. But Diane and I had already had run-ins at that stage. She thought I was cavalier. I was just young and trying to make some noise. Your dad suggested bringing you in to try and talk Diane around. I was the one who told him no.' Nathan lowered his head into his hands. He broke down. 'If it wasn't for me, he might have called you that night...and all of this would have been different.'

Novak appreciated the self-criticism, but it wasn't an entirely comforting admission.

'That was when your dad told me about some precautions he had taken. A dead man's switch. I thought he was overreacting. But thank god he'd used it.' Nathan wiped away his tears with his sleeve, the way a little boy does. 'We were talking on the phone, when he told me that the power had gone out in his house. I didn't like it at all. So I told him to run. That's how I knew he didn't kill himself.'

Novak let out a long puff and looked to the ceiling in despair. Rebecca's burner phone evidence had already formed a picture in his mind of his dad being hunted. But hearing Nathan's testimony made it feel much more immediate and real. All he could think was how badly he wished he had been there to help.

Fighting back tears, Novak said, 'Why didn't you *tell* me? Why didn't you tell anyone? The police?'

'I was scared,' Nathan cried. 'The next day, when I heard that your dad had killed himself in the woods, I knew what had really happened. I thought, if they could get to your dad, then they could get to me. You had just lost your dad which was painful enough. I didn't want to risk your life too. I knew you would figure it out once you'd gone through all of your dad's papers. It was all in there the whole time. I kept waiting and waiting. And it's not like I could ask you if you had found anything. I needed you to come to it by yourself. If you knew then that your dad and I had been working together, and that I thought he had been murdered...Honestly? I was worried you would get scared and ditch the story.'

Novak said, 'I don't know why you thought I would do that.'

'You were a pretty selfish person back then, Tom. Egotistical. Narcissistic. I really didn't know I could trust you not to drop it.'

Novak scoffed. '*You* couldn't trust *me*...that's a laugh.'

As he walked away again, Nathan went after him. 'But I saw what you did with the NSA Papers, Tom. And Goldcastle. I could tell that you had changed. That you weren't the same reporter anymore. When I cooked that story for Diane, I had been running myself ragged trying to find a silver bullet that would prove what had happened to your dad. But I didn't have access to the technology like Rebecca does. Or the contacts you and Stella have. Technologically, it was a different time then. I had no idea what could be proven or asserted with phone locations, and pings. Or about the extent of Hilderberg's influence over the political landscape then. So when Diane fired me, I couldn't see a way back. In an instant, all my infrastructure was taken away from me. All my expenses to travel and nail a story down. So I gave up.'

Novak shut his eyes, restraining anger from resurfacing. 'You let me believe a lie. For years, Nathan.'

Nathan knew he had plenty to be contrite about, but that was one sword he wasn't willing to fall on. 'Let you believe?' he fired back. 'Where the hell were you, Tom? I was waiting. For months, years, for you to just look through your dad's things and put the pieces of the puzzle together. Where were you all that time?'

Novak raised a hand, begging for him to stop. 'Okay,

okay. That was a cheap shot. But why bring it all back? Why now?'

'Because of Angela Curtis. Tucker Adams. But mostly because of Diane. I let her down. I let you down. And I let Seymour down. I couldn't live with the truth anymore. I tracked down some of your regular hang-out spots from your Instagram, and I hung out there, waiting to bump into you. I had to hang out six nights in a row in that bar before you showed up. The plan was to give you a little taste of what Seymour and I had been working on. Just a hint. Enough to let you realise something shady had gone down. It had to be enough to convince you it was more than just some story. But not so huge that you didn't believe me. I knew I had to earn back your trust. When we got talking and you offered me the job to deal with your dad's archives, I couldn't believe my luck. I could organise exactly what you saw and when.'

'Then why wait until the day of the archives launching to tell me about the Saratoga booking? And everything else? You could have told me that weeks ago.'

Nathan exhaled, struck by his own calculated callousness. 'I knew you would be more emotional and have a stronger reaction if I left it to the day of the launch. It was my last shot to make you see, Tom. I couldn't risk you walking away. In any case, it took time to earn back your trust.'

'By *lying* to me?'

Nathan looked solemnly at the floor. 'If I had it to do all over again, I swear I would have done things differently.'

'But wait,' said Novak. 'What about the dead man's switch? Where are the files on that?'

'I've had them all along,' Nathan admitted.

Novak threw his head back in anguish. He had been within a few feet of them multiple times and never known.

'I had to be sure,' Nathan pleaded. 'If I gave you the dead man's switch files, there was a good chance you would either refuse to believe them because they came from me, or worry they could get you killed. I had to be sure.'

'Are you sure now?' Novak asked.

Nathan went to a box that he had been monitoring ever since the material had been transported to the archives room. No matter the mess or chaos of the filing system, he always knew where that one box was.

'This obviously isn't the only copy,' Nathan said, taking out a plastic sleeve with a few documents inside. 'But it is the original that your dad had kept in the fireproof box.'

Novak took hold of it like it was the original Magna Carta. A glow seeming to emanate from the page. 'What is this?'

'This is something your dad found independently. When we figured out where Storm Capital was sending the majority of their money, we started investigating what seemed special about the politicians. We were both experienced politicos, for both D.C. as well as London, but neither of us had heard of Angela Curtis. The more digging we did, the less remarkable she seemed. At that time, she was being touted for the Home Office, but no one we spoke to thought she'd be any good. We were right as it turned out. She disappeared into the wilderness after her stint as Home Secretary in the UK. Only an organisation as powerful as Hilderberg could have manufactured her path into Downing Street from that kind of inauspicious starting point. There had to be something else, your dad thought. That's when he found out that Curtis had changed her surname when she was twenty-one. An Angela Kertész was once a director in some minor small business run by a family member. The address listed was the same as the one provided by Curtis to HMRC when she was first elected as a politician three years later. So your dad began tracing the lineage of the Kertész name. It didn't go back far – but it went far enough.'

Novak shook his head in disbelief as he realised what he was looking at. 'Where did he get this?'

'It's just sitting there available on ancestry websites, waiting to be discovered. Even Hilderberg couldn't remove every mention of a family name going back generations. Without knowing that Curtis had changed her surname, there was little chance of anyone discovering her true family lineage.'

The document showed a family tree going back to the Second World War. The Kertész family origins were in Hungary. Hungarian Jews to be precise.

There was one name, however, among all the Kertész relatives that stood out to Novak. And would have stood out to anyone who had paid even minor attention to the news in the last few years. Friedrich Hilderberg.

Novak remonstrated with the document. 'This proves that Friedrich Hilderberg was Angela Curtis's grandfather. It's evidence of a motive to kill my dad. No wonder they got rid of him.'

Nathan agreed. 'He was going to expose Angela Curtis as bought and paid for by Hilderberg. It would have exposed their entire enterprise long before the Goldcastle conspiracy, and long before Curtis could reach Downing Street. She was an investment worth billions to Hilderberg.'

Novak said hushed, overwhelmed, 'He found it before I

did. We ended up working the same story without realising it.'

Nathan nodded. 'That's not all. Look underneath.'

Novak shuffled the family tree document to the back. He knew what it was the moment he opened the first page.

Nathan said, 'This, I didn't know he had until after the dead man's switch was triggered. This is why we're standing here right now.'

In Novak's hands was a list of every Hilderberg operative in every realm of modern life. 'It's just like Wolfgang Tibor described.'

'Look at the back,' said Nathan, enjoying the dazzled look on Novak's face. All of the risk to get to that point suddenly felt worth the effort. 'It goes all the way back to the early seventies. Every operative they've ever had.'

Novak looked up to meet Nathan's eyes. He was speechless.

Nathan said it for him. 'Your dad found the Directory.' He reached over to grab hold of the document. 'This is it, Tom. It's over. This is everything we need to end them. For good this time.'

CHAPTER THIRTY-EIGHT

LEON SAT at a white metal table, his hands cuffed to a metal loop welded into the tabletop. The room was kitted out like a police interview room, but it felt different inside. It still had a fresh paint smell. There were no cracks or scratches or marks on the table or floor. It was like a showroom interrogation suite.

Leon had no idea where he was, as a black hood had been placed over his head once Counter Terror had handed him over. Though judging by the travel time in the car, he was still very much in central London.

The door opened, and in stepped a man in his fifties with greying hair, a paunch, and a stack of paperwork.

Leon said, 'I want to speak to a lawyer, or my union rep.'

The man smiled. 'That's nice,' he said. 'But we don't worry about any of those rules. Not down here. Not on these charges.'

He didn't want to give the man the satisfaction of wriggling about in his restraints, fighting them. 'Where am I?' he asked calmly.

'Somewhere not many people have seen,' he answered. 'You can call me Roger, by the way. And the room you're sitting in is three floors below the entrance to Thames House. You should soak in the atmosphere, because you're going to be here a while.'

'Based on what?'

'Based on your girlfriend's fingerprints and DNA being found at the scene of Wilson Kipchoge's murder.'

For a moment, Leon thought he had been the victim of an elaborate practical joke. 'Don't be ridiculous.'

'I'm not being ridiculous.' Roger slid a copy of a forensics report across the table. 'It's there in black and white. Rebecca Fox threw up in the hallway. It's her DNA.'

Leon shook his head as he realised it was serious. 'No, this can't be happening. You can't possibly–'

'On the plus side, two hundred thousand will buy you a pretty decent lawyer.' Roger flashed a sudden, and brief, grin.

'What are you on about? Two hundred thousand what?'

'The savings account you opened last month.' Roger slid the documentation proving it to Leon. 'The two hundred thousand pounds that's now in there was deposited last night. Was that once the hit team knew they were going ahead? Is that your reward for leading them to Stanley House?'

Leon kept shaking his head. He was in a nightmare he couldn't wake up from.

Roger continued, 'Let me tell you a story, and you let

me know where I'm wrong. A young ambitious cop finds his way by pure luck into the life of a rather brilliant intelligence analyst, who's just been knee deep in one of the biggest political conspiracies in British history. She's got power and access beyond anyone's wildest imagination. That's got to be worth something on the dark markets. You could make enough money to set you up for a good few years off that.'

'This is crazy,' said Leon. 'This is all a terrible mistake.'

Roger ignored his pleas. 'I think you got Rebecca into Wilson Kipchoge's flat on false pretences. When she saw you murder Wilson and his flatmates, she threw up in the hall. Who wouldn't? She's a programmer by trade. Nothing like your background. Which looks pretty rough.'

Leon wasn't going to take anymore without fighting back. 'So what happened next?' he retorted. 'After witnessing a murder she wanted no part of, she went off to work, where she made no mention of what had happened to anyone there. Didn't call the police? Didn't make any attempts to get help?'

Roger kept on, 'I think you convinced her that there were some bad people in that flat. No doubt spun a convincing story. It didn't matter. It only had to hold up for a few hours, until your hit man friends could penetrate Stanley House – no doubt off the back of intel you could have accessed from Rebecca at any time – and kill everyone there. Including the one person who could point the finger at you.'

'And I assume that Rebecca is corroborating this particular fairytale.'

'Don't you worry about what Rebecca Fox is telling us.'

Leon stared him down, then he smirked. 'You don't have her, do you?'

Roger said nothing.

'You're guessing.'

'You'd bet your future on that, would you?' Roger's eyes narrowed, just as there was a knock at the door.

Roger answered, met by a junior operative who looked fresh out of university. 'I told you no interruptions,' Roger complained.

A man with his arm in a sling and wearing the same suit he'd been shot in earlier, pushed past the junior operative into the interrogation room. He flashed his badge with his spare hand.

'DCI Warren Bell,' he said. He pointed to the chair next to Roger's.

'We're not opening this up to external units yet,' said Roger.

Bell pushed his chair back from the table to allow himself to stretch his legs out, and stop the exit wound on his side from pulsing with agony. Anyone else would have been laid up in a hospital bed, but DCI Bell was made of stronger stuff.

He said, 'Then you'd better read paragraph six of the Domestic Crime and Terrorism Act of last year, which grants full powers to me to sit in this room.'

Reluctantly, Roger nodded to the junior operative who scuttled away. 'Fine,' he said. 'Where were we, Leon?'

'I think I can help you with that, Roger,' Bell said. 'It is Roger, isn't it? It's much simpler at the Met. You see, officers like DC Leon Walker don't hide behind a failure to identify themselves to suspects who are innocent until proven guilty.'

'Whose side are you on?' Roger asked, taking his seat again.

'The truth doesn't have any sides,' Bell said. 'Does it, Leon?'

Leon couldn't understand what Bell's game was. It sounded on the face of it that he was there to help. But it was hard to tell.

'See,' Bell continued, 'I came here because I want to know what a cardiac specialist was doing in the forensics wing of St Thomas' Hospital this morning. The esteemed Dr Linda Upshaw.' He leaned towards Roger. 'Who, incidentally, has just been found in the boot of a car in Battersea. She'd shot herself in the head. Then very tidily wrapped her entire body three times over in plastic sheeting. Which ranks as either the most considerate suicide I've ever encountered, or yet more evidence that what we're dealing with here are highly motivated, professional killers. All the same, it's a tragic turn of events for a doctor who was so trusted, that she was signed into the forensics ward where evidence samples from Wilson Kipchoge's flat were being rushed through for analysis. So trusted, that Superintendent Sue Thornley herself signed Upshaw in. Some very esteemed friends.' Bell now turned fully in the direction of Roger. 'Can you tell me, what on god's green earth, Upshaw was doing in there, in a unit she didn't work for, in a speciality she didn't have? And who, hours later, conspired with persons unknown to murder Detective Inspector Sofia Molina, and attempt to murder DC Leon Walker. We know she conspired, because two different nurses saw her opening the blinds in Lee Patterson's room on a dark evening. The very window that shots were fired through by an assassin who is still in the wind.' He put his hand out to stop Roger interrupting. 'I know what many in your position would say. It was probably Damian Oxley, the second Stanley House shooter who fired the shots. But it wasn't. The reason I know that, is that Oxley was fifty miles away at a farmhouse in Buckinghamshire, shooting me while attempting to gun down for the second time today, Director Rebecca Fox of Ghost Division.'

Leon jolted forward, testing the limits of his restraints. 'Is she all right?'

'I'm flattered by your concern for me, who was *actually* shot, but yes, Leon, she's safe and well. She's currently safely hidden away with Stella Mitchell in a house in Romford. Bloody hard to vanish without a trace these days.' He turned to Roger, 'Though you'd know more about that than me. Or are you more of the desk-bound, inactive type that MI5 has so many of these days?'

Roger's mobile rang, which he was only too pleased to answer, taking it to the corner of the room.

Leaping on the first opportunity to do so, Leon said, 'I'm so sorry about DI Molina, sir. It happened so quickly. I did everything I could to go after Upshaw.'

'I know,' said Bell. 'I saw the CCTV. I also saw you not resisting arrest. As well as out running by the Thames this morning alongside Rebecca.'

Leon sighed in relief, his shoulders dropping. 'Are you getting me out of here?'

'There's a car waiting upstairs.' Bell nodded towards Roger. 'That's the director of MI5 acting on direct orders of the Home Secretary to release you, and expunge the falsified forensic evidence against you and Director Fox in the Wilson Kipchoge murder case.'

'What about the bank account?' Leon asked, panic

rising in his voice again. He didn't want any loose ends in the circumstances. 'You've got to believe I had nothing–'

Bell motioned for him to calm down. 'The account was opened at the same time that you were interviewing a suspect in a robbery case last month. You're on video and audio. You're in the clear.'

Leon sighed again. 'Thank god.'

'The question remaining is, why did someone go to a lot of trouble to frame you and Rebecca on murder charges? My suspicion is that the proof that's exonerated you would have been tampered with or removed had Specialist Protection been slower to act.'

Leon said, 'Someone wanted us out the way, or discredited at the very least. It's pure luck I didn't suffer the same fate as DI Molina.'

Roger finished his phone call, then approached Leon. 'DC Walker. Will you please accept my apologies?' He unlocked Leon's handcuffs. 'You're free to go.'

Feeling his wrists, Leon said, 'Thank you.'

Once he and DCI Bell were alone, Bell said, 'Linda Upshaw gave Lee Patterson an injection to bring on cardiac arrhythmia. Someone instructed her to make sure Lee Patterson didn't say a word. The only evidence that Patterson said your name is from Upshaw herself. I'm not inclined to believe her word over yours at this point.'

'I appreciate that, sir,' said Leon.

In the corridor outside, Bell stopped Leon, then took a step closer to him, lowering his voice. 'Leon, I need you to convince Rebecca to come back in. We can't break this thing working in factions, journalists versus police. We have to work together.'

'I'll see what I can do, sir. But you've seen for yourself

that the police can't keep her safe. Whoever's behind all this is bigger than what we are.'

'Then let's not fuck it up.' Bell winked, then urged Leon on. 'Come on. I know a quick way to get to Romford.'

CHAPTER THIRTY-NINE

Novak and Nathan strode through the empty newsroom towards Mark Chang's office, a swagger and a sense of purpose about them, despite it being the middle of the night.

'What's Mark like?' asked Nathan.

Novak asked, 'Wasn't he around when you were here?'

'If he was, I don't remember. Any pointers?'

'Focus on what you have, not what you're still looking for. Anything negative these days, and he'll use it to shut the whole story down.'

'He can't possibly shut *this* down, can he?' asked Nathan.

'That remains to be seen.' He glanced at Nathan. 'Get that smile off your face. This isn't a home run yet.' Taking a look around the office, he said to himself, 'I'm worried we should have waited until morning.'

'Tom, I've been sitting on this for six years. I know the value of what I have. There's no way he can say—'

Novak snapped, 'Don't finish that sentence. If he's

drinking a coffee, we're at least in with a shout. If he's still wearing his coat, then he's just biding time until he can go home again.'

The wait to see which Mark Chang they were going to get stretched until they were past the newsroom, where Chang's office came into view through the glass walls of the conference room.

Novak tutted. 'Shit.'

Mark was sitting at his desk, scrolling through his phone looking half asleep. He was still wearing his coat.

AFTER HALF AN HOUR of summary between Novak, Nathan, and Stella on video call, Mark weighed up everything he had heard.

He rocked back and forth in his chair, making a tent with his hand and placing the tip of it under his chin.

Novak couldn't take the wait any longer. 'What are you thinking?'

Mark rocked his seat forward to its upright position. 'I think...I need a coffee.'

Novak made a head flick in the direction of the staff room to Nathan, then he winked.

Post-coffee, Mark had taken his coat off and was now pacing back and forth behind his desk. 'Okay,' he said. 'What do we have that's verifiable. Tom?'

Novak lifted the Directory up off Mark's desk. It was still in its protective plastic sleeve. 'We've got this for one thing. Hilderberg's greatest hits.'

'That's exactly the problem,' said Mark. 'We've seen

this before. In the UK, Angela Curtis. In the US, Tucker Adams. We've been there. Done that.'

'There are new names in there,' Nathan said, leaning forward, relishing being a part of proceedings again. Having thought he'd never be in an editor's office again, he was having the time of his life. 'New, but not unfamiliar. The President, and the British PM.'

Mark reached forward for the document. 'And you're saying this is incontrovertible proof that these politicians are linked to Hilderberg?'

Novak said, 'We have a source who can verify that Jozef von Hayek's personal secretary testified that this list existed, and what it was.'

'Is the source Rebecca Fox?' asked Mark.

Novak paused. Wondering if it was a good or a bad thing. 'Yes,' he replied.

Mark pushed his lips out. His expression was unreadable. 'How about the veracity of the document itself. It's genuine?'

Nathan answered, 'There are names going back to nineteen seventy-five in there, which von Hayek maintained personally. You can actually see the typing transition from typewriter to word processor over the years.'

'You want more?' Novak asked.

'Try me,' said Mark.

'Seymour had evidence linking Angela Curtis to a change of surname from her family's native Hungarian spelling. He uncovered proof that Friedrich Hilderberg, the founder of the group, was Curtis's grandfather. Our theory is that Seymour was killed for it. Then when Rebecca Fox began searching for the same directory, she and her entire agency were targeted by hit men. Anyone who comes into possession of this list becomes a target.'

Mark nodded slowly. Still appearing ambiguous. He turned to Stella on his computer screen. 'What about you and Ralph, Stella? What have you got?'

Stella looked to be talking from Ralph's kitchen. His kitchen table, to be precise. She kept her voice low, so as to not wake the children upstairs, though in reality it would have taken an earthquake to waken them. She said, 'Ralph has internal financial documents that show there's money missing from SCX's books which tallies with donations made to the President and the PM's election campaigns.'

Mark said, 'Rough numbers, or numbers with arrows between them, pointing to SCX?'

'The numbers aren't rough,' Stella replied.

'Well, stick a pin in that for now. What else?'

Having expected a home run on the donations material, Stella was thrown by Mark's cool response. 'Um...okay, we can link Seymour's death and the Ghost Division attack to a man named Damian Oxley. Rebecca found phone data points that link Oxley to the murder of a former Marine turned private contractor called Eric Bogossian. Bogossian was killed the same night as Seymour, and we can place him within metres of the location of Seymour's house around the time of his death.'

'What do we know about Bogossian?' asked Mark.

'His body was found near where a burner phone was discarded in the Hudson River. He was in a unit with Damian Oxley, which is how Rebecca recognised him. She saw him during the Ghost Division attack and instantly recognised him in a group photo of Bogossian's troop in Iraq. Now, if we also have evidence that shows politicians linked to Hilderberg, and campaign funding for them coming from only Storm Capital and/or SCX, then that makes a strong argument for saying that Storm Capital are the financial wing of Hilderberg.'

Mark looked through all the material the team had acquired. A long, nervy pause followed. 'You don't have it,' he finally said. 'Not on Storm Capital. It's conjecture. We can't risk it.'

Not helped by a minor time delay in Stella's video feed, she and Novak argued back against Mark, talking over one another.

Mark interrupted them. 'Even if I could make out what both of you are saying, the answer would still be the same. It's not here in black and white. What are you expecting me to publish? Storm Capital funded politicians backed by Hilderberg, and paid a former Marine contractor to carry out hits on anyone who threatened to uncover their plans?'

Stopping short of admitting they didn't have it, Novak suggested, 'I don't think we're a million miles away.'

'Then you need to get there, or it's not going in. I think we need to focus on Seymour. There's much more documented with that.'

'The point,' Nathan said, 'is that this is happening again. Yes, we want to tell people what happened to Seymour. But in a way, they've already got away with that. This, what's happening now, we can still do something about.'

Novak looked at Nathan with admiration. He'd forgotten how passionate Nathan had been as a reporter. It made him sad to think that Diane never got to experience his positive side, or the story that he had found out of nothing that would have knocked her socks off.

Mark held firm. 'We need to shore up the autopsy side. If the report was changed, let's get the original on record. I'll send someone in the morning to Westchester Hospital to pull the original. Our only source on what was in the original is you, Tom. We need hard copy on something like this. If we're going to say that doctors lied, and the police collaborated with them on it – like the death of this Dr Blackford that sounds so suspicious – we'd better be airtight.'

Novak said, 'Actually, it will have to be me that gets it. It needs to be a family member.'

'It's not a good use of your time...but we need it.' Mark nodded, as if reassuring himself. 'We get it, we print it.'

Stella raised her hand to get Mark's attention. 'I'd just like to say that I agree with Nathan on this. My concern is that we're cutting and running. Everyone knows what Hilderberg was up to. What we're planning on publishing just redefines the scope of it all. But it avoids the bigger story of what Storm Capital's role is in all of this. That's a conspiracy that could be ongoing.'

'What's your theory?' asked Mark.

'You take this, Tom,' Stella said.

Novak said, 'Storm Capital hired Damian Oxley to stop Rebecca digging any further into finding the Directory, because it's full of people they've given money to. It indelibly associates them with corruption, and opens them up to any number of campaign finance lawsuits. And if we can demonstrate that they were involved in the Ghost Division attack, we can damn well link them to the murder of my dad as well.'

Mark rubbed his eyes. Only half joking, he said, 'Stella, I think I understand why you wanted to go back to reporting now. Tom, you don't get to make accusations like that with hearsay. I understand what it looks like. But do you have a contract from Anna Storm to the shooters? Someone on tape demanding Ghost Division and Rebecca are targeted? Your story amounts to no smoke without fire. We're not that type of publication.' He stood up and shuffled into his coat. 'No. We publish what we've got. You've got tonight and the morning to tidy it up. We publish in forty-eight hours. If you don't have it by then, it's not going in.'

Still unsatisfied, Stella asked, 'What about Damian Oxley? He's still on the loose.'

'That's a police issue, not ours.'

Novak chimed in, 'And what about Storm Capital? We've got their fingerprints all over this. The political donations done through SCX–'

Mark sighed. 'Can you *prove* that Anna Storm forced her son to make those donations?'

Novak didn't reply.

'Then we can't print it,' Mark said. 'Tell me Diane would have done anything different.'

Novak shrugged. 'You're right. We don't have it yet.'

'Will someone, at some point, get someone on the record here. Or we're going to end up publishing a story with just prepositions.'

Novak said, 'I'm trying Anna Storm later today. It could be a blowout but it's worth a shot.'

Stella warned, 'Even if she pulls up the drawbridge afterwards? You only get one shot at someone like Anna Storm.'

Nathan suggested, 'What about the next best thing?'

Stella said, 'Zach?'

Novak laughed. 'SCX is a dumpster fire right now. You think he's going to go on the record?'

Nathan said, 'I think Storm Capital is the reason SCX is burning down. Ralph already had financials leaked to him from someone on the inside. You never know. If Zach's got an axe to grind, he might name names.'

Mark gave them the nod. 'Do it.' He checked his watch, which was showing half past three in the morning. 'Christ... I'm going to get home, walk a loop around my kitchen, and then come boomeranging back. I think we'll call that a full day.'

As Novak and Nathan said goodbye to Stella and prepared to file out, Mark stopped in his doorway. 'Hey guys...great work. Diane would have been proud of you all today.'

Nathan looked down, thinking Mark was done.

Then Mark added, 'You too, Nathan.'

When Mark was gone, Nathan told Novak, 'Six years. I've been waiting six years to hear someone say that.'

'You'll hear it from me too tomorrow, if we can get Anna Storm on the record.'

CHAPTER FORTY

THE PROJECTIONS on Zach's Bloomberg terminal were getting worse by the hour. The crypto market was going into freefall, and no amount of desperate tweeting could stop it.

It was a position Zach wasn't used to finding himself in. He had always enjoyed immense privilege and influence thanks to his parents' positions. Get a job straight out of college in one of the most sought-after trading firms on Wall Street? No problem. Raise $100 million by getting celebrities to endorse SCX as a trading platform? Easy. There was no problem in life that he couldn't solve by throwing some money at it. But this was different. And if he couldn't course-correct it, he wouldn't have any money left by the end of the week.

Zach was in the middle of firing off another round of tweets to project optimism and stability – as suggested by Anna via a series of texts – when an email popped into his inbox.

It was from his dad. The subject line caught his attention. "*200k WTF??*"

He clicked into the message:

"*Hey son, just had confirmation of my salary through for work done recruiting for SCX. I don't know what to say. When we talked about money, 200k wasn't anywhere near what I expected. Do you not actually value what I bring to the company? I'm pulling in business every day off the back of my reputation. Is this how you treat your own father?*"

Zach called him straight away. 'Hey, dad, it's me.'

'Yeah, hi,' Noah replied, short and sharp.

'I wasn't trying to low-ball you with the salary thing.'

'Well, it sure felt like that, son. It's not just about the money. It's the whole...deal.'

'What deal?'

Noah paused. 'Was it your mother's idea to fob me off with this pittance of 200k?'

'Why would you even think that?'

'Oh, don't play innocent, Zach. You've always been your mother's. Everything we do, it's all about her.'

For a moment, Zach forgot he was speaking to a grown man. He hit refresh on his screen showing the current crypto price and the value of SCX tokens. When the page reloaded, the value had dropped another four per cent from fifteen minutes ago. Zach looked up to see one of his main numbers guys standing in his doorway. Zach squinted and mouthed, 'You okay?'

He shook his head gravely.

Zach told his dad, 'I'm sorry, dad, I'm going to have to go. But I'll sort the contract for you, okay? You pick the number you want.'

Noah sighed. 'Okay. Thanks, son. Oh hey...I love you.'

Zach nodded. 'Okay, bye.'

The numbers guy was Gary, who had been right by Zach's side since chess club in high school. 'We've got a major problem,' he said.

Gary had studied jet propulsion theory at college, which technically made him a rocket scientist. Whenever Gary told Zach there was a problem, Zach always listened.

'Let's go to your desk,' Zach said, eager to escape the misery of his office.

Gary led him across the hall, then stood with hands on hips, pointing at his computer screen like someone had died. 'Look at this.'

Zach leaned down. 'What am I looking at?'

'Obviously, we're in bad shape,' Gary said. 'So I started tracking what exactly we've got on our books. Did you know about this?'

Impatiently, Zach snapped, 'Know *what*? What is this?'

'I was looking at our overall holdings, to get a clear picture of our position. Look at this number here...' He pointed to the screen.

'What is that number?'

'That's how much is missing from our books.'

Zach looked up at him with a baffled expression. 'We've mislaid a billion dollars?'

Gary held his hands out in defeat. 'That's what it says. It's been replaced with a billion dollars of SCX tokens.'

Zach stood up, taking a steadying breath. He patted Gary on the arm. 'Don't worry about it.'

'Don't worry about it? Zach, that's a billion dollars of customers' money that's disappeared. And if the value of our tokens keeps dropping, that billion dollars of tokens is going to be worth about $50 million in a few days. Did you okay this?'

'I said don't worry about it. The market will bounce back. It always does.'

Gary didn't think he had a choice but to say it in the starkest possible terms. 'Zach, our projected losses are greater than the overall value of this company. And with each hour the market falls, those losses are just going to get bigger and bigger.'

Zach walked back to his office. 'It's going to be fine, Gary,' he called back.

On the way past Georgia's desk outside his office, he told her quietly, 'Hey, Georgia, why don't you take the rest of the day off.'

'Really?' she said, oblivious to what was going on across the office.

'Yeah, take off.' Zach closed his door behind him, then drummed his fingers on his desk, watching the market collapse.

He shut his eyes in despair. 'Mom...what did you do?' he said to himself.

The ping of an email notification made him open his eyes.

"FROM: *TOM NOVAK*

Hey Zach...let me know when's good to follow-up."

Zach drummed his fingers some more. Then he tapped out a reply. "*Hi Tom. You should come out here and we can talk face to face. Excited to share some things.*"

CHAPTER FORTY-ONE

ANNA STORM HAD SPENT most of the evening's performance of Wagner's *Ring* cycle at New York's Metropolitan Opera House on her phone. The only part of the multi-hour epic she liked was the four-minute opener "Vorspiel". Everything after that was a real slog. For someone who had been to as many operas as she had, Anna disliked them immensely. The Italians, especially Puccini. She couldn't stomach all those slushy arias, and the insistence on singing what otherwise would have been simple dialogue if it had been a movie. There was something faintly preposterous singing lines about shutting a door, or going out to buy some bread. At least Wagner had some guts about it.

Her face was lit up by her phone screen throughout the performance, but not a single person dared say anything to her. They knew who she was.

At intermission, she hobnobbed around the bar, being pulled this way and that by New York's cultural elite. Gallery owners. Painters. Writers. And, of course, the ones in finance for whom going to the opera was part of the penance of being rich. In New York money circles, if you wanted to stay rich, you had to go where other rich people were. It's how you found out what stock was hot. What venture capitalists were coming on the scene. Anna just wished there was a way to cram all the socialising into the first part of the night – that way she could disappear home at intermission.

As the lights overhead flashed on and off again to signal the imminent end of intermission, she felt an elbow go into her back. She whipped around, ready to unleash a volley of insults. Then she realised she knew the man in question.

'Henry?' she said.

'Anna,' he replied with a smile, then raised his arm, ready to accept a hug in profile, which Anna dutifully delivered.

She wasn't the only one to be surprised to see Henry Self. His appearance had been causing ripples all night – whispers of gossip, comments overheard at the bar. Once the publisher and owner of *The Republic*, his stint in prison had done nothing to blunt his style, dressed as he was in a brown Tom Ford suit that elevated him miles above the drab navies and greys on show amongst the other men his age.

'You're looking well,' she said.

'Thank you. You too,' he replied.

She paused. Hesitated.

'Anna Storm tongue-tied,' he cooed. 'Whatever next. You can ask me. I don't mind.'

'When did you get out?'

'About six months ago.' He looked up, taking in the

breathtaking surroundings. 'I used to dream of having nights like this again.'

'I can imagine.'

He looked cautiously towards the stairs which were full, as people made their way back to their seats. 'I'll be honest, I'm not loving this. You want to get out of here?'

They took a slow walk to Henry's car. His driver was waiting for him on Broadway.

Anna said, 'I don't see any neck tattoos. Are you sure you were in jail?'

Henry laughed. 'I'm certain.'

The crime he had committed – violating a federal gag order by revealing to rival publications that the government was censoring a story of theirs, and handing it over for them to print instead – had seemed an honourable sacrifice to make at the time. But just a few weeks in to his eighteen-month sentence, Henry regretted his decision.

He'd had plenty of opportunity to discuss it with his most frequent visitor Tom Novak, who had only missed a handful of visiting days in the whole length of Henry's sentence.

Approaching Henry's car, Anna asked, 'Is this work or personal?'

'A little bit of work. I'm trying to rebuild my social network post-incarceration.'

Pausing at the back door, Anna leaned in to whisper in Henry's ear, 'Are you going to give me a rolling around in there, Henry? For old time's sake?'

The back door opened up. But not by Henry. From the inside, where Tom Novak was sitting.

Anna shot Henry a withering look.

Henry defended himself, 'I told you it was a *little* about work.'

'Anna Storm,' Novak said. 'You're a hard woman to get on the phone.'

'That's how it goes when someone you don't want to speak to keeps calling.' She looked back towards the Met. 'Well, I've missed the start of the second half, so I might as well get in. You've got as long as it takes to get to Hudson Yards.'

Henry remained on the street. 'Call me?' he asked Anna.

'If only impoliteness was a parole violation, Henry.'

He shut the door with a grin, then gave his driver the instructions for where to go.

Anna made clear, 'We're off the record, by the way.'

Novak gestured humbly that he was fine with that.

'We're only a short drive down 10th Avenue, Mr Novak. You'd better be quick.'

Novak said, 'I've come into some documents that show Storm Capital was funding the election campaigns for two politicians who couldn't have been less consequential. Angela Curtis and Tucker Adams. Why those two back then? There must have been twenty prospects either side of the Atlantic that were substantially more attractive.'

'Why not?' Anna replied.

'I ask, because Storm Capital must have a lobbying budget the size of most countries' GDP. Yet you only funded two campaigns. And boy did you throw your weight behind them.'

'It's what we do at Storm, Mr Novak. When we find people we believe in, we back them all the way. That's how SC got where it is today.'

Novak looked over both shoulders. 'I'm sorry, are there cameras in here or something? Of the top twenty MPs backed for Cabinet positions within the next election cycles, Angela Curtis wasn't even mentioned in political commentary. And Tucker Adams was nothing more than a pinstripe suit and a haircut. How did they even end up on Storm Capital's radar? And, not only that, draw financial backing that rendered all other donations practically invisible by comparison?'

Anna smiled. 'You've clearly made up your mind about what we do. In my experience, it's pointless to argue with naysayers.'

'Were you surprised when the two candidates your fund had actually backed both ended up implicated in the Hilderberg conspiracy? I mean, what were the chances of that? Bad luck isn't something that appears to affect Storm Capital in any other way.'

'I don't condone some of the things that people affiliated with Hilderberg did. But not everyone associated with them was a murderer or a dictator. You're reaching, Tom. Did you really think you could just bully me into a confession?'

A quick survey of the geography outside told Novak that he was running out of time. 'I think Storm Capital is part of Hilderberg. And my dad was going to expose you, and your cronies. That's why you got rid of him, wasn't it?'

Anna leaned forward towards the driver and knocked on the glass. 'Pull over. I'm getting out.'

The driver ignored her.

'Annoying, isn't it?' said Novak. 'When people won't listen. My dad knew your whole game. And he would have blown it sky high.'

Anna looked horrified. 'Tom, what do you take me for? You think Storm Capital had anything to do with your dad's death?'

'It's not even in doubt,' Novak replied. 'I'm inches away from linking Damian Oxley to you. And when I do, you're going down for good. I don't care how much money you have. Who you've got in your pockets.'

Anna knocked more insistently on the driver's glass.

Novak called forward. 'Hey, man. Can you pull over?'

The driver did so immediately.

As Anna got out, she paused on the sidewalk. 'Keep pushing us like this, Tom, and you'll regret it. I promise you.'

She walked quickly – or as quickly as she could in her tall heels – towards Storm Capital's offices in the 50 Hudson Yards building, overlooking the Hudson River. She called her assistant, who was still working upstairs, and had been since five that morning. Anna barked, 'Get me the numbers of as many board members of *The Republic* as you can.'

CHAPTER FORTY-TWO

STELLA WAS WOKEN in the spare room at six by Molly and Matilda jumping up and down in their beds and laughing next door. Now Ralph's wife, Christine, was shepherding them around downstairs, trying to keep them out of Ralph's way, who was already up and working downstairs at the kitchen table.

They kept yelling, 'Daddy, daddy, daddy...' until Ralph couldn't take it any longer.

He shut his laptop and put his arms out. The two girls ran towards him, taking an arm each to cuddle. 'Ah!' Ralph called out in elevated surprise. 'My two little ladies!'

Stella came to, and immediately whipped over to her left where Rebecca had been sleeping. Her bed was now empty. She shot to her feet and called out, 'Rebecca!' The fear was evident in her voice.

As she ran along the hall, Rebecca came out of the bathroom and walked straight into her.

Stella let out a sigh of relief. 'Thank god. I didn't hear you get up.'

'Sorry,' Rebecca said casually. 'Have you checked your phone?'

'No, I'm literally just up.' She retrieved her phone from the spare room and found the same message that Rebecca had received from Novak.

"*Anna Storm was a washout. Plan B time.*"

'Damn,' Stella said.

Downstairs, there was a loud knock at the front door.

Apart from the girls, all chatter and activity instantly stopped.

Stella instinctively put her arm in front of Rebecca and pushed her back out of the sight line of the front door.

Ralph hurried along the hall and looked up the stairs towards the two women. He put his finger to his lips. 'Who is it?' he asked, without opening the door.

'It's Leon,' came the reply.

It took Rebecca a moment to process the voice and the name. She set off down the stairs, almost slipping on some toys that she hadn't spotted. She fumbled with the chain, and the latch, then pulled the door open.

She threw her arms around Leon, holding him tighter than she had ever held anyone before.

Rebecca jolted when she saw DCI Bell standing a few steps behind Leon on the garden path.

'It's all right,' Leon said, as Rebecca let him go. 'He's helping us.'

'I know,' Rebecca said, looking at Bell. 'You saved my life, chief inspector.'

Bell held his hand out to shake, but Rebecca hugged him instead.

'Thank you,' she said.

Squirming from the minor intimacy, Bell released

himself from her. He said, 'If I found you here, then there's a chance Damian Oxley can, as well. I need to get you moved to a secure location.'

Stella stepped forward into the doorway. 'Yeah, I was thinking about that last night.'

As Rebecca tidied the bed upstairs, Leon stood close by.

'You're sure you want to do this?' he asked.

'I want to go on the record about Wolfgang Tibor.'

'And what about Ghost Division? The investigation?'

Rebecca plumped up the pillow she'd been using, then put it back tidily, straightening the edges of the duvet. 'Ghost Division is over, Leon. There won't be any political will to bring back an agency started by Angela Curtis. Especially after this. In any case, they've got no one to run it.'

'What do you mean?' he asked.

She sat down on the edge of the bed. 'I mean it's over. I don't want to do this anymore. I want to get out for good this time.'

Leon sat next to her and took her hand. 'You're resigning?'

'Effective immediately.'

'Can you still talk to Tom and Stella about Tibor? What about the Official Secrets Act?'

'Tibor's testimony doesn't fall under the law.'

Leon shook his head disconsolately. 'You know I can't come with you to New York. I have to work.'

'I know,' said Rebecca. 'It's okay.'

'But you need armed protection until Damian Oxley is found. Who's going to do that?'

Stella appeared in the doorway behind. 'We know someone,' she said, then retreated to allow the pair to say goodbye – not knowing how temporary it may or may not be.

———

In DCI Bell's car on the way to the airport, Bell glanced at Rebecca in the back via the rear-view mirror. 'You're trying to flush him out, aren't you?'

Rebecca and Stella said nothing.

Leon in the front did likewise. Despite how much he disapproved of Rebecca's plan.

Bell looked at the road again. 'I won't ask too many questions. But promise me, if you catch him...' He trailed off.

Rebecca leaned forward and laid a hand on Bell's shoulder. 'We will.'

'For DI Molina, at least,' Bell added.

He and Leon watched Stella and Rebecca check in at Heathrow Airport, staying as long as they could before they entered the cavernous security clearance zone.

Leon waved as Rebecca looked back at the last possible moment. Once she was gone, he didn't move. 'And you're sure GCHQ have checked the flight log?'

'They've done background checks on every other passenger on the flight. They're all cleared. Damian Oxley is not on that flight.'

'But he could be on any number of other flights. I mean, someone like him has access to multiple identities.'

Bell shrugged. 'I'm afraid it's inevitable. Rebecca knows that this isn't without risk.'

'What if he thinks she's still here in the UK?'

'I'm almost certain Superintendent Sue Thornley is involved in this somehow. She provided Linda Upshaw with access to forensics to try and frame you and Rebecca. I made sure it was leaked to her that Rebecca was leaving for New York.'

Leon shook his head. 'I don't like this.'

'You and me both,' Bell said. 'Come on. We've got work to do.'

Halfway across Terminal 3, checking in at an American Airlines desk for a flight to Philadelphia, was a man wearing a baseball cap with only a small carry-on bag.

The desk clerk gave him a brief smile, but could tell from the man's lack of reaction that he wasn't interested in pleasantries. He was dressed to be anonymous. Forgettable. Dressed like thousands of others that would pass through the terminals that day. And he had the demeanour to match. Not too talkative. Not too quiet. If he was a colour, the clerk would have called him grey.

After checking his boarding pass and passport, the clerk handed both back to him and said, 'Thank you. Enjoy your flight, Mr Watkins.'

His passport named him as 'Michael Watkins', but the photograph was unmistakably that of Damian Oxley.

CHAPTER FORTY-THREE

As he had predicted, Mark had barely had time to get home when it was time to come back in. He had woken to a message from several board members calling an emergency video meeting that morning – and it didn't appear to be good news.

Mark's first thought was that another round of layoffs were being handed out. But after barely two and a half hours sleep, he wasn't thinking clearly about much at all.

When he logged onto the video call, he got the impression that the rest of the board had been talking for some time already.

Chairman of the board, Louis Sullivan, led the discussion. 'Mark, we've woken up to the news that Storm Capital is pulling all of its advertising with us immediately. Basically, every product or company associated with them is being pulled. As you can imagine, that's a lot of a companies.'

Mark didn't panic. 'Okay,' he said carefully. 'What exactly is the nature of the complaint?'

'Did you send one of your reporters round to harass Anna Storm at the opera last night?' asked Sullivan.

'The reporter was Tom Novak, and he wasn't actually *at* the opera. They were in a car together. They talked. That's it.'

'Well, she's screaming bloody murder, Mark. We have to make this right.'

Mark paused. 'What does that mean?'

'You know. Do the right thing. Or our lights will go out for good.'

Another member added, 'We can't survive without their advertising, Mark.'

'You mean your annual dividend depends on their advertising.'

'Excuse me?'

'I'm chief editor. I've looked at the numbers, and I'm telling you, yes it's a hit if they leave us, but it's not terminal. Far from it.' Mark shook his head. 'They're bluffing.'

Sullivan said, 'I'd love to know how you've arrived at that conclusion.'

Mark replied, 'If Storm Capital were to pull all their ads with us, we'd be expected to put out a press release to clarify our position and explain why Tom was talking to her in the first place. Pulling their ads guarantees that the story gets out there. I can't imagine that that's what Anna Storm wants. She can't have thought it through. I say let's hold off until lunchtime, and see if she has a change of heart.'

'If we leave it that late, Mark, they might not ever come back. You've never been in advertising. I have. As soon as you take one foot out the door, it's harder to put it back in again.'

Mark spoke with his hands, emphasising the depth of

his feeling on the matter. 'Look, Tom, Stella, and Ralph have done great work on this story. I back their assertions one hundred per cent. We won't go to print with anything that can't stand up. But we can't allow ourselves to be blackmailed like this by a major advertiser.'

There was a long silence, as none of the other members wanted to say what would happen next. They hoped it wouldn't have to be said.

Sullivan finally spoke. 'I'm very sorry to hear that, Mark. I think we all know where we each stand. Maybe it's best we let the lawyers handle things from now on.'

'Lawyers?' said Mark.

'It's the only sensible course of action. The board has got a fiduciary responsibility to do what's in the best interests of *The Republic*. Unless you pull the plug on the story.'

Mark was adamant. 'I can't do that,' he answered. 'I won't.'

'Then we should let the lawyers handle this now.'

'We want to thank you for service, Mark,' said one member.

A few more chimed in with similar sentiments.

The call might have ended amicably, but when he made his way to his office, Mark had a rocket up his backside. He called Tom and Stella, and told them stridently, 'We need to get these fuckers. Do you hear me? Make big fucking plays today, guys.'

CHAPTER FORTY-FOUR

THE CHAIN of islands that made up the Bahamas were spread out across five hundred miles to the east of Florida, and north of Cuba. The most populous island lay to the east of the chain. New Providence, where Novak and Nathan were bound.

They landed at Lynden Pindling Airport on the banks of Lake Killarney, the greenest lake that Novak had ever seen. The airport was impeccably clean, if dated. Much like most of New Providence. The pockets of wealth that were present on the island were highly concentrated around protected, privately owned areas along the coast. Most notably the Four Winds Club, where SCX had set up their headquarters.

The taxi driver that took them from the airport was surprised to hear their destination. Neither Novak nor Nathan looked wealthy enough to be staying at the Four Winds. Taxi drivers always had high hopes when a passenger asked to be taken there. It often meant a sizeable tip that was chump change to the tourist, but a windfall to a local.

Novak and Nathan were both open-mouthed at the luxury on display at the Four Winds.

Novak hung his arm out the window. He took a deep breath. 'Even the air smells different here.'

Nathan couldn't believe his luck. From down-and-out reporter, to having a shot at getting back on staff at *Republic* if he played his cards right, and now this.

The main base of the club consisted of eight crystal-white apartment buildings arranged in a horseshoe shape around a super-yacht marina. It was everything Novak had imagined an exclusive gated community to be.

Nathan tapped Novak gently on the leg. 'Tom. Look,' he whispered, then pointed out two burly men in suits with earpieces in, trailing behind a couple who were about the most beautiful human beings Nathan had ever seen in real life. They were like cartoons of beauty.

'A lot of celebrities around here, apparently,' Novak said, spotting a sign outside a coffee shop advising customers not to photograph celebrities there. The menu advertised a basic Americano at $10.

Nathan remarked, 'Some people just live in a different world.'

'Kind of makes a mockery of Zach's whole effective altruism thing,' said Novak. 'This should be the antithesis of the sort of place he would want to come to.'

'I guess he justifies it by telling himself he'll give away much more by the end of his life.'

'Yeah, but what if it's a grift? The only reason to move your business here is if you want to get away with things you'd never get away with in the States, or even China.'

Nathan did a quick check on his phone. 'Are we sure he's going to be in a fit state to do an interview?' He showed Novak the current value of SCX.

'Holy hell,' Novak said.

The value of SCX had dropped sixty-three per cent in just two days, the majority of which had happened in the last twenty-four hours.

Zach met them in the lobby and took them to his apartment via his private lift. He didn't say much, other than to comment on the weather.

Novak and Nathan couldn't believe Zach's mood. Either he was dangerously disconnected from reality, or he knew something that no one else did about the situation.

They set up for the interview in the sprawling lounge area, which was fitted with corner sofas, and oversize TVs for Zach and his employees to enjoy gaming into the small hours of the morning.

Only then did the journalists realise that the apartment block was both a work and living space for employees, with Zach having the penthouse to himself.

Novak noted a black, well-worn beanbag next to Zach's desk. He had heard rumours that Zach did all of his sleeping there, getting only three hours a night.

Zach took a seat on one of the sofas, sitting compactly as if he had to share it with several other people. His body language hunched and afraid.

'I suppose you've seen the share price,' Zach said.

'Yeah,' said Novak. 'Is there a plan for a turnaround?'

'No,' Zach said emphatically. 'It's over. We're going down. All that's left is to do the right thing.'

'Why did you want to talk to us?' Nathan asked.

Zach fidgeted with his hands. 'I know I'm probably going to jail for a long time when this is over. I want to get some things on the record. While I still can.'

Novak edged forward in his seat. He showed Zach his phone screen, which was set to the audio recorder and wasn't recording yet. 'Zach, are you scared that you're in any kind of danger?'

'Not yet,' he said. 'But by the time we're done talking and you publish, I will be.'

CHAPTER FORTY-FIVE

Novak's audio recorder now running, Zach was going on the record. Every word that came out of his mouth could be published in full by *The Republic*.

Novak said gently, trying not to spook him, 'Zach, I'm going to ask you some yes or no questions. Okay? Just yes or no. For clarity.'

Nathan couldn't believe that Zach had agreed to it. It was a bold but clever move. One that Nathan had never seen before.

It was a trick that Diane Schlesinger had taught him to get a bare minimum of answers to your most pressing questions, so that if the interview went south in a hurry, you would still have enough answers to form the basic architecture of a story.

Trying to underplay the scope of what he was asking, Novak said, 'Were customer funds transferred out of SCX to Storm Capital?'

Zach gave a firm nod. 'Yes.'

With just one word – and his first on the record for the

interview – Zach had admitted to a felony. Something Novak was all too aware of.

Novak asked, 'Were the funds replaced by SCX tokens?'

'Yes.'

'Were the funds used to finance the election campaign of Peter Hoyle, now the President of the United States?'

'Yes.'

'Were the funds used to also finance the election campaign of Amanda Channing, now the British Prime Minister?'

'Yes.'

Internally, Novak and Nathan were doing cartwheels, but they couldn't let on. They were less than thirty seconds into the interview, and Zach had just caused potentially fatal damage to his own mother's hedge fund, and potentially started the process of bringing down both the current US President and the British Prime Minister, months into their first terms. And all it took to create the spark that started it was four uses of the word "yes".

Novak asked, 'What was the purpose of funding those particular candidates over others?'

Nathan suddenly spoke. 'Uh...Tom, could I have a quick word?' He motioned towards the back of the room.

Novak looked like he wanted to set fire to Nathan. Once they were a safe distance away and Zach was busy scrolling on his phone, Novak whispered, 'What the fuck are you doing?'

'Me? What are you doing with that question? You're trying to get him to link Storm Capital with Hilderberg, aren't you?'

Novak paused. 'Not exactly.'

'What if he doesn't know? We'll have put him on record issuing a denial of knowing any link between the two. If he might not know, don't ask the question.'

'We might not get another chance, Nathan. You saw the stock price. It's only a matter of time before Bahamian police come in here, acting on a tip-off from the FBI. And good luck getting access to Zach after that.'

'If you swing at this and miss, it doesn't matter if he later claims to know of a link between Hilderberg and Storm Capital. You'll have to tell Mark that he at first issued a denial. And if Mark knows that, he'll never run with the second answer.'

Novak said, 'You're right. I know you're right.' He walked back towards Zach, then turned to tell Nathan, 'But it's a chance I'm willing to take.' When he got back to his seat, he said, 'Sorry, Zach. I asked you about–'

'I remember the question,' Zach said. He picked at some fluff on his baggy cargo shorts, thinking about what he was going to do. He looked more like a penniless student than someone with a net worth of billions. Everything would be different once he'd answered the question. There would be no going back. 'Those particular candidates were targeted because I was directed by my mother, Anna Storm, to do so.'

'Hoyle and Channing were the only candidates SCX donated to. Did Anna say why those particular candidates were so vital?'

Zach snorted, remembering the conversation. It was the moment he found out that his mother was corrupt. 'She said, they're as good as family. And that as family, they would in turn look after us.'

'What family was she talking about?'

A look came over Zach that made Novak and Nathan believe for a few seconds that he was actually going to confirm it was Hilderberg. Then, despite the decades-plus of her tyrannical mother behaviour, some deeply buried loyalty to her took over.

Zach shook his head. 'I don't...I don't really know what she meant. God knows the family is not us. My mom and dad and I, we're not a family. We're just a series of ongoing transactions. Even my name was a transaction. When my mom married my dad, she demanded they take her name. Of course, my dad, who's never stood up to anyone in his life, caved like he always does. I might be known as the CEO of SCX, but it's in name only. I mean, I invented the exchange and coded it all. But my mom is the one who really runs it. She has as much access to the backend of the platform as I do.'

Novak's eyes widened in surprise. 'I'm sorry?'

Zach repeated it, as if it was no big deal.

Novak asked, 'Does that mean she has access to customer and company funds?'

'Yes. For her, it's as simple as withdrawing funds from the bank. She replaced the cash with our SCX tokens, so the company didn't look like it had lost a stack of its assets overnight. Which was fine, provided the value of our tokens didn't drop below a certain point. We sailed past that point, and then some, last night. As the market continues to drop, people cut and run. They withdraw their money from our exchange. And if we only have SCX tokens that are worth a fraction of the cash they gave us, then we don't have the funds to pay them. It's like going into your bank and you ask to withdraw from your account, and they hand you over Monopoly money instead.'

'But why use SCX for this?' asked Novak. 'Storm Capital controls trillions in assets globally.'

'And part of the security in the plan was that no one ever found out it was Storm Capital who financed those election campaigns. That's why your father got himself into trouble.'

Novak's face darkened in an instant. 'Do you know of evidence that connects the people who killed my dad to Storm Capital?'

'I've never been allowed deep enough inside to find out. But my suspicion is yes.'

'What's the ultimate play for Storm Capital in all of this?'

'The same as it always is. Money. Tons and tons of money. They buy the politicians, and in return they create laws that help us – like the upcoming Financial Regulations Bill.'

Nathan said, 'But the politicians themselves don't really profit, do they?'

Zach snorted. 'Is that a joke? Storm has got half the financial services committee lined up to join the board within the next five years. Have you ever looked at the boards of major financial firms? They're all filed with former politicians for a reason. Do you know how much a Storm Capital board member earns compared to a US senator? Not to mention the lucrative connections they make during their elected terms. It's a system that feeds itself. A perpetual motion machine that can never be turned off. With the right regulations – or lack of them – Storm stands to make hundreds of billions over the next ten years. That's hundreds of billions of reasons to kill or remove anyone who stands in the way of that.'

Novak drummed his fingers on his leg. He only had one more question left. 'Zach, I'm going to ask this, and you might not like it.'

Zach waited.

'Do you think your mother ordered a hit on my father, and on Rebecca Fox of Ghost Division?'

Nathan turned his head slightly, watching Zach carefully.

Zach showed no sign of not knowing who Rebecca was, or what Ghost Division was. Which, in itself, was notable to both Nathan and Novak.

Zach thought long and hard, before finally settling on an answer to Novak's question. 'I think my mother is capable of anything.'

When Novak and Nathan packed up their things to get the next flight back to JFK, Novak asked, 'Are you sure you wouldn't consider coming back with us? I mean, forget about any story. Just on a human level. I don't know that you should be on your own right now.'

Zach replied, 'I'm sure. There's nowhere I could go where trouble wouldn't eventually find me. It might take a little bit longer here though. If I'm lucky, I'll escape much in the way of hard jail time. Wire fraud and money laundering won't be easy to avoid though.'

'What will you do next?'

'We'll declare bankruptcy tomorrow.' Zach looked down. 'After that, I don't know. What I *do* know is that whatever happens, Storm Capital will survive. Unless you go back to Regis Point.'

Novak heard the words, but after several seconds he still hadn't reacted. There was no logical reason why Zach knew about the tiny hamlet where his father's autopsy report had been kept. 'What do you know about Regis Point? Why would you know about it?'

Zach turned to go back to his office. 'Call me when you find it.'

'Find it? Find *what?*'

'You'll know when you see it.'

Nathan and Novak stared at each other in disbelief.

Nathan shook his head. 'How can he know about that? No, seriously, Tom. How can he know about Regis Point? SCX and Storm Capital don't have any links out there.'

Novak replied, 'Apparently they do. We need to find out what they are. I think this thing goes deeper than we imagined.'

CHAPTER FORTY-SIX

WALTER SHARP MET Stella and Rebecca at the arrival gate in JFK. He was treating the task of protecting the two women with the utmost seriousness, switching to a mode he called being "on". It was akin to what sports stars call "getting in the zone": another level of concentration, mixed with ability, composure, and rational decision-making. He calmly evaluated everything – and everyone – he saw with a ruthless efficiency. At a glance, he could either dismiss a threat, or zero in on the possibility of one.

When Stella and Rebecca came through with their carry-on luggage, he upped their speed to get them to his car as soon as possible.

On Grand Central Parkway passing LaGuardia, Manhattan got bigger and bigger in the distance ahead. He told them, 'I should warn you. There's only so much I can do. I'll defend life if anyone is in danger, but I'm not an assassin. I'm still a Specialized Skills Officer with CIA. That trumps any other measure of loyalty.'

'We understand, Walter,' Stella replied.

Checking the rear-view mirror for what felt like the hundredth time, Sharp asked, 'What's going to happen to Ghost Division now?'

Rebecca said, 'I'm sure it will disappear.'

'The White House wasted no time getting rid of our incarnation of it. No one really wants to know what's hiding in the intelligence community.'

'I suppose I should be grateful to have survived this long.'

'What will you do?' asked Sharp.

Rebecca said, 'Play Scrabble? Read books?'

Sharp smiled knowingly. 'I'm not talking about hobbies. Distractions. Leisure. I'm talking about your *life*. What are you going to do?'

'Who says I need to do anything?'

Stella remarked, 'Your bank manager, I expect.'

Sharp added, 'I always wondered about those people who win the lottery. People get so jealous. They want it so badly for themselves. As if the aim of life is to get to the point where you do nothing. People like you, Rebecca, and you, Stella, you have a greater purpose than that.'

Rebecca countered, 'I only ended up in Ghost Division, firstly, because Angela Curtis thought she could control and manipulate me. And because of what happened to my dad. I wanted revenge. I wanted to expose the people who imprisoned him, and stole so many years of him from my life. I did that. They want to keep fighting, but I don't. I won my fight.'

A MAN who looked like a younger version of Sharp, along with a woman whose strong physique was evident underneath a trouser suit, were waiting outside the front doors of a ten-storey sandstone in midtown Manhattan that was home to *The Republic* offices. The pair of them looked like law enforcement, hands clasped behind their backs, waiting dutifully for their former colleague.

'Don't worry,' Sharp said, 'they're with me. And they're damn good.'

Their backs straightened when they saw Sharp approaching.

Sharp said, 'Stella and Rebecca, this is Drew and Martha. We used to work together, but they're in the private sector now. They're going to be helping me out on our little security detail here.' He turned to them. 'We good?'

'All set, Walter,' said Martha.

'We're good,' said Drew.

Rebecca felt it only polite to say something to strangers offering to protect her. 'Thank you.'

The thanks didn't seem to register with them.

On the lift up to the fifth floor, Sharp began, 'It's time for me to tell you about some monitoring I've had done today. An NSA buddy of mine tapped into some systems to have a look for me. There was a Michael Watkins who arrived in Philadelphia not long after your flight landed. My buddy tells me that Watkins' photo is a positive match for Damian Oxley. I expect he'll be in the city soon, if not already. Phillie's only an hour or so drive from here.'

Stella extended a hand to Rebecca. 'You sure you want to do this?'

'I trust Walter,' Rebecca said.

'This guy's good, ladies,' Sharp said. 'But I'm better.'

Mark had set up the conference room for everyone to help with information sharing, as the plan was to have the final story written between Tom, Stella, Nathan, and with an "additional reporting" credit for Ralph.

Sharp kept his distance, remaining near the edge of the newsroom, where he could monitor all traffic in and out of the office, as well as keep a close eye on the conference room thanks to its glass walls.

Rebecca took a seat on the outer edge of the conference room, trying to stay out of the way, as Mark, Novak, and Nathan were in the middle of an animated discussion about the conversation they'd had with Zach in the Bahamas earlier in the day.

Novak was leaning over the table, remonstrating with Mark. 'What else can it mean?' demanded Novak. 'What the hell does Zach know about a tiny hamlet in Northern Westchester? I've got to get back out there.'

Stella took off her coat and tossed it aside. 'The hell you are. We've got a story to write. A bloody big one. There's no time.'

Mark, leaning back in his chair like an army general considering troop movements on a map, said, 'Actually, Stella, I need Tom to pick up a copy of the other autopsy report. For comparison with the one he and Nathan collected yesterday.'

'Damn,' said Stella. 'I forgot about that.'

'Right,' Novak said, 'I'm taking off.' Like a baseball coach telling a player to sub in, he pointed at Nathan, who was sitting in the margins, unsure of how involved he would be permitted to be. 'Nathan, you get started on my piece – from the Zach interview.'

Nathan didn't know what to say.

Neither did anyone else. No one wanted to be the one to question Nathan's abilities – especially while Nathan was in the room.

'I trust him,' Novak assured them.

Mark shot Stella an accusatory look. 'What about you?'

'I'm done,' Stella said. 'I sent it to you somewhere over the mid-Atlantic.'

Mark double-checked his email. 'Ah, yeah. Thanks.'

He and Nathan huddled at one end of the table, going over their notes on Zach.

'I'm getting coffee,' she told them.

While the kettle boiled in the staffroom, Stella's eyes drifted towards reception, where a large glass cabinet housed every single edition of *The Republic* ever printed. She lodged her tongue into her cheek. 'I wonder...' she said to herself. Then she set off towards reception.

She peeled down every issue she could find with a Nathan Lugati story in it. She made a pile of them and walked with the stack back to the staffroom.

Then she began to read.

CHAPTER FORTY-SEVEN

ZACH'S LEAD on Regis Point had proven so ethereal, if the entire town had grown legs and walked ten miles east, it still wouldn't have been enough to satisfy Novak's expectations.

The little town was as normal as ever when Novak arrived. He slowed to ten miles an hour, looking carefully out each side of the car for a clue – any clue – that would reveal itself as important.

After a few minutes of frustration, Novak began to shake his head. 'I don't get it, man...I don't get it.'

Then he got it.

Zach was indeed right. Novak knew it when he saw it.

He was looking at the location of the doctors' surgery and didn't understand what he was seeing. As Zach had instructed, Novak called him and slowly got out of the car.

'Hi Zach,' said Novak. 'It's Tom Novak. So I'm here in Regis Point like you suggested.'

'What do you see?'

'I was hoping you could tell me, because I'm currently

looking at a building whose windows are boarded up as if it's been closed for years. A building I was standing in yesterday.'

Taking the opportunity of what appeared to be a local walking past, carefree, carrying some shopping bags and walking an energetic little terrier dog, Novak told Zach to hang on.

Lowering the phone, Novak extended a hand towards the passerby. 'Excuse me,' he said. 'Sorry, I'm just wondering about the doctors' surgery.'

'Oh yes?' came the reply. 'It's not been that for a while. Well, it's not been anything. Though, now you mention it, I thought I saw it open a few days ago. Seems they've gone already!' The passerby allowed their dog to pull them on.

Novak said, 'No, hang on! Please...I was in there yesterday.'

The local laughed. 'That place has been out of commission for three years, son.'

Novak returned to the phone call. 'What can you tell me?' he asked.

'All I know,' said Zach, 'is that a mention of the property came across my desk a few days ago. If you give me an hour I'll find the details on it.'

Novak hung up the phone and took in the sight of the former surgery building. The windows were all boarded up, and the small car park at the rear was closed off by a thick chain stretching across the entrance.

He checked the time, then cursed, 'Shit.' He had so much writing to do, and he hadn't even got the alternative version of the autopsy report Mark had sent him after.

Novak's phone rang with a piercing shrill tone. In

Manhattan, it was necessary to cut through the noise of the traffic and people. In Regis Point, it was overkill.

'Mark,' said Novak. 'You're not going to–'

'I need you back,' Mark said. 'There's a problem with the story.'

Acid flooded Novak's stomach, hitting him with a wave of nausea. He was almost scared to ask. 'What's the problem?'

'It's the Directory,' said Mark. 'Get back here.'

CHAPTER FORTY-EIGHT

Novak returned in a haze of anxiety about the story. He tried to prepare himself for anything as he walked into the conference room.

The Directory was sitting on the table in front of Mark, along with his laptop, which was hooked up to the projector screen.

Stella hit the button to darken the walls.

Rebecca excused herself to make a phone call.

'Shit,' said Novak. 'It must be serious if we're going dark.'

Mark replied, 'I want you to be able to see what Ralph has not long shown us.'

On the video wall was a still shot of a page from the Directory. Not a random page, as Novak first assumed. Quite the opposite.

'What am I looking at?' he asked.

Stella had her arms folded, head tilted back against the wall. 'The end of this story,' she said.

'What?'

Mark stood over his laptop. 'Are you there, Ralph?'

'Yeah,' Ralph replied. 'Ready.'

Mark said to Novak, 'Okay, Tom. We've got a bit of a problem. Ralph's going to walk us through it.'

Controlling the image on the video wall, Ralph's voice came through the speakers in the conference table.

'As you can see, Tom,' Ralph explained, circling elements with his cursor, 'these are the names in the Directory we're all familiar with. Angela Curtis. A number of others. As well as a number of ones we're not quite so familiar with.'

He changed the image to a different page. But instead of politicians' names, they had all been replaced with the names of characters from *The Simpsons*.

'Is this meant to be funny?' asked Novak. 'I've got honest-to-god shit to deal with right now. Serious shit, and–'

Mark was miles away from laughing. 'This is serious, Tom.'

Novak pointed to the wall. 'Other than the names, that looks identical to the real Directory. How did you do that, Ralph?'

'Oh, it was quite hard,' he replied. 'Took me about five minutes with Microsoft Word and a scanner.'

Novak paused as he looked around the room. Then he let out a single burst of laughter. Then he clapped his hands in relief. 'Thank, god, for that. You really had me there. I thought you were actually saying the document's a fake. Of course you can recreate the document in Word. My laptop's got about ten fonts that look like an old typewriter font.'

'No, Tom,' Ralph said. 'This example is to show you

that I can create a document that looks just like the Directory very easily. I created the one with the politicians' names on it as well.' He switched to another example. This time alternating between a loop of a page of the original Directory document this time, and a very similar-looking version of it. The same words. The same sentences. 'If you look at this, you can see I've recreated this original page almost exactly.'

Novak pouted. 'Hardly, Ralph.' He pointed at the screen. 'There! I can tell that second page is different. The font's much cleaner. Doesn't look as aged. It's obvious.'

Stella and Mark both looked down. They had made the same error as Novak.

'It's not about the effect, Tom,' Ralph explained. 'The point is about the spacing of the font. That's all.'

Novak squinted as the document changed on a loop.

Ralph went on, 'See how each letter lines up perfectly in both versions? The first version purports to be from the seventies, created on a typewriter. We know this because it's been dated as such. The second version is a mono-spaced font taken from a modern version of Word.'

Mark cut in. 'If that page from the Directory is genuinely from the seventies, Tom, then the fonts shouldn't line up like that.'

'It shouldn't be possible,' Ralph added. 'It's the typesetting equivalent of playing a VHS tape in a Blu-ray player.'

Novak tried to laugh again, but couldn't quite match the enthusiasm of the previous time. 'Okay, will somebody please explain this to me as if I'm just a small child. What are you saying?'

Stella delivered the gut-punch conclusion. 'The Directory's a fake.'

No one said anything. Everyone waiting for the truth to hit home.

'But what about the age effects?' said Tom. 'It *looks* so real.'

Ralph said, 'I created the same aged effects running the modern Word version of the document through a scanner a dozen times.'

Flailing for an explanation, Novak said, 'What about the names...there are names on here that we know are Hilderberg operatives.'

Stella said, 'I think someone's trying to trick us into publishing something that's wrong. They put Angela Curtis and Tucker Adams in there to convince us that it's real. Two people we knew were Hilderberg operatives. All the other names we're not familiar with, so we can't be sure. Not now. Whoever put this together thinks that we'll go ahead and print this based on their association with Curtis and Adams being in the same document. That's how they're going to get us, Tom. That's the play. They're not trying to kill us. They're trying to get us to destroy our careers by going all in on a huge story. Remember what happened to Dan Rather on *60 Minutes*? One innocent mistake, and you're fake news and out of a job.'

Mark came closer to Tom and Stella. 'The question is: where did Seymour get this document from?'

Novak gulped hard. 'We don't actually know who–'

Stella interrupted, 'Nathan was the one who found it in your dad's archives, Tom. Something he'd been sitting on for six years according to him.'

Novak nodded rapidly. 'No, I get it. I get it. This ties in with the surgery.'

'Surgery?'

'Nathan and I managed to pull a copy of my dad's autopsy report that was vastly different to the one I was shown at the time my dad died. The surgery's in a tiny town called Regis Point in Northern Westchester. When we were talking to Zach Storm this morning, he ended by telling me to go back to Regis Point.'

'Why would he know anything about Regis Point?' asked Stella.

'That's what I said. So I go back there today, and...the surgery's gone. The building's all boarded up like it's been that way for years.'

'What do you think's going on?'

'The surgery Nathan and I visited was a setup. A fake. Like the autopsy report I was handed. Sure, my dad didn't die by his own hand. But whoever's behind all this wanted me, *needed* me, to believe.'

Mark interjected, 'But I thought there *was* foul play? Why would conspirators who killed your dad hand over evidence that contributes to proof that he was murdered?'

'They don't care about what I can prove or not prove about my dad's death. All they care about is us printing a story about that.' Novak pointed to the Directory. 'A big part of that, is me believing that hostile forces murdered my dad because of a staggering secret he found out about. It makes sense when you find out who actually owns the property that housed the surgery.'

'Who?' asked Stella.

'It's owned by a subsidiary linked several miles down the road to Storm Capital. The director is listed as N.Bergman. In the car coming back, Zach confirmed to me the first name of that subsidiary.'

'What is it?' asked Mark.

Novak replied, 'Noah.'

'Who the hell is Noah Bergman?'

Stella put a hand to her head as she realised. 'Oh, god...'

Novak flicked through pages of the Directory, stopping when he reached a page from the modern end of the document. 'Noah Bergman. Zach confirmed it to me. His dad changed his surname when he married Anna Storm. He kept it very private. But there are still traces of evidence, such as this, that are around. It's only easy once you know what the name was.'

Mark shook his head. 'Noah Bergman's a member of Hilderberg.'

'Hang on,' said Ralph, frustrated to be stuck behind a computer so far away. 'We already demonstrated that the Directory is a fake.'

'It's a question of language,' said Novak. 'I agree, Ralph. You've shown that there are problems with the Directory. But I don't think it's fake. I think it's counterfeit. Fake denotes something that's not the real thing. But counterfeit merely implies deception. All they had to do is throw up President Hoyle and Prime Minister Channing's names up there to seduce us into thinking we were exposing something huge.'

As Rebecca returned to the room following her phone call, Mark raised his hands in defence. 'Can I just say, that we don't actually have anything definitive to say those two are not involved.'

'No,' said Rebecca. 'But I wouldn't advise you to name them. Wolfgang Tibor just retracted his whole testimony about the Directory. He says it's bollocks. Or, words to that effect.'

'We've been played this whole time,' said Stella, looking around the newsroom. 'Where the hell is Nathan?'

CHAPTER FORTY-NINE

SHARP HAD SETTLED into his surroundings, getting a feel for how the place moved. What people went where. What the process was for visitors coming into reception.

He walked the long corridors either side of the newsroom, always leaving himself with a vantage point on Rebecca in the conference room.

He pressed the speaker for the radio on his wrist. 'Drew, check in, please.'

Several seconds went by without an answer.

Sharp repeated the process. Same result.

He did it again, this time with Martha.

After that failed to get a response, Sharp jogged to the conference room, nipping in quietly to tell Rebecca that he was going downstairs, and that she was to remain with the others in the room until he returned.

Sharp took the stairs to limit the chances of a radio dropout. His voice was getting increasingly desperate. It was a simple job, and they were good operatives. There was no reason for them to fail to respond.

'Drew, Martha, check in...'

He quickened his pace, instinct telling him that something serious had happened.

When he reached the lobby, he saw the building security guard at a desk near the front door. But no sign of Drew or Martha.

The guard hadn't seen anything of them in the last twenty minutes.

Sharp cursed himself. He should have arranged more frequent check-ins.

He showed a picture of Damian Oxley to the guard. 'Have you seen this man come in here?'

'No, not here,' said the guard.

Sharp pocketed the photo, and was already on his way back to the stairs.

Then the guard added, 'Out the back earlier.'

'What did you say?' Sharp ran back, showing him the picture again. 'You saw this man at the back of the property earlier today?'

'Yeah, it was about half an hour ago...'

Sharp sprinted past the lifts, narrowly avoiding a postal cart being wheeled out of the service lift. Then he bounded through a maintenance door which led to the rear entrance of the building. It had been Martha's task to secure the area.

When Sharp got there, the rear entrance door was flapping open when it should have been locked.

'Oh, shit...' he said, gathering his breath. Then he noticed a shoe sticking out of a door. He opened the door, finding Martha and Drew's bodies one on top of the other. Each with a gunshot wound to the forehead.

CHAPTER FIFTY

DAMIAN PERFORMED the final checks on his M4 assault rifle in an empty office on the vacant floor above *The Republic*.

Spread out in front of him, which he had been memorising were the floor plans for *Republic*, annotated to show where each individual reporter's desk was.

Damian clutched his weapon and shut his eyes. Walking the floor of the office below, imagining what every sense would experience down there. Just as he had done when running ops in the Marines. It helped him attune to his environment, in situations where things changed rapidly. And the quicker you adapt to the change, the better your chances of not only completing the mission, but staying alive.

The performative aspect to his preparation had earned Damian the nickname of the Jihadi Whisperer. No one in his unit had anywhere close to the number of kills as he had.

Like in Marines ops, the *Republic* offices would throw

up the unexpected. Every mission did. You can make all the right plans, which is fine if you encounter everything as you anticipate it should. Warfare didn't work like that. He didn't kid himself that what he was about to walk into was anything like warfare. But the principles were the same.

He opened his eyes as soon as he heard the triplet knock on the door, as arranged. Still, Damian took no chances, placing a handgun up against the inside of the door at chest height, to maximise his chances of incapacitating an enemy if needed by striking the largest target on the human body: the torso.

'It's me,' Nathan whispered.

Damian opened the door, keeping himself hidden behind it. 'What are you doing here?' he asked. 'I told you to not risk coming up here.'

'I've got good news,' Nathan informed him. 'It's a stop.'

'A stop?'

'They're going to publish. They're about to discuss the Directory, but Novak thinks that's a home run already.' He held his hands out as if it was obviously good news. 'So there's no value in killing Rebecca now.'

'I'm here to do a job,' Damian said.

'Her death was meant to be another piece of the puzzle to make Novak believe. There's nothing to be gained from going ahead now.'

'I'll be the judge of that.'

Nathan reached out for Damian's submachine gun, and pulled the barrel down and away. 'I don't think so.'

Damian stared at Nathan's hand. 'Take your hand off. If you make me say it twice, you'll be pulling back a stump.'

Nathan removed his hand from the barrel, then turned his palms towards Damian. 'I'm sorry, all right. But I'm telling you the job is over. Novak's about to bring me back into the fold, I think.'

'That's got nothing to do with me. I've been paid to finish a job by an employer. Who is, frankly, a lot scarier than you'll ever be.'

Nathan chuckled nervously. 'Please, Damian. Okay? Please. You saved my life in Basra. I will never forget it. But I have a second chance now. If you go down there, you destroy my life all over again.'

Damian had heard enough. He placed his M4 down carefully on the ground, then when he stood up again, he reached for his sidearm, which he had fitted with a suppressor.

Nathan saw his life flash before his eyes. All he could get out was, 'No, no...'

Then Damian fired two rounds into Nathan's forehead.

Nathan's body crumpled, but Damian caught it in time before it could thud on the thin-carpeted floor.

CHAPTER FIFTY-ONE

STELLA HAD BEEN STANDING over her computer for five minutes, having asked for time to check something. She then beckoned everyone from the conference room to reception, where she had stacked a pile of back issues of *The Republic*.

'What's this all about?' asked Novak.

She explained, 'I was looking through Nathan's old stories while you were gone, and I came across one about him being embedded with a Marine unit in Basra during the second Iraq War. It got me thinking about Eric Bogossian.'

'The guy killed the same night as my dad?' said Novak.

'*Why* was Eric killed that night?' asked Stella. 'We know that Damian is the link between both Seymour's death and the Ghost Division attack. It couldn't be coincidence that the one person we knew to be involved in the attack was in a Marine unit with a guy who had a proven phone connection to Seymour's murder. I think Eric was part of a hit team that night, but something went wrong, and he was ditched. We probably will never find out what happened, but the point is that it reminded me of the Marines in both cases.'

Novak reached for the magazine Stella had been waving around for emphasis. He quickly handed it back to her. 'You've got no names or photos here.'

'Not published, anyway,' Stella said. She scrolled on her phone to a photo she had not long taken. She showed each person one at a time, so that they had a chance to appreciate it. 'I pulled up the background notes for the story. And found this.'

On Stella's phone was a photo of Eric Bogossian and Damian Oxley, standing next to Nathan.

Stella explained, 'Based on the metadata embedded in the photo, this was taken the day they saved Nathan's life.'

Mark said, 'Some bonds are hard to break.'

Novak let out an anguished cry. 'Shit!'

Then the lights went out.

'That's not good,' said Stella.

The other reporters in the newsroom had no idea the malevolent nature of the power cut, with some chuckling or whooping in delight – though some were panic-stricken about losing work. The last power cut in the block had lasted three hours, and cost a combined loss of two hundred thousand words.

The only one prepared for this event was Walter Sharp, who had a torch clamped by hand against his gun, lighting the way ahead as he exited the stairwell. He stalked through reception, ensuring the newsroom was clear.

Sharp's voice boomed through the darkness. 'My name is Walter Sharp, I'm an officer with CIA. This is emergency! Find an office you can barricade yourselves into. Lock the door, and stay quiet. There's a gunman in the building. This is not a test or a drill...'

He ran back towards reception, and beckoned Tom, Stella, Rebecca, and Mark back into the depths of the office. There was no point getting into a face-off on the stairs. Damian had territorial advantage coming from higher up, which improved sight lines and angle of attack.

For Sharp, the smart thing to do was to try and protect his friends, and hold out for the police arriving.

CHAPTER FIFTY-TWO

THERE WASN'T time to try and evacuate staff. There was only one route in or out of the office through reception, and Sharp wasn't willing to take the chance of someone being caught up in a crossfire. An attempted evacuation would almost certainly be part of Damian's plan.

With Mark's help, Sharp corralled the rest of the newsroom staff into any office space available. Unaware of the imminent threat, it took Sharp's firmest tone of voice to communicate the danger. All it took was one word to spread through the newsroom to get everyone moving at pace: gunman. The whispers grew with each person who repeated it, but there was no frantic stampede, or selfish shoving. The reporters looked after each other, performing head counts for each of the desk groups they sat in, accounting for every last soul. *The Republic* didn't have a large bureaucracy for management. The individual offices were small, and now completely rammed.

'Quick,' Sharp told them, running from office to office, relaying instructions for how best to barricade the door.

Once Sharp and Mark had secured everyone into an office, or under a desk, Mark joined the other senior staff in his office. Though it had glass walls, Mark demanded that they take the risk of hiding there, rather than risking Damian going office to office in search of them. Tom, Stella, and Rebecca were unanimous on that point. They wouldn't have anyone else end up in the firing line.

Sharp helped create a dam of furniture behind Mark's desk where they could all hide, on the blindside of the office as Damian would approach it – then he told them to lock the door behind him.

Rebecca leaned around the desk, crouched on the floor. 'Wait, Walter. Where are you going? You can't go out there yourself.'

'I have to,' he replied. 'Sometimes attack is the safest option.'

With his back pressed up against the table, and shielding Stella, Novak remarked, 'I can't say I agree with that, Walter.'

'Call the police,' Sharp said. 'Tell them there's a gunman roaming the newsroom.'

'Are you nuts?' said Stella. 'They're going to end up shooting *you*.'

'Don't worry about it.'

Sharp asked no one in particular, 'Is there a backup generator around here?'

'Yeah,' said Mark. 'In the maintenance cupboard beside the staffroom. Tom knows where it is.'

'Me?' Novak said in surprise. 'Maybe as editor you should try volunteering yourself for suicidal tasks, Mark.'

'Listen to me,' Sharp said. 'Tom. I need you to come

with me, and get ready to turn on that generator when I say.'

'How will I know?'

'Trust me. You'll know. I don't really do ambiguous.' Sharp turned to leave, then stopped in the doorway. 'Mark, barricade the door behind me.'

Mark sprang into action, tipping a filing cabinet onto its side with a crash. But he found it too heavy to push along the carpet to block the door.

Seeing what was happening, Rebecca dashed out from behind the desk, and helped give the extra weight necessary to get it moving.

Now it was a matter of hoping and trusting in Walter.

CHAPTER FIFTY-THREE

HOLDING the torch against his gun, he lit the way through the darkened maze of desks and office chairs. They had been turned this way and that in the rush to find a hiding spot. He looked for any visible sign of a figure entering from reception, which was the only way in or out, but the darkness was so complete he could barely see his own gun in front of him.

Somewhere ahead, he heard the floor creak. He rolled his shoulders, trying to remove tension in his arms, which would spread to his fingers if he held onto it too long.

A reporter attempted to peek out from under his desk.

Sharp whispered in a low, urgent tone, 'Out of sight!'

Everyone in the office now felt their lives were on the line. Especially Sharp, who felt exposed and vulnerable creeping through the newsroom.

He was convinced that Damian would have night-vision goggles to boost his advantage. And there wasn't anything Sharp could do about it.

At reception, Damian was able to creep inside stealthily, with full view of everything around him thanks to the night-vision goggles that Sharp had correctly predicted him having.

He caught a glimpse of movement near the conference room, and knew that it must be Sharp. A man of his experience, expertise, and character wouldn't be sitting this one out, hiding under a desk somewhere.

Dressed in black from head to toe, Damian moved silently past reception. The only sound accompanying him was the faintest of creaks from the night-vision goggles each time he turned his head.

Sharp kept low, making much slower progress than Damian. His senses heightened in the darkness, reacting to any tiny sound coming from the street outside.

Blending seamlessly with the darkness, Damian entered the open space of the newsroom and took aim at Sharp.

The office, normally such a hub of activity and noise, was now totally silent.

Damian called out, 'I just want Novak.'

Sharp refused to reply. But judging from the direction that Damian's voice had come from, Sharp knew that Damian had the upper hand and must have had clear sight of him from where he was.

Sharp dived behind a desk, landing on his front. There was no longer any positional advantage to be had. Now it was going to be a straight shootout.

Damian repeated, 'I just want Novak! Then this all ends. And all these people can go home.'

Then a voice called out from near the maintenance cupboard.

'It's too late,' Novak told him. 'You can shoot everyone

in the building. It won't change anything. We know about Nathan. And the story he fed us.'

As long as Damian was being pulled into a negotiation, Sharp tried to reason with him.

'The police will be coming up the stairs as we speak, Damian,' Sharp told him. 'It's over.'

Damian flashed a look back towards reception, and saw a white glow massing by the lifts. He had no way out.

But Sharp wasn't going to take any chances. He yelled to Novak, 'Now, Tom!'

Novak hit the lever to turn on the backup generator, which kicked in quickly. The newsroom was suddenly flooded with what seemed like blinding light, even to those not wearing night-vision googles.

But to Damian, it was even more intense. It was a fallacy that wearing night-vision goggles when lights were turned on caused pain. What they did, though, was "bloom out". A sudden and complete wash of greenish white filled the lenses, making Damian stagger backwards, as the goggles' amplification plate was overwhelmed by photons pouring in.

As he recoiled, he involuntarily raised his weapon, pointing it at the ceiling,

He was a sitting duck in the wide-open space of the newsroom floor, standing in bright office light.

Sharp shot to his feet and fired off two rounds into Damian's chest. Then he got off a further headshot before Damian fell to the ground.

Sharp knew it was over, but he didn't take any chances. He covered Damian the whole way with his weapon, ready to fire again if necessary.

Novak ran over to see what had happened, as Sharp hadn't said a word.

'Walter!' Novak cried out, terrified that Damian had been the one to shoot first. He let out a cry of relief when he saw Sharp closing in on Damian, who lay sprawled on the ground. Limbs limp. His threat over for good.

Sharp motioned for Novak to stay back all the same.

Reacting to the shots, the police charged in, weapons drawn, a dozen demands and yells for hands to be raised ringing out through the office.

Satisfied that Damian was dead, Sharp held his hands aloft, demonstrating that he was surrendering his weapon to them.

'I'm CIA,' he declared, squinting against the brightness of the overhead lights.

Terrified that the police might fire at Sharp, Novak shouted in a panic, 'Don't shoot! Don't shoot!'

Sharp identified himself to the police unit's principal, who reacted with composure and control, calling off his team once he had established Sharp's identity from his official CIA cover.

Now that Damian was down, and Sharp was safe, Novak allowed himself to fall to the floor, resting like an athlete who had finished an exhausting race. 'It's safe,' he yelled to the others. Increasing in volume. 'It's safe!'

Stella was the first to emerge, dashing to Novak's side. She had no idea what had happened, and thought that by Novak's position on the floor that he might have been shot.

'Tom!' she cried out. 'Are you okay?' When she reached him, she refused to believe his claims that he was fine, running hands over him to check for wounds.

'I'm fine, Stel,' he insisted.

When she was certain he was, she threw her arms around him.

They each closed their eyes and embraced.

The rest of the office emerged from their hiding spots, slowly filtering back out onto the newsroom floor.

Mark and Rebecca soon reached Tom and Stella.

'Is it just Damian down?' Mark asked.

Sharp was deep in conversation with the police chief on site, explaining who he was, and what had happened.

'Just Damian,' Novak said, relinquishing his hold on Stella.

'Come on,' Stella said, helping him to his feet. 'We need to get out of this building.'

But Novak wanted to get a look at the man who had killed his dad. He needed to stand over him and know he was never getting up again.

He thought he was in control of his emotions now that the threat was over. But the second he saw Damian on the floor, he felt a rush of something primal and overwhelming take over his body. He was no longer in control, seeing a dark red mist in his peripheral vision.

The police, reacting to Novak's sudden burst of movement, didn't fully understand what was happening and reached towards their weapons without actually pulling them out.

Sharp was the one to stop Novak's charge towards Damian's body. 'Hey, hey, hey...It's over, Tom,' he told him.

Novak didn't stand a chance of getting past Sharp to get any closer, but it didn't stop him trying.

Sharp was taken aback at Novak's strength, driven by the sort of pure emotion that only the loss of a family member can create.

'You bastard!' Novak railed with tears in his eyes. 'You took him from me, you bastard!'

Sharp felt Novak's strength fade, then let him drop gently to the ground. Both Sharp and Stella comforted him, crouching beside him as Novak finally cried the tears for his father that he should have cried so many years ago.

'Bring him back,' Novak cried. 'Just five minutes...that's all I want.'

Stella had never seen him in such a state, and made her eyes well up too. 'It's all right, Tom,' she said.

Novak's voice weakened as he repeated, 'That's all I want...'

EPILOGUE
TWO WEEKS LATER

NOVAK STOOD at the lectern of the lecture hall where a fortnight earlier, he had frozen so dramatically. Now, he was a different person. Freed from the past, and unburdened of the guilt of his dad's loss, Novak was able to give the speech he should have made the first time.

Reaching the section where he had previously faltered, he now commanded the stage and the entire School of Journalism lecture hall.

He said with warmth and love resonating in his voice, 'Seymour Novak is the reason I became a journalist. Without him, I wouldn't be standing here in front of you tonight. That is why opening this archive means so much to me. This archive is a testament to him, and his career as a journalist.'

That should have been the end of it. At least as it was written on the page in front of him. But something about looking off to the west wing and seeing Stella standing on her own, where Fitz should have been standing alongside her, prompted Novak to make an improvised addition.

'Since I started at *The Republic*, I've seen a lot of people come and go. Stella Mitchell came into my life on a story that would change me forever. Nothing's been the same since. Together, with our close friends and contacts, we've all lost people along the way. Diane Schlesinger. Stanley Fox. And in just the last week, the great, great Martin Fitzhenry.'

Novak had to stop for the spontaneous applause that almost took the roof off the hall.

Stella joined in, clapping as hard as she could. She looked behind her, where Mark was standing in the shadows. He was looking down, turning his wedding ring gently in his finger, experiencing a similarly overdue catharsis with thoughts of his wife Caroline. Stella held her hand out for him to join her.

As she pulled him in closer, she whispered to him, 'She would be so proud of you, Mark.'

Never comfortable displaying emotion publicly, Mark pursed his lips and nodded.

Once the applause subsided, Novak continued, 'Opening this archive has meant stepping into the past. Which has not always been the easiest place to go to. I've had to confront a lot of complicated emotions about the relationship I had with the man that created all of what you'll find in the archive room. I realised that for a lot of my life, I got my dad all wrong. He never stopped being the journalist I thought he was. It was inside him all along, and he proved it right up to his final days. With nothing but his own talent and eye for a story, Seymour Novak helped expose a story of corruption and corporate fraud within the biggest hedge fund the world has ever known. Exposing Storm Capital's greed and criminality seems a fitting final act for a man whose greatest compliment to someone was to call them honest. If the past weeks have taught me anything, it's that it's often easy to believe a falsehood if you find it comforting. If it explains the world in a way that reinforces what you already believe. Looking back through this archive, and all of my dad's previous work in the last few days, I can see that he never stopped looking. Never stopped digging. No matter how things appeared on the surface. I can only hope that there's more of him in me than I used to think.' He dropped his head momentarily, then announced with arms out, as if beckoning friends into his own house, 'Ladies and gentlemen, I now declare the Seymour Novak archive open.'

AT THE DRINKS RECEPTION AFTERWARDS, Novak was swept up with well-wishers and congratulations for *The Republic*'s comprehensive exposé of the SCX bankruptcy scandal, and the monumental collapse of Storm Capital that followed along with the arrests of Zach Storm, Anna Storm, and Noah Bergman on multiple counts of wire fraud.

Stella had experienced similar, and felt lucky to get a few minutes alone with Novak outside in the university garden.

He was holding the same glass of champagne that someone had given him half an hour ago. Realising he wasn't in the mood to drink it, he poured it onto the grass.

'That's a very expensive champagne you just threw away,' said Stella, walking towards him.

Novak said, 'I would have given it to you if I'd known you were there.'

She kicked up a foot to demonstrate. 'The beauty of wearing flats. You doing okay?'

'Yeah,' he said, sure of himself. 'Relieved more than anything. It's been such an intense couple of weeks. With the story. Everything with Nathan. And then Fitz. Mark getting his contract as editor secured. It's a proper changing of the guard. We're done with Hilderberg once and for all.'

'Rebecca's moving on too,' said Stella.

'Oh yeah?'

'She messaged earlier. She's taken a research fellow position at Cambridge in the maths department.'

Novak grinned. 'So solving puzzles, then?'

'Yeah. How perfect for her.'

'What about Leon?'

'He's staying in London. DCI Bell's taken him as a Detective Sergeant in Specialist Command. It's only ninety minutes in a car. That's shorter than some people's commute into London.'

Novak puffed. 'It feels a bit like a blank slate.'

Stella nodded in agreement. 'I think it's a good time to move on, don't you?'

'Yeah. It just feels strange to say that. So much of our lives the past few years has been tied up in this one story. And now it's over.'

'Sometimes it's good to say goodbye, though. What's that dreadful word you Americans use? Closure.' She smiled affectionately.

Novak said, 'I just don't know what I'm going to do with myself until something new comes along.'

'That's the simple part, Tom. You don't sit around and wait. You get out there and go find it.'

Novak shook his head, looking up at the clear night sky above. 'What if I can't find anything else? What if this is all I was meant to do?'

The pair were distracted by the sight of Mark appearing at the patio door, evidently in a hurry, holding a phone aloft. 'Guys...you're going to want to take this.'

Novak and Stella shared a look together, equal parts mischief and curiosity.

Stella said, 'It's like what Diane used to say. There's always another story. The truth will never die.'

ALSO BY ANDREW RAYMOND

Printed in Great Britain
by Amazon

35850711R00179